TELL ME
I'M YOURS

A BRITISH BILLIONAIRE NOVEL

Book Two

J. S. SCOTT

Tell Me I'm Yours

ISBN: 9798570973060 (Print)
ISBN: 9781951102425 (E-Book)

CONTENTS

PROLOGUE

(Just in case you missed this part in
Tell Me You're Mine, Book 1)

Kylie

"WHO IN THE fuck are you, and why are you here? Never mind. Just go away and stop pounding on my door."

I lowered the fist I'd been using to bang on the door since Dylan Lancaster had finally decided to open it.

I'd rung the doorbell for two minutes straight, and then resorted to hammering on the door for several more minutes before Dylan had finally popped his head out.

I wasn't about to…go away.

Not in the near future, anyway.

I plowed past him and into the foyer of the Beverly Hills mansion, a rolling suitcase in tow, and my miniature beagle, Jake, cuddled against my body.

I took a deep breath as I turned to face him. "I don't really have to ask if you're Dylan Lancaster. You do look a lot like Damian. Although I do have to say that your brother looks a lot...healthier."

I stared at Dylan, assessing his bloodshot eyes, unkept attire, and his general malaise.

His eyes were the same color as Damian's, but Dylan's didn't seem to have a single spark of life in those pretty irises. What a shame, because I'd always thought Damian's eyes were one of his best features.

Dylan slammed the door. "I'll ask you again. Who in the fuck are you? And what do you mean that Damian looks...healthier?"

I smirked because I knew I'd hit a nerve. Obviously, Dylan didn't like being compared to his elder identical twin.

Jake squirmed in my arms, so I put the miniature beagle down on the floor. He was well potty trained, and he wasn't a chewer. "I mean that you look like the anti-twin. Your eyes are bloodshot, you're way too skinny, probably because you prefer to drink your meals instead of eating them, and your general sense of style with your clothing is horrible. Not to mention the fact that you need a haircut, and possibly a shower because I can smell you from way over here."

Okay, I really *couldn't* smell him, but I'd much rather nip the cleanliness thing in the bud. There was absolutely nothing worse than a guy who reeked, and I was going to have to be around Dylan every single day.

"I do not stink. I shower every single day." His answer was haughty, and he sounded somewhat offended.

Since I wasn't about to get close enough to him to sniff for myself, I ignored his comment. "Don't you have caretakers here?"

I could have sworn that Nicole had mentioned a couple who lived here, and managed the estate.

Dylan glowered at me. "They're on vacation somewhere in the Caribbean. I didn't expect to be back here so soon. Now tell me who you are and what you want, or I'll throw your ass out of here."

"Oh, yes. I forgot. You *were* staying at Hollingsworth House until your mother decided that it wasn't appropriate behavior for you to fuck a female under her roof while she was throwing her gala. Not to mention the fact that you broke Nicole's heart. Is that why you ran back here like a coward instead of telling Nic that you were sorry?" I plastered an innocent look on my face while I waited for his answer.

Bastard!

He had no idea how much I wanted to put my knee in his balls for making my best friend cry.

"I was in a private bedroom, for fuck's sake. It wasn't like I knew that she was going to come and watch," he said testily.

I folded my arms over my chest. "But you apparently had no problem if she wanted to join you and your girl-toy."

Dylan glared at me. "She wasn't a girl. The *woman* was thirty years old, and as for Nicole, I thought the more, the merrier. How was I supposed to know that my brother was madly in love with her? Damian has never fallen in love with any of the women he's shagged."

Don't do it, Kylie. Don't punch the bastard in the face so hard that he can't talk anymore.

I was usually more patient, but Nicole was my best friend, so it fried my ass to hear Dylan referring to her like she was just another fuck for Damian.

Since it wouldn't exactly start us out on a good footing if I punched Dylan, I resorted to insults. "Seriously? I doubt you could handle one woman in the shape you're in, much less two. And by the way, Nicole *is* my best friend, so if you say anything bad about her, I'll put my knee in your balls until you sing soprano. Do we understand each other?"

Dylan's expression turned dark. "The shape I'm in? What in the hell does that mean? I'm thirty-three years old. I'm perfectly capable of handling any number of women in one night."

I snorted. "I noticed you didn't say you could actually *satisfy* them. You probably are capable of *pawing* them, but not much more than that."

The visual for *that* whole scenario wasn't exactly pleasant, so I made a face and shut down the image of Dylan petting a harem of women.

He let out a low, throaty sound as he moved toward me. "You know nothing about me. I don't really think I even care anymore who you are. I just want you to leave. I don't even know why I'm having this unpleasant conversation with you. I don't give a damn what you think. Go. And take that miserable excuse for a hound with you."

I tilted my chin up as he got close enough to grab me. "I'm not going anywhere."

Dylan started to crowd me, so I stepped back, even though I didn't really *want* to back down.

Really, he wasn't *terribly* skinny, and he *was* extremely tall. I was five foot seven, over the average height for a female, but Dylan towered over me. I didn't like his menacing expression, either.

With my back against the wall, I put my palm out to keep him from moving any closer. "Back off."

Dylan smirked as he took another step closer. "Could it be that you're only brave from a distance, Red?"

God, I hated it when people made fun of my hair. "Fuck off, Lancaster."

"Is that an invitation?" His voice became low and seductive.

I wouldn't say I was afraid of Dylan Lancaster, but I was more uneasy with this new, provocative Dylan than I had been with the asshole.

He's trying to throw me off-balance. The bastard is trying to make me nervous.

I met his gaze and refused to look away, even when he placed his palms against the wall, trapping me between his arms.

"It's not even close to an invitation." I scoffed. "I wouldn't screw you if you were the last man on Earth, and my hormones were running rampant."

I'd be damned if I'd back down from someone like Dylan Lancaster. He was a man-whore, a spoiled rotten billionaire who treated women like their only purpose was sex, and to plump his already over-inflated ego.

"Is that right, Red?" His deep baritone was captivating now.

I took a breath and released it slowly, determined not to give an inch. Unfortunately, I realized that Dylan had been right. He definitely didn't *stink*. His scent was musky, masculine, and he exuded something that reminded me of sex, sin, and hot, sweaty nights of carnal pleasure.

Shit!

"Get off me, Lancaster," I insisted, never allowing my gaze to waver.

"I'm not on you yet, Red," he answered huskily.

I was wrong about his eyes!

I froze as I noticed that his irises were darker and filled with something that looked like...sheer, unadulterated lust.

Holy shit!

"Last chance. Back the fuck off." I hated the fact that my voice sounded slightly panicked.

I was honest enough with myself to admit that it wasn't fear that was making me edgy.

It was Dylan's eyes, his sexy British accent, and the way that he was looking at me right now.

I could handle the asshole.

I wasn't so sure about the sexy Brit persona.

I took another deep breath, and then bit back a groan as I was overwhelmed by Dylan's I-want-to-fuck-you-into-multiple-orgasms scent.

He lowered his head until I could feel the warmth of his breath on my lips. Those puffs of air smelled minty and fresh, making me want to grab him by the hair and yank his head down until I could taste that hint of peppermint on my tongue.

"What are you going to do if I kiss you, Red?"

"Don't do it," I warned him.

No matter how much my body was clamoring for Dylan's touch, I wasn't about to let this asshole manhandle me like he'd done with countless women before me. Dylan Lancaster was playing with me. I was simply his...entertainment.

He grinned, and the action lit up his entire face. "Now that sounds like a challenge," he said.

I pushed against his chest. "It's not," I snapped.

My entire body tightened as his mouth landed on mine, and his lips coaxed me to respond.

For a moment, I couldn't fight the attraction, and I opened, allowing Dylan's lazy but thorough exploration.

My arms snaked around his neck, and I answered every blatant caress of his tongue.

He teased.

He tempted.

He tantalized.

And oh, my God, the man could provoke a reaction from an inanimate object with a kiss as sinful as his.

Kylie! What the fuck are you doing? He's a male slut, and you know it!

I squeaked as I tried to move away from temptation by turning my head, and breaking lip contact. "Let go of me."

Dylan's body stayed exactly where it was, and he tried to connect our mouths again.

If he doesn't move, I'm screwed. I'd let myself get sucked right back under his spell again.

So I did what I'd already thought about doing earlier.

My knee came up in a quick motion of desperation, and connected directly with my target.

"*Fuck!*" Dylan let out a groan as he let me go. "Bloody hell! Why did you do that?"

I scrambled away from the wall and moved until there was nothing behind me but air. I watched Dylan as he clung to his family jewels and sucked air in and out of his lungs like it was the most difficult task he'd ever done.

"I told you to let go." Honestly, I *did* feel a little bit guilty. I had led him on. A little. Not on purpose, but my hormones had gone from zero to overdrive in less than a second when he'd kissed me.

It had taken my brain a little longer to catch up.

"You wanted that as much as I did," Dylan accused.

"You caught me off guard," I argued. "And then I remembered that you were a man-whore, and I *definitely* didn't want it. I didn't knee you *that* hard. It could have been worse. You're still a baritone."

Dylan's breathing evened out, but his hand was still protectively holding his junk. "I don't give a fuck who you are—leave this house. Now."

I shook my head. "Not happening, big guy. We never really got around to introductions, but I'm Kylie Hart. My best friend is going to be marrying your brother in approximately six weeks. I'm here to make sure nothing goes wrong, and there's no more negative press, here or in the UK, before that happens. Damian and Nicole deserve this time stress-free to plan their wedding, and spend some quality time together without having to put out fires that *you* create."

"I'm not planning on raining on their parade," Dylan grumbled.

I beamed at him. "Good. Then we'll get along fine."

Dylan grimaced as he stroked his crotch like he was trying to decide whether or not I broke something vital before he said, "I don't need a goddamn companion."

"Oh, I'm not planning on being your companion, Dylan." I reached down to scoop up Jake. "In six weeks' time, you're going to clean up your act, and then you'll fly back to London for the wedding. After that, I don't give a damn what you do because Damian and Nic will be on their honeymoon."

"I'm not going to the wedding."

Oh yes, you are.

I curled my fingers around the handle of my suitcase. "I assume the bedrooms are upstairs?"

"You're not going upstairs," he growled. "Leave."

"This isn't your house, so technically, you're a squatter," I informed him. "This place belongs to Damian because you signed everything over to him. And I highly doubt he's going to kick *me* out. Believe it or not, he likes me."

He raised a brow. "I highly doubt that. You're a thoroughly unlikable female."

I laughed. "I'd be completely likable if you weren't such an asshole."

I could see the muscle in Dylan's jaw twitch, and I knew he was losing his patience, if he ever had any to begin with, so I said, "I'll just show myself upstairs."

"If you think you can tolerate six weeks with me, you're delusional," he said.

There was something in his voice that stopped me from tossing back a smart-ass reply.

Something desperate.

Something vulnerable.

Something...tormented.

I hated the fact that I couldn't completely harden my heart when it came to Dylan Lancaster. I didn't exactly like him, but he *had* suffered significant loss.

I headed for the stairs with my suitcase in tow. "We can do this easy and friendly, or you can make it hard. Your choice."

"What are you, my mum?" he taunted.

"No, I'm your new babysitter for the next six weeks." I kept heading for the stairs without looking back at him.

"You'll be gone in twenty-four hours!" he called after my retreating figure.

My heart ached because I could hear a little bit of fear in his tone, like everyone before me had abandoned him, so he just expected that everyone else would, too.

I'm not going anywhere, big guy.

I wasn't just here to make sure Dylan stayed out of trouble, although that was definitely one of my goals.

Nicole had given me a partnership in ACM, even though I didn't have the funds to buy in.

In return, I wanted to do something to thank her for being more like a sister than a friend. And for trusting me to take care of her mom's business. I really wanted to give Damian his brother back. The *real* Dylan Lancaster. Not the asshole who was currently inhabiting his body.

It was the one thing that would mean everything to Nicole and Damian.

I smiled as I climbed the stairs.

I couldn't think of a better wedding present than that.

CHAPTER 1

Kylie

"OKAY, THIS IS perfect," I muttered to myself as I unpacked my suitcase. "It even has a sitting room with a desk that will double as an office."

I didn't want to admit that the suite I was making myself comfortable in upstairs was...slightly intimidating.

Yeah, I was a California native, and I was used to seeing ridiculously expensive real estate, but I'd never actually *stayed* in any of those pricy mansions.

The enormous bedroom, sitting room, and en suite bathroom were bigger than the entire one-bedroom apartment I rented in Newport Beach.

I frowned as I turned back to the bed to grab some underwear from the suitcase. "I'm not so sure you should be making yourself at home on *this* bed, Jake."

My canine had taken the temporary move in stride. He'd come a long way from the abused, frightened shelter dog he'd been two years ago when I'd adopted him. Jake opened one eye from his place on the gorgeous teal comforter, but he didn't move.

I shrugged as I went to the dresser and stuffed my panties and bras into a drawer. I let Jake sleep on my bed at home, and I kept him well-groomed. The last thing I wanted was to confuse him. I'd already brought him to a strange home in Beverly Hills to live with a guy who obviously *wasn't* a dog lover.

If Jake gets the pretty comforter dirty, Dylan Lancaster can well afford the dry cleaning bill.

I sighed as I started to hang up some of my stuff in the closet. It wasn't like I hadn't known that this endeavor was going to be difficult.

Dylan Lancaster was a selfish billionaire with an attitude problem, just like I'd expected.

I just didn't prepare myself for the unlikely event of being attracted to him.

God, why would I have *ever* imagined that I would be?

He was a total jerk.

He was a man-whore who indulged in orgies and other hedonistic behavior.

Ultimately, he had no redeeming qualities at all that were readily apparent or obvious. It was highly possible that none existed. Not even ones that were deeply buried in that smoking-hot body of his.

It's strictly physical. He smells good. He has a drool worthy body, and he's drop-dead gorgeous. That silky smooth baritone with a sexy British accent adds to his appeal, too.

Yep. I was simply reacting to hormones, but I was completely turned off by his character.

My best friend was marrying the "good" twin, Damian Lancaster, a guy who was actually worthy of respect.

Oddly, I could appreciate the fact that Damian was incredibly attractive, but he'd never once made a single one of my female hormones twitch.

Unlike his identical twin, who had practically made those hormones get up and dance the second I'd walked through the door.

I hated the way I'd reacted to Dylan. Did I have some kind of secret affinity for bad boys that I'd never known existed?

I felt like an idiot because, for a few moments, I'd literally lost all of my ability to think or speak.

Me! A woman who made her living as a public relations crisis manager. I was successful at what I did because I had the ability to talk my clients out of trouble, and I never lost my reason during that process.

What in the hell is wrong with me? Why am I always attracted to the jerks?

The hair stood up at the back of my neck before I actually heard Dylan's voice. "Did Damian send you here?" he asked flatly.

I turned to see Dylan leaning against the doorjamb of the bedroom, his expression angry, but as I caught his gaze, I could also sense some defeat in those gorgeous green depths.

"No," I told him honestly, not looking away. "This was *all* me. Nicole and Damian have been through hell, and I don't want their wedding to be ruined if you decide to pull another asinine stunt like you did when you got caught by reporters and photographers during your drunken orgy."

"It was a setup. I was drugged," he said defensively.

"You were bare-ass naked," I reminded him. "For God's sake, you're one of the richest men in the world, and co-CEO of one of the largest corporations on the planet. Don't you people learn to lock your damn doors, so you don't have to deal with the press? Or were you just okay with letting your kinder, nicer brother take the fall for every stupid thing you did?" I took a deep breath as I turned my back on him to continue unpacking. "It hurt Damian, you know. He pretended every ridiculous thing you did was *his* mistake. He was loyal to you to the very end, and that nearly killed his relationship with the woman he loves."

Luckily, when Damian had needed to make a choice between the brother he'd protected for two years and the love of his life, he'd made the right decision.

"Damian should have told her that he had an identical twin," Dylan scoffed. "If he had, there wouldn't have been any misunderstanding in the first place. I never asked him to pretend he was me or take any of the blame for my actions."

My blood started to boil. "He did it for you, to protect you, although I have absolutely no idea why. You obviously don't have the same loyalty to him. God, do you really *not* give a damn about your own twin?"

Yeah, Dylan had suffered a loss, which had obviously caused him to become a different man than he'd been before. But that was no excuse for the way he'd shunned his entire family after it had happened.

I caught his furious expression out of the corner of my eye. *Good!* Let him be pissed off. It was better than the dead expression I'd seen in his eyes when he'd first come to the door.

Something or someone needed to penetrate this man's armor, and I didn't care if I had to irritate the hell out of him until he finally broke. There had to be some of the old Dylan still left inside of him, and I was determined to find it.

"He never told me that he was masquerading as me every time I made…an error in judgment," he snarled.

I dropped a pair of jeans onto the bed and swung around to face him again. "Please! Damian was covering for you for over two years. You didn't know because you were just too self-absorbed to notice. Meanwhile, he was screwing up a relationship to keep his promises to you about letting you disappear from the public eye for a while. Well, if that was what you wanted, why in the hell did you keep showing up in the dumbest of ways?"

"I admit, I did some nonsensical things—"

"Foolish," I corrected, unwilling to let him squirm out of his outrageous actions over the last two years. "Behavior that was more than newsworthy to the gossip columns, which makes no sense when all you wanted was your damn privacy, according to Damian."

He folded his arms across his broad, muscular chest and sent me a glare that probably should have had me running for the hills, but didn't.

I didn't back down to idiots.

"Those events only happened when I drank too much," he grumbled.

"Which was apparently way too often," I commented drily.

Dylan released what sounded like an exasperated breath as he walked into the room and sat down on the end of the bed. He eyed Jake's snoring body sprawled out on the comforter before he said, "That really is a sorry excuse for a hound."

I grabbed the jeans and folded them before I shoved them into a drawer. "Jake is an amazing dog. I'm so sorry he offends you because he isn't a purebred, perfect specimen," I said in a snarky tone.

Dylan ignored the comment. "I do care about Damian, which is why I'm not planning on getting into trouble or attending his wedding," he informed me grimly.

"And you think that's going to make him happy?" I snapped out the question. "Even though you don't deserve it, he still loves you. Do you really believe that he wants to experience one of the happiest days of his life without his twin brother there?"

"He made it perfectly clear how he felt about me after that little incident at the gala in England," he answered harshly. "I haven't heard from him, my mother, or my younger brother, Leo, since that night."

"Do you really blame them?" I asked. "You propositioned the woman he loved. You asked Nicole to join your orgy while you were staying at your mother's country home. During a formal gala. And she had no idea you existed. Nicole thought you were Damian."

"Technically, it would have been a ménage, not an orgy," he answered coolly. "There was only one woman in the bed at the time, and it wasn't like we were in the process of intercourse. The liaison was still in the early stages of foreplay when Nicole walked into the bedroom."

"Whatever," I replied sharply. "What in the hell possessed you to hit on Nicole to join your little twosome?"

"Shock value, I suppose," he answered nonchalantly. "One look at her had already told me she wasn't the type."

"Of course she's not," I huffed. "Nicole has more class in her little finger than you possess in your entire body. Not to mention the fact that she's madly in love with your brother. It destroyed her when she thought you were Damian, and that he was already cheating on her."

"Obviously, she doesn't know my twin all that well," he drawled. "I knew when he finally fell for a woman someday, he'd fall hard. Apparently, I was right, and he isn't the cheating type. He's absolutely obsessed with Nicole. I doubt he even sees another woman."

I slammed the empty suitcase closed. "How was she supposed to know that? She didn't even know he had a twin brother."

He shrugged, which made me want to slap him. "If it makes any difference, I hated myself after I understood what had happened."

"It doesn't," I informed him as I shoved the empty suitcase in the closet. "Has it ever occurred to you that you'd be far better off cleaning up your act than burying yourself in self-loathing? It's a hell of a lot more productive."

"That idea did occur to me just recently," he answered in a bitter tone. "You can go home, Kylie. I don't drink myself senseless anymore, and I don't want you here."

I put my hand on my hip and stared at him, wondering if I could believe what he'd just said. Truthfully, he looked like crap, but I hadn't caught a single whiff of alcohol on him, and God knew I would recognize it if I had. "I don't trust you," I said bluntly. "How can I when you've been behaving like a selfish jerk for the last two years?"

He shot me an annoyed look. "Believe me when I say I haven't enjoyed a single moment of that life."

Oddly, I didn't doubt that, and even though Dylan Lancaster was a complete asshole, there was something about his pain that touched a long-buried part of me.

No one seemed to know the entire story about the loss he'd suffered, which was obviously the catalyst for his prolonged, erratic behavior over the last two years. According to Damian, his twin had been a fantastic human being *before* his sudden turnaround two years ago.

No orgies.

No drunken episodes.

No anti-social behavior. In fact, Damian swore that Dylan was a charmer, and far better with people than he was.

I wasn't entirely certain what he'd been through. Even Damian only knew the basics, but I had to wonder what his family *didn't* know about Dylan's suffering.

Grief and sadness aside, what in the hell had happened to Dylan Lancaster?

I shook my head slowly. "I'm afraid you're stuck with me for now. Let's just try to make the best of the situation. Maybe I can eventually forget that you tore my best friend's heart out since she and Damian are blissfully happy now."

"And what about that kiss, Red? Can you forget about that, too?" he asked in a husky voice.

My breath hitched, and I tried to push aside exactly how it had felt to be consumed by Dylan Lancaster. "Yep. Absolutely," I answered in a casual tone. "Like I said, I was caught off guard. It was nothing."

Did I really believe that? *No.*

Would I pretend like hell that it was true? *Yes.*

If I gave an inch to a man like Dylan, he'd take a mile, and then some.

He smirked, like he knew I was lying. "Suit yourself," he said as he rose from the bed. "Just don't expect me to entertain you unless you'd like me to do it while we're both naked."

I took a deep breath, and then let it out, trying to do a mini-meditation to calm myself down.

It didn't work.

"If you tease me one more time about my hair color, my knee will end up in your groin again," I warned him. "I've had to put up with that bullshit my entire life, and now that I'm an adult, I don't put up with bullies. Also, I make it a rule not to sleep with a guy who has slept with half the women on the planet. So let's get one thing straight. I will never be desperate enough to sleep with a man like you, Dylan Lancaster. Remember that, and I think we'll tolerate each other just fine."

I turned and headed for the door.

"You sound somewhat defensive, Kylie," he said, not sounding the least bit daunted. "Where are you going?"

"I'm starving," I called over my shoulder. "I'm sure this place has a kitchen. I intend to find it."

"That's probably not a good idea," Dylan said in a warning voice as he followed me down the stairs.

"Finding the kitchen first in a new place is always a good idea." I snorted. "I like to eat. My body doesn't run well without any fuel."

My mission was to find the kitchen, and that was that.

CHAPTER 2

Dylan

"OH, MY GOD. What happened to this kitchen?" Kylie said as she gaped at what had once been a spotless chef's kitchen.

It wasn't like I hadn't thrown up the caution signals *before* she'd gotten here. If she chose not to listen, it was *her* fault.

"I did warn you," I said defensively. "Clarence and Anita were gone by the time I got back to the house. They'll be gone for another six weeks since they had no idea I'd be returning to the house much earlier than expected. I'd planned on spending a few months in England."

"Which gives you permission to be a complete slob?" she asked. "Surely, even a billionaire knows how to clean up after himself."

I shrugged. "It's not like I was expecting company. I would have done it at some point."

I resisted the urge to call her *Red* again, and I wasn't quite sure why since it was my mission to get her to leave. It obviously irritated her, but for some reason I didn't completely understand; I didn't actually want to…hurt her.

Kylie rolled her eyes. "When was that going to happen? When you couldn't see the kitchen counters anymore?" She picked up one of the pans in the sink carefully. "Were you trying to cook?"

"In the beginning, yes," I admitted reluctantly. "Eventually, I just gave up and ordered out."

I watched her as she started to fill the pans in the sink with water.

"I'll let them soak," she explained. "I think I can get the burned food off the bottom. This is really high-end cookware. I've been lusting after a set like this forever."

I'd much prefer that she was lusting after *me.*

It was rather deflating that she found those dirty pots and pans more desirable than kissing me again.

Does it really matter what she thinks?

It's not as though I'd really cared how anyone felt for the last two years. There was really no point in starting to let anyone's opinion matter at this point.

"Just leave it," I instructed as I started to throw away the trash on the counters. "I'll buy more pots and pans."

She turned to me, her eyes wide. "Are you insane? You don't just toss cast-iron pots and pans like these."

I shrugged. "I would."

I frowned when a wet dishrag collided with my head as Kylie requested, "Would you mind wiping the pizza sauce off the granite on the island?"

It wasn't really a request, even though she'd technically *asked* me to do it.

Rather than argue, I started cleaning the island.

Really, I had to admit that the kitchen *was* a mess.

It was sad that it had taken an annoyingly bossy female to point that out, but cleaning up hadn't been a priority for me.

I straddled one of the stools at the island once the cleanup was done. "If this doesn't prove that I'm not a good housemate, I'm not sure what will," I grumbled. "You might as well pack up that suitcase if you like to eat. There isn't much food in the house."

I watched as she opened all the cupboards, and then rummaged through the refrigerator and freezer.

"Nice try," she answered in a much too cheerful voice. "There's plenty of food here, and there are grocery stores everywhere for the fresh stuff I need. I'm not going anywhere, Dylan, so you might as well give up on trying to make me go. Nicole is like a sister to me, and she just made me a partner in ACM, the crisis management PR firm where I've worked for years, even though I couldn't afford to buy my part of the business up front. I also happen to like your twin brother. So I'm going to make damn sure the two of them have a fabulous wedding without any hassle."

I heaved a beleaguered sigh, not sure if I was terrified or relieved that she wasn't easily intimidated.

Granted, I'd been behaving like a wanker for a while now, but I was *still* Dylan Lancaster. It was a name that instilled respect in almost everyone—with the exception of my family.

Well, the Lancaster name demanded admiration in everyone except *her*, apparently.

I wasn't certain if I liked the fact that she wasn't impressed or if it annoyed the hell out of me.

I certainly didn't want her here, but maybe it *was* easier to just ignore her, for the most part.

Did I really need to let myself get this annoyed with someone that I didn't even know?

If nothing else, I *could* use her for information to satisfy my curiosity. "So how did Damian and your friend meet in the first place? I'm going to assume they don't exactly have mutual friends in the same social circles."

She turned around and glared at me. "Why? Because your family is so much wealthier and better connected than Nicole?"

Christ! Did the woman have to defend even the smallest perceived slight when it came to Nicole? "She's American. Damian is British. It just seems highly unlikely that they bumped into each other at some kind of gathering. My twin isn't exactly a frequent attendee of social events."

Her fierce expression softened. "Your mother never told you?"

"We didn't speak often, and no one mentioned Nicole before that gala. Lately, we don't talk at all," I said tersely.

For the first time in my life, even my mum was so angry with me that she never called anymore.

"Have you tried to call her?" Kylie asked in a kinder tone.

"No," I answered stiffly. "She always keeps in touch with me. Obviously, she doesn't care to chat. I think my entire family is done speaking to me."

She opened her mouth to say something, then closed it, as though she had changed her mind about what she'd meant to tell me. After a moment of hesitation, she explained, "They met while Damian was taking a commercial business flight on Transatlantic Airlines. Nicole was coming back to the States after completely bombing a pitch to Lancaster International. News of the orgy, complete with pictures, broke just before her presentation. Everyone at the meeting was too preoccupied with that scandal to pay much attention to her, and she was upset that she'd failed. Damian sat next to her and talked her off the ledge. Nicole didn't recognize him and didn't realize who he was until after the flight was over."

"He's still doing that?" I asked, not particularly surprised that Damian was flying commercial on our airline instead of using his private jet. He'd always felt he needed to fly Transatlantic occasionally as a passenger to make sure standards were being met.

She nodded, sat down at a stool near the island, and went on to explain how Damian had sought Nicole out later to apologize. And how he'd subsequently hired her to try to diminish the gossip over the naked orgy pictures that had been taken when I was drugged.

"So the entire relationship was a ruse?" I asked once Kylie had given me all the details. "I've seen the pictures online of the two of them at various events in London. Charity events, galas, and other high-exposure affairs that Damian wouldn't normally attend. They actually looked…happy."

"Even back then, I don't think either of them was pretending," Kylie said in a softer voice. "I think they were already crazy about each other, even though those appearances were planned as a diversion tactic."

I raked a frustrated hand through my hair. "I still don't understand why he didn't just tell her the truth. That he had an identical twin, and none of those actions were his."

"He'd planned to confess right after your mom's gala," she informed me. "Unfortunately, she discovered you in the bedroom with a woman who wasn't her before he got that chance. In a bed that Damian had used for the beginning of their stay in London, so it wasn't a stretch for her to assume you were Damian."

My mind flashed back to that exact moment, and I tried to brush away the horrified, betrayed expression I'd seen on Nicole's face.

I also remembered what had happened only moments later, when Damian had looked at me with nothing but disgust. That was the second I'd realized that my identical twin despised me for what I'd done and always would.

I'd gone too far, and I'd known it that night.

"I can't change what happened," I said tightly.

"Would you have changed it if you could have?" she asked.

"Bloody hell! Of course, I would. Do you really think I *wanted* to hurt my brother or Nicole?"

"Then maybe you should call all of your family and apologize," she suggested.

"I think it's rather late for that," I replied irritably.

"It's never too late. They love you, Dylan. They just don't like your behavior," she said quietly. "Do you really blame them for that?"

I slammed a hand down on the granite. "No! Do you really think I like the fact that I made my brother choose between Nicole and me? In my opinion, he made the right choice when he decided Nicole was more important than his twin brother."

"He was angry, and rightfully so," she said with a sigh. "But that doesn't mean that he won't get over it. They were just words, after all. It's not like you attacked Nicole. You broke her heart, but Damian mended it."

Easy for her to say. Kylie hadn't seen the look of contempt and revulsion in Damian's eyes that night.

I *had* seen it, and I'd hated it.

I would have rather Damian had slugged me rather than look at me like a total stranger that he abhorred.

"You don't know Damian," I said brusquely. "And you sure as hell don't know me. I don't need advice from someone who has probably never had an unhappy moment since she was born."

She was way too upbeat.

Too naïve.

Too idealistic.

What in the hell could she understand about a cynical bastard like me?

I added, "Keep your opinions to yourself. You know nothing about me, Kylie, or why I'm such a prick. I don't want to talk to my family or anyone else for that matter. I just want everyone to leave me alone."

I ignored the disappointed look in her beautiful hazel eyes as I turned to leave the kitchen.

"I may understand more than you think," she called after me.

I kept walking until I hit the stairs.

There was no possible way she could comprehend my actions when I rarely knew what I was doing myself most of the time.

CHAPTER 3

Kylie

F OR THE NEXT several days, I actually saw very little of Dylan, but his routine was always the same.

He got up early, used the home gym, and then left the house until he arrived home in the afternoon.

At first, I'd been tempted to follow him to make sure he wasn't doing anything outrageous, but he always arrived home completely sober every day. Since there hadn't been any breaking news about his antics, something had told me to give him his space.

In the afternoon, he disappeared into his home office and didn't surface until the evening.

He'd generally order out for dinner, and eventually headed up to his bedroom after reading in the evening or taking a swim in the pool.

It wasn't like it was difficult for the two of us to avoid each other since there was plenty of room in the ginormous mansion to put some distance between us.

I got up early every morning to do some yoga and meditation. There was a sundeck outside of the pool room that was a perfect space outdoors for my usual routine.

After that, I spent most of my day working in the office I'd made for myself in my suite of rooms.

My evenings were the same as they were in Newport Beach.

I'd done the grocery shopping, so I cooked myself some dinner, took Jake out for a long walk, and read a book or watched some television in one of the many entertainment areas of the mansion.

I had to admit that my stay in Beverly Hills wasn't exactly what I'd expected.

No orgies to stop.

No wild behavior.

We co-existed in the same large space with very little interaction.

It's been five days, and it doesn't seem like Dylan is likely to invite a harem into his house.

I stirred the marinara sauce I was making for dinner and put some water on to boil for the noodles.

Was it possible that I really *didn't* need to be here at all, and that Dylan had been telling the truth about changing his ways?

That was unlikely, right?

Why would he suddenly stop behaving like a jerk?

And what was he doing when he went out for the better part of the day?

Rather than harassing me, Dylan basically tried to ignore my existence. No more propositions or rude comments, either.

The few brief interactions between us had been short, abrupt, and matter-of-fact.

Part of me was relieved, but I was also…intrigued.

I had no idea what made Dylan Lancaster tick or why he seemed more regimented and serious than I'd expected.

I guess I'd thought that he'd piss away his days sleeping and spend his nights partying and indulging himself in every imaginable way.

But he didn't.

Which made me curious about how he was spending his time.

I had no doubt he was working in his home office. The few times I'd caught a conversation when I was passing by his office door, he'd sounded like he was discussing business.

Damian had said that Dylan was totally uninvolved in Lancaster International, but that didn't appear to be the case now.

I was startled when the object of my thoughts suddenly appeared in the kitchen.

I watched from my place at the stove while he started to search for something in the drawers.

He was dressed casually in a pair of dark jeans and a jade T-shirt that hugged his muscular body and matched his mesmerizing eyes.

I had to stifle a sigh as my eyes roamed over him.

Dylan Lancaster was hot, and even though I didn't like him, it was hard not to notice a guy who was physical perfection.

His features were still drawn and somewhat harsh, but that slightly edgy part of him did nothing to lessen his appeal.

"Do you need some help?" I asked politely.

"No," he said gruffly. "I was looking for a menu, but I can look something up online."

As he turned to leave, that should have been the end of our discussion.

Leave it, Kylie. Don't do it. Everything has been just fine without any discussion between the two of you.

"It's spaghetti night," I told him. "If you don't want to order out, I have plenty if you want to join me."

Dammit! I wanted to kick myself for opening my mouth. Now, why had I felt compelled to offer him *that*?

I took in a deep breath as he stopped short near the entrance to the kitchen.

Oh hell, I knew why I'd done it.

There was something about Dylan that drew my empathy, whether I wanted to feel it or not.

Maybe it was the occasional despair or loneliness I could sense whenever he was close.

Yeah, he *was* a jerk, but I couldn't help but think that there was more to Dylan than just his defensive exterior.

"Smells good," he said as he turned around. "You sure you don't mind?"

"Not at all," I said as I reached for the noodles in the cupboard. "Do you like garlic bread with your pasta? I already made some salad, and I have some tiramisu for dessert. Not homemade, though. It came from the bakery."

Okay, Kylie. You're rambling just a little too much here.

I had no idea why I was so nervous, but dealing with Dylan felt a little bit like trying to wrangle an ornery bear.

"I'm good with whatever you have," he said. "Since I'm not cooking, I can hardly be picky, and I do like any kind of bread with pasta. Can I help?"

Okay, so that offer was a surprise. "No. I'm good. There's really nothing else to do."

"Then I guess I showed up at the right time," he said drily. "In time to eat without any tasks left to be done. That's rather brilliant."

I laughed. "I'm sure you didn't plan it that way."

"I didn't," he answered. "But it sounds like me."

Once the noodles were done, I made both of us a plate and put the salad on the kitchen table.

Dylan got us both a bottled water and sat down across from me.

"How was your day?" I asked as we started to eat, hoping he might tell me what he did when he wasn't at home.

"It sucked. Yours?" he responded politely.

I decided not to push him. "Being a partner is a lot different from being a director. Nicole might not have known a lot about the PR business, but since she was a corporate attorney, some of this business stuff was a snap for her. But I really don't want to bother her right now. I'm...struggling a little."

I'd hesitated to admit any of my weaknesses to Dylan because it could end up being used as ammunition in the future.

I might be willing to share my food with him, but I still didn't trust him.

He was silent as he took a few gulps of water. As he put the bottle down, he said, "I have a few business skills. I could probably help you."

I nearly choked on a sip of my water.

A few business skills?

"I think your advisory fees would be a little too pricy for me," I said lightly.

"Not at all," he replied. "Right now, I'll work for food since I'm getting bored with the same takeout places every night."

I eyed him for any evidence that he was playing with me. Yes, I'd definitely do anything to pick his brain, but I had no idea whether or not he was sincere.

He was one of the best businessmen in the world, so it was hard to believe he was serious. After all, he didn't like me, and he didn't want me here. So why was he offering to help me?

"Do I get credit if the desserts come from the bakery? I'm not exactly Betty Crocker," I said warily, trying to figure out what his game was right now.

He shrugged. "I'll let you know as soon as you let me try that tiramisu."

Dammit! His expression was so guarded that I still couldn't figure him out.

I gave up and just asked. "Are you messing with me, Dylan, or are you really willing to answer some business questions for me?"

He looked up, and our gazes locked.

The dead look in those beautiful green eyes was gone, but that old saying about the eyes being the window to the soul didn't apply to Dylan Lancaster.

That window was definitely nailed closed in his case, but I didn't see any animosity.

"I'm willing if you are," he said hoarsely. "And I was joking about the tiramisu. I'll stop by your office tomorrow when I get home. Or I'll come up after we're done eating if it's urgent."

I shook my head. "It's nothing that has to be done right now. Tomorrow is fine."

"Good," he answered. "Now tell me what's on the menu for the rest of the week. I don't think I've eaten this well in a long time."

I looked at his plate and noticed that he'd already emptied it.

Judging by the way he'd devoured the food, I didn't think he was messing with me about the fact that he'd enjoyed his dinner.

"Stir fry? Quiche? Mushroom chicken and rice? I have no idea what you like," I told him.

I had to believe he was serious, but I was still handling this situation with some caution.

"They all sound good," he said. "I don't expect you to go out of your way. Whatever you normally make for yourself is fine."

"There's more spaghetti if you want it," I offered.

"I'll get it," he said as he picked up his plate. "Finish your own food."

I picked up my fork and started to eat, wondering if Dylan and I had just come to some kind of truce.

Or if it was just the beginning of some kind of twisted game for him.

As I started to eat, I was guessing I'd find out exactly what his real intentions were soon enough.

CHAPTER 4

Dylan

"THOSE ARE JUST a few things I see that could help your bottom line. I thought I'd mention them, even though you didn't ask for my advice on that," I told Kylie the next afternoon.

She swiveled her office chair around to face me. "Thank you. I honestly didn't mean to take up so much of your time. I just meant to ask you a few things about the profit and loss, but I appreciate the advice. I can implement so many of the things you suggested that I never thought about before."

"Glad I could help," I replied, realizing that I was actually sincere about that comment. "You already knew what you were doing. I think all you needed was a second opinion."

Kylie actually had a savvy business mind, and she absorbed information like a sponge. All she'd really required was some guidance.

She smiled, and her entire face lit up.

Fuck! It had been a long time since anyone had looked at me as though they actually...liked me.

And I wasn't quite sure what to do with that.

She's grateful, which is entirely different from her actually being fond of me.

It wouldn't do for me to start thinking that she didn't mind my company.

The problem was, I was actually getting used to *her* being around.

Granted, we didn't speak often, but just hearing another person moving around in the house was better than total silence.

I wasn't about to say that I *liked* her pathetic canine, but I didn't *dislike* it when he sought me out and decided he'd grace me with his presence.

Jake was fairly unobtrusive once a person got past the fact that he tended to snore rather loudly at times.

"Right then," I said. "If that's all you need, I'll just pop down to my own office."

There was no need to ruminate over whether or not Kylie could tolerate being in my presence any longer.

"Dylan?" she said in a questioning tone.

I didn't rise from my chair as I replied, "Did you need something else?"

She shook her head. "No. I just wanted to ask why you're helping me. You don't want me here, yet you spent a couple of hours of your time working on my business with me. I thought you hated me."

How was I supposed to answer that? I hardly knew why I was doing it myself. "I don't hate you, Kylie."

Well, at least *that* was true. I hated myself far more than I disliked her.

Honestly, I didn't dislike her presence at all anymore.

True, she was annoyingly blunt and outspoken, but it wasn't like everything she'd said about me *wasn't* true.

I'd just resented the fact that she'd pointed out every single one of my failings.

She sighed. "I don't hate you, either, Dylan. Maybe I do detest some of your actions, but I really don't know you."

I shrugged. "Is there really a difference between those two things? It's nearly impossible to like someone when they've acted like a complete idiot."

"It depends," she mused. "Sometimes a person can act out of character for a lot of different reasons."

"You don't want to know me. Take my word on that one. That would mean going to a very dark place," I cautioned her.

She tilted her head in an adorable way that completely fascinated me, like she was trying to figure me out and find some kind of redeeming qualities in my personality.

I should probably let her know that she was looking for something good in the wrong place.

"Are you really all that scary?" she asked. "I've actually been in a pretty dark place myself, so I'm not really afraid of the dark anymore."

She had no idea how terrifying my mind could be, and I highly doubted that she actually knew what pitch-black actually looked like.

Kylie was all light and happiness.

And I was doom and gloom.

Those two things rarely mixed well.

"I'm totally fucked up," I confessed. "I would think you would have recognized that by now. I think it's best if we avoid getting personal with each other."

"Why?" she asked.

"Why what?" I growled, hoping to get her to stop asking questions.

"Why are you fucked up? It's not like you've always been that way. Something caused it, right?"

I folded my arms across my chest and glared at her, but she just kept looking at me like she expected some kind of answer.

Jesus! Was there no way to intimidate this woman into silence?

Strangely, I couldn't force myself to say anything that would hurt her feelings.

Fuck knew I wanted to because that was my normal response when I wanted to push someone away.

"Why is this something you need to know?" I asked in a surly tone. "We had a deal. Food for business advice. Period."

She shrugged. "I have no idea. Maybe I want to get to know you. Maybe I want to try to understand."

"You can't," I said shortly.

She folded her arms over her chest, refusing to back down. "Try me," she challenged.

"Only if you're willing to get naked," I replied, knowing it irritated her when I went down that road.

Not that I *didn't* want to get her naked, but the only reason I'd actually voiced that desire out loud was to make her back off.

She lifted a brow. "That's not going to work anymore. I know you're just saying that to change the subject. You don't mean it."

Maybe so, but I certainly wouldn't argue if she changed her mind and decided she wanted to have this discussion without our clothes on.

I'd been attracted to her from the moment she'd walked through my door, and my desire to fuck her until she begged for mercy was unrelenting.

My comment might have been a desperate attempt to distract her, but the actual urge to get her into my bed was very, very real.

"Try me," I repeated her challenge. "I'd be more than happy to show you just how much I mean it."

She rolled her eyes. "God, why do you have to be so stubborn? I'm just trying to get to know you."

I found myself trying not to smile over *that one* since I'd never met a more obstinate female in my entire life. "Did it ever occur to you that I may not want you to know me?"

I watched as a moment of uncertainty crossed her face, and I instantly hated myself for putting it there.

After all of the reasons I'd given her to hate me, why in the hell was she still trying to get to know me?

"Okay. Forget it," she said tersely. "I thought you might want somebody to talk to, but you obviously prefer to just be a jerk."

Her disappointment roiled in my gut and compelled me to speak. "I don't *want* to be this way. Do you really think I like being the man I've become? You're right. I wasn't always this way, and I want to change so damn bad that I spend hours in different types of therapy every day to try to get my life back. I started the day I got back from England. Am I feeling somewhat better? Yes. Do I feel like I can find the man I used to be? No. But I'll keep on trying until my head is on straight again. I don't know exactly what that looks like, but it has to be a hell of a lot better than the last two years."

I was breathing heavily by the time I'd finished, still astonished that I'd blurted all that out at all.

Kylie looked taken aback, but her tone was warm as she asked, "Do you want to talk about your therapy?"

"No," I grunted.

"Do you want to talk about what happened two years ago?" she tried again.

"Hell, no," I answered. "I spend enough time talking about it every day. I'm not good at spilling my inner emotions until I want to vomit."

"Okay," she agreed readily. "Then I'll tell you about what happened to me and why I'm not afraid of the dark anymore—if you want to hear it."

Hell, anything was preferable to me having to talk about myself, and I was curious. "Tell me."

"I'll make it short because it was a long time ago," she started. "I got married when I was nineteen, and my husband was a control freak who criticized every single thing I did or said. In his mind, nothing about me was attractive. My red hair was ugly. My freckles were hideous. I ate way too much for a female. My breasts were too small. My ass was too big. My cooking was inedible. I was stupid, ridiculous, and…well, you get the idea, right? I wanted to work, but he wanted me to stay at home. I turned myself inside out to please him. I dyed my hair. I tried every freckle cream on the market and covered what was left with makeup, but I still wasn't enough, no matter how hard I tried. But I stayed for over three years, until I found out he was fucking someone else. I finally got up the courage to file for divorce, and when he found out, he beat me up so badly that I could hardly get off the floor."

I was so astounded and furious that any man would treat Kylie that way that I could hear my heart pounding in my ears.

"Jesus! Kylie—"

She held up a hand. "Let me finish. I don't talk about this part of my life anymore, so I just want to get through it. Kevin was a police officer, and when he went to work after leaving me bloody and bruised, he was shot and killed in a gang-related incident. He was a hero, and there was nothing I could do except sit through the funeral services in heavy makeup to hide the marks he'd left. Through that entire service, I didn't know if I was mourning or if I hated him, and that confusion didn't go away, even after he was buried. My whole marriage, his death, and my confusion messed with my head pretty badly. So I drank a lot to escape because I went through a really bad period of anxiety and depression. I had panic attacks that I couldn't control. It was a difficult climb out once I'd gone down that rabbit hole. My mind went to plenty of dark places, but it wasn't until I sat in my apartment one night with a bottle of pills, wondering if I should just put myself out of my misery, that I finally realized I needed help. That I couldn't do it alone."

"What happened?" I asked gruffly, my brain still trying to take in all that had occurred with a woman who seemed like nothing but light and happiness.

"I was fucked up, too, but I got treatment," she said with a sigh. "And I slowly pieced my life back together. I told Nicole and Macy, and my friends supported me through the treatment. So yes, I do know what it feels like to be in a really bad place, which is why I could probably sense that you might need someone to talk to right now. I'm not sure what happened to you, Dylan, but I'm glad you're getting help. Just know that if you ever do feel like talking, I kind of know what you're going through. If you don't want to talk about that, maybe you could just use someone to hang out with and have some fun. That's probably something else you could use, too."

I clenched my fists, and I felt physically sick that any man had laid a hand on Kylie, and had subjected her to years of making her feel like she wasn't good enough. "If he wasn't already dead, I think I'd be willing to kill him for you," I rasped.

She shot me a melancholy smile and rose from her chair. "That part of my life is over, thank God. I know that maybe you don't feel like it will happen, but you'll come out the other side of this, Dylan. I'm going to go start our dinner."

My entire body was humming with so many emotions that it was almost painful. After being numb and detached for so long, it was difficult to sort them all out.

I wanted to say *something* to her, anything to let her know that I appreciated her sharing a story that painful just to help me.

"Kylie?"

She turned back to me as she reached the door. "Yes."

I struggled to try to utter the things I wanted to say, but in the end, all I could say was, "Thanks."

She shot me an encouraging smile and nodded as she said, "Don't be late for dinner. It's mushroom chicken and rice night."

After she left the room, I sat there for a few minutes, still thinking about everything she'd said.

Jesus! How had someone so young coped with so damn much, and then finally made that choice to get help instead of taking the easiest way out?

Looking at her now, no one would ever know that she wasn't always the bold, outspoken woman she was today.

And the fact that she still had so much warmth, compassion, and empathy was pretty remarkable, too.

I finally stood up and shook my head. As I went toward my office, I had to admit to myself that not only was Kylie Hart stunningly beautiful, but she was also the most incredible, determined woman I'd ever met.

CHAPTER 5

Kylie

"I SHOULD HAVE BEEN able to win that match," Dylan grumbled a week later as he devoured the dinner I'd cooked. "I guess I'm out of practice."

I snorted after I'd swallowed a bite of my own stir-fry dish. "Don't be a sore loser, Lancaster," I teased. "Did it ever occur to you that I might just be a better tennis player than you are?"

"Never. Not until I lost," he answered. "I grew up playing the game. I had private lessons when I was younger, and I rarely missed an opportunity to get out on the courts as an adult, either. Maybe that's why it surprised me so much that I actually lost the match to you tonight. I didn't lose very often, but now I am willing to admit that you're an amazing player and that you are better than I am. Where in the hell did you learn to play like that?"

I smiled as I took in his disgruntled expression from my seat at the kitchen table across from him.

I wasn't sure if Dylan didn't like losing at all or if it was especially painful because it was a female who had kicked his ass.

My guess was the former. After nearly two weeks of observation, I'd noticed that Dylan didn't like to be bested at anything. Period. And I'd never heard him imply that a woman couldn't do anything just as well as a man could.

He was stubborn, which seemed to be a trait we shared, but at least he could admit that he'd been beaten, however grudging that admission might be.

Truthfully, Dylan had surprised *me,* too, because he was a much better tennis player than I'd expected. He'd had me on my toes to eke out my win.

I shrugged as I took a sip of my water and then put my glass down again. "I've been playing since I was a kid," I explained. "By the time I was fifteen, I had enough points accumulated to qualify for the Junior Grand Slam tournaments."

He looked at me and lifted a brow. "Then you were beyond just a good player. What happened at the tournaments?"

I sighed and pushed the rest of my food around on my plate absently. "My dad didn't have the money to send me, but I managed to raise enough money and get sponsorship for the Australian Open. Unfortunately, I got the flu the day before I was supposed to leave for Australia. Two weeks later, I started getting some weird symptoms after I'd gotten over the flu bug. Long story short, I was put out of commission for over a year with Guillain-Barre syndrome. I missed the entire year of competitions, and I was never as good as I was before that happened."

"What exactly is Guillain-Barre syndrome? I've heard of it because Mum once had a friend who had it," Dylan admitted. "I just don't know much about it. From what I understand, it's pretty rare, right?"

I explained that it was pretty poorly understood *why* anyone developed the disease but that it usually happened after an infection or virus. And that it was a rare disorder where the immune system started attacking the nerves.

"I spent two months in intensive care, and a total of three months in the hospital," I told him. "After that, it was months of occupational therapy and physical therapy just to get back to normal again. I lost all my physical conditioning and my mojo," I ended in a lighter tone.

"And your sponsorship, I suppose," Dylan mused.

I nodded. "There are no second chances for a girl who couldn't really afford to play competitive tennis in the first place. I'd hoped for a tennis scholarship at UCLA, but I was almost seventeen by the time I could actually play again, and I wasn't good enough. Plus, I was going to age out of juniors. I was disappointed about everything back then, but I'm not complaining. I'm happy with being a partner in an up-and-coming PR agency now. I love what I do, and I love the team at ACM."

Every word I told Dylan was true. Maybe my heart *had* been broken over my lost opportunities as a teenager, but I was truly content with the way my life had turned out now.

"Really?" he asked in a doubtful tone. "You'd rather be doing what you're doing now than be a filthy rich tennis pro?"

"Who's to say I would have been successful as a pro?" I questioned him. "All it takes is one injury to end a career. Or some off days during some big tournaments. Nothing was guaranteed. So yeah, I'd rather be where I am than a washed-up pro player who couldn't reach elite status. It takes a lot of skill and some luck to be at the very top, but just because I didn't go that direction, that doesn't mean I don't still love to play. Really, I have the best of both worlds, right? I can still enjoy some matches and have a career I love at the same time."

He shook his head as he went back to eating. "Bloody hell, woman, are you always nauseatingly positive? That has to get completely exhausting."

Since I was used to his cynical sarcasm, I just smirked as I started to polish off my food. "I'm a glass-half-full kind of person now, I guess. Life is short. What's the point of lamenting over what could have been if I'm happy with my life?"

Dylan Lancaster had been hardened by his own life experiences, and he hadn't taken me up on my offer to talk about what happened two years ago, so there was still so much I didn't know about him.

However, he did talk about his treatment occasionally, and it sounded pretty intense, which was probably why he seemed to look less haunted and slightly more upbeat every day.

Most of the time, we just hung out together because he seemed to prefer having company rather than being alone.

Honestly, he wasn't a difficult man to get along with when I was able to cut through all the bullshit.

Yeah, he'd been an asshole in the past, and he was still derisive. But there was something inside me that could sense the pain he was trying to hide beneath that somewhat jaded exterior.

I just wasn't entirely sure how to reach that tormented Dylan Lancaster that he didn't want anyone to see.

"So what happened after your destroyed hopes and dreams of a scholarship and a tennis career?" he asked.

"I got a job during my last year of high school as a hostess in a restaurant. I went full-time after I graduated and took community college classes at night. My dad moved to Florida once I was eighteen. He met someone, and wanted to relocate, so I had to support myself," I shared as I pushed my empty plate aside. "You know what happened after that. I got married way too young, gave up my job, and stopped taking classes."

"So, did you eventually make it through college?"

"Later," I said. "I finished a marketing degree once I came to work for Nicole's mom at ACM. She hired me once I got my shit together after Kevin died and supported me in finishing my degree. Nobody else would have adjusted my hours to fit my school schedule like she did. She was an incredible woman, and Nicole is so much like her."

I'd already told Dylan a lot about Nic since he seemed curious about the woman his twin brother was going to marry.

I got up and started to clear the dishes.

He rose and grabbed his own plate and dirty utensils.

Since I'd started to cook for him, he'd gotten into a routine of helping me clean up every night. Plus, he still checked in with me every day to see if I needed any help with my business before he went to his office.

I was actually making out like a bandit on the whole exchange deal we'd made.

I got Dylan Lancaster as a consultant when I needed him, *and* he helped me clean up the kitchen.

I wasn't about to tell him that his negotiation skills had been lacking in that particular agreement.

Dylan followed me to the dishwasher, and I took his plate.

He leaned his fine ass against the kitchen counter right next to me and crossed his arms over his muscular chest while he waited for me to start the dishwasher.

God, he was close, so close that I could smell that masculine, earthy, unique fragrance that clung to him wherever he went.

I breathed in, drowning in the tantalizing scent, even as I chastised myself for being so attracted to Dylan Lancaster.

All the man had to do was stand next to me, let me breathe him in, and I was ready to get him naked.

What in hell is wrong with me? He's still the guy who hurt my best friend and participated in orgies.

I let out a long breath. The problem was, there were some qualities about Dylan that were really...likeable.

He didn't drink himself into oblivion anymore, so I never saw that asshole side of him. I was even starting to believe that those orgy pictures had been a setup.

He was highly intelligent, and he wasn't letting that brilliant mind go to waste anymore. Dylan was in his home office every day, working with his Los Angeles team on some projects he said that he and Damian had put aside because there were too many complications involved.

He seemed to hate being totally idle.

I also had to admit that Dylan had a droll, ironic sense of humor that amused me most of the time.

It would be impossible to deny that Dylan Lancaster was physically the hottest guy I'd ever seen.

And God, he smelled good.

How could my female hormones not rejoice every damn time he got close to me?

If he'd stayed a complete jerk, it might have been easy to ignore how attractive he was, but really, he *wasn't* a complete asshole.

He was bossy sometimes, but there were thoughtful things that Dylan did that kept him from being overbearing.

He went faithfully to his therapy every day, even though I knew there were times that he was emotionally spent.

Dylan was trying, even though he apparently hated every moment of those sessions, and I had to give him credit for his tenacity.

I couldn't help but laugh every time he told me that he'd had to talk about his emotions until he was nauseous and knackered.

I was slowly getting used to some of his British lingo, so I didn't have to ask him every time he used a word I hadn't heard before.

Honestly, his sexy British accent was just one more thing that made the man almost irresistible.

After closing the dishwasher and turning it on, I rotated until I was face-to-face with Dylan.

I wasn't sure where it came from, but there it was, that raw, tormented look in his gorgeous eyes that made my heart ache for him. It appeared and disappeared out of the blue, and regardless of everything he'd done in the past, it got to me.

Dammit! I couldn't help myself.

"Are you okay?" I asked quietly.

He was visibly startled like he'd needed to give himself a shake to come out of some deep thoughts.

He nodded. "I'm good. I was just wondering why you're still so damn nice to me after all the things I've done in the past. My own family doesn't even want to talk to me."

My heart started to race, and my fingers twitched with the desire to smooth my palm over his tight, slightly scruffy jawline.

I had to force myself not to touch him as I said, "Almost everyone deserves a second chance, Dylan. Just don't screw this one up. You did hurt my best friend, so another chance isn't in the cards for the two of us, even though she's ecstatically happy now. I can be your friend or your worst enemy. Your choice."

My voice was firm, but I held my breath as I waited for his reply.

I was surprised by how much I wanted Dylan to gain my trust, and vice versa.

His full, delicious lips turned up just a little at the corners as he drawled, "It seems I have little choice after the way you kicked my ass on the tennis court earlier. You're pretty fearsome, regardless of your slight stature, so I wouldn't dare disappoint you."

I released my breath. I knew that was the biggest bone Dylan was going to toss me for now, but it was enough.

I smiled at him as I said breathlessly, "Good choice."

CHAPTER 6

Kylie

"OH. MY. GOD," I crooned right after I closed my eyes and swallowed. "I think I'm having a foodgasm. This is one of the most delicious things I've ever eaten."

Dylan actually chuckled a little from across the table in the swanky restaurant. "Feel free to continue. Watching you would be highly…entertaining."

I opened my eyes and smiled at him as I said, "Thank you for this. I'm a Southern California native, but I've never eaten here. Everything has been amazing."

Dylan had offered to take me out to dinner several times over the last week, so I didn't feel like I always needed to cook, but I'd brushed him off until this evening.

I'd been feeling drained after spending the entire day trying to put out a couple of fires at ACM, and dinner out had sounded like a great idea.

I just hadn't planned on ending up at one of the most iconic Michelin-star restaurants in the Los Angeles area.

I'd balked because it was a little rich for my blood, not to mention the fact that this restaurant was always booked and hard to eat at on short notice.

Dylan had overridden my arguments, telling me he ate here occasionally and would have no problem getting a reservation. He'd also jokingly said he thought he could handle the bill.

After reminding myself that he was one of the richest guys in the world, it hadn't been hard to convince me to eat here.

I'd always wanted to but had never had the opportunity or the spare cash when I'd lived in Los Angeles. Now that I probably could afford the occasional expensive dinner splurge, I hadn't really thought about it since there were plenty of good restaurants in Newport Beach.

Dylan shrugged. "You cook all the time. It's not as though I'm doing you a big favor."

I shook my head. "You don't understand. This is a big deal to me, Dylan. I'm a regular person who doesn't get to do something like this very often."

Luckily, I'd had the handy *little black dress* that I'd been able to accessorize with some cute costume jewelry.

My heart had skipped a beat when Dylan had strolled down the stairs, looking good enough to eat in a pair of what looked like custom slacks and a light-blue polo shirt that fit his massive body perfectly.

Of course, I'd quickly reminded myself that we weren't going on…a date.

It was just two friends having a meal together.

"You did look like you were enjoying your Spanish octopus," Dylan teased. "I'm actually impressed by how much food you can manage to put into such a small body."

I flushed a little. I *had* eaten a lot, and I wasn't even close to finished with my rich cream, pastry, and strawberry dessert that was sitting in front of me. "I'm sorry. I've never been a dainty eater. I'm a foodie."

"Don't you dare apologize," he demanded gruffly. "It's refreshing to see a woman who isn't afraid to eat. I'll have them bring you everything on the menu if you want it. I like it, and I definitely love the way you enjoy your food."

I lifted a brow. "Then prepare to be refreshed while I demolish the rest of this dessert."

I was relieved that he didn't seem the least bit repulsed by my hearty appetite. My deceased husband used to be horrified that I could actually outeat most men.

"I'm ready to be delighted with your food orgasm," he joked. "It would be the most action I've seen in a long time."

I snorted before I took another bite, savored it, and then swallowed. "Please. Says the man who indulges in wild orgies."

I didn't really have to guard my words since the enclosed patio was empty, something Dylan had probably arranged when he'd made the reservations, so we'd have some privacy.

I almost regretted giving him a hard time when his eyes darkened as he said grimly, "I told you that was a setup. I *was* drugged, Kylie, and I'm certain I never shagged any of those women. I suspect they were actually after Damian, so they could tarnish his image with a company that prides itself on being squeaky clean. There were a lot of competitors who desperately wanted the deal he eventually made, despite that debacle. They got me instead of Damian because I was idiotic enough to let it happen."

"Maybe so," I mused before I took a sip of my French press coffee. "But please don't try to tell me you've had a long dry spell. It hasn't been long since the incident with Nicole."

I actually did believe him regarding the orgy situation, but he was no angel.

His laser-sharp gaze locked onto mine, and my heart somersaulted inside my chest. His eyes were dark and earnest as he asked, "Do you really want the truth?"

Jesus! Did I really want to know about Dylan's promiscuous sex life?

No. No, I really didn't, but I was compelled to nod slowly because the moment was so damn intense.

His eyes never left mine as he said, "Most of the time, I was too thoroughly pissed to even care about a shag. It's difficult to have sex when you can't stand up straight. The orgy situation was a setup, and my behavior at the gala was a mistake. I would have walked away before all the clothing came off. I was impaired enough that I wouldn't have been able to get to the finish line." He lifted a hand before I could speak. "I'm not saying that I've ever been averse to great sex, and I sure as hell didn't turn it down as much as Damian did. I'm just saying that it hasn't happened over the last two years, despite the evidence that would make you think just the opposite."

God, was what he saying actually…true? Given his logic, it was highly possible. A guy really *couldn't* perform all that well when he was wasted.

Something flip-flopped inside my belly as I looked into a pair of gorgeous eyes that looked like they desperately wanted to convince me that he was sincere.

It was the most earnest and personal thing Dylan had ever divulged, and I wasn't about to discourage him. So I tried to lighten the mood. "So, are you saying that you were all promises and no action at the gala?"

He looked relieved as he shot back, "That doesn't mean I'm not able to completely satisfy under other circumstances."

Oh, Lord. I'm very sure you can, Mr. Sexy.

49

I swore that Dylan Lancaster oozed an aura of hot, sweaty, multiple orgasm sex with every single breath he took.

That slight edginess that surrounded him did emanate a hint of danger, but it was the kind of peril a woman wanted to fall into and wallow in rather than avoid.

My forehead was dotted with perspiration just thinking about him naked and showing me just how orgasmic a little bit of riskiness could be.

I broke eye contact and took another bite of my dessert as I squeezed my thighs together before I finally squeaked, "I have no doubt you're totally capable."

That's putting it mildly!

"I'm more than just capable," he said, sounding slightly offended. "What about you? Is there a guy in Newport Beach who's missing you in his bed?"

I nearly choked on my torte.

He'd asked that intimate question so casually that he sounded like he was talking about the weather.

I took a sip of water before I was forced to cough, and then replied, "It's been a little bit of a dry spell for me, too," I said vaguely, not willing to tell Dylan that it had been way too long for me.

Even longer than his two-year dry spell.

I was far from being a prude. I liked good sex. Loved it. It had just been a few years since I'd met a guy who inspired enough lust in me that I couldn't go without it.

He grinned mischievously, a full-fledged, sexy smile that I'd never seen on his face before, and it wrecked me.

I melted into a puddle on the concrete patio floor as he said, "Then I guess we can commiserate. Although it's very hard to believe that you aren't fighting off a tosser or two every single day."

I smiled because he looked disgruntled about the idea of me needing to supposedly beat off guys off me all the time. "This is

Southern California, Dylan. There are stunningly beautiful women everywhere. It's not like men are panting to have sex with *me*. You've seen me without makeup in the morning. I'm a redheaded, freckle-faced female who is incredibly average compared to a lot of women in this part of the country." I was in good physical shape, but I was otherwise pretty boring. Even my breast size was mediocre.

"You don't actually believe that nonsense, do you?" he asked, sounding slightly confused. "Makeup or no makeup, you're absolutely ravishing, Kylie. You must know that. Your hair color is stunning, and your freckles, which are barely noticeable, are completely adorable."

I snorted. "Women want to be sexy, not adorable."

Secretly, I loved the way he was protesting my comment about being extremely ordinary, but I knew he was probably trying to be polite.

"Your freckles are extraordinarily sexy," he clarified.

I laughed as I pushed my empty plate away. "Now I know you're crazy. I'm not a girlie girl. I never have been. I was teased a lot in school because of my bright-red hair, my freckles, and my tendency to be more athletic than ultra-feminine."

"I'm not sure how any man could miss that you're female," he answered in a husky voice. "I certainly can't seem to ignore it."

My eyes flew to his face, only to find nothing except sincerity in his expression. And there was something else in his eyes as they swept over me...

Something hot and immensely sensual.

Stop it, Kylie. Stop this right now!

Oh, God, I didn't need to start believing that Dylan Lancaster actually found *me* attractive.

Not when I knew he could be surrounded by a bevy of goddesses if that's what he wanted.

I wasn't ugly.

I wasn't hypercritical about my appearance.

However, I was realistic, and I wasn't the type of woman a man like Dylan Lancaster would lust after.

He was a billionaire, highly sophisticated, and educated, and most men like him would end up with a hot, blonde supermodel in their beds.

Possibly more than one.

Not some ordinary, redheaded, working-class woman like me.

I shrugged. "I'm actually okay with who I am now," I told him honestly.

Maybe I hadn't been the grand prize winner in the gene pool lottery, but I liked the woman underneath my average exterior most of the time. That was more important, and something I couldn't have said a decade ago.

Oh, hell, maybe I *still* couldn't take a compliment well.

It had taken me a long time to get over the beating my confidence had taken during my marriage, and I wasn't used to men as slick as Dylan when it came to outrageous compliments.

"Thanks for saying such nice things, though," I added, not wanting him to think his kindness went unnoticed.

"Kylie?" he queried.

"Yes?"

"I didn't tell you that you're beautiful just to be polite. I meant every word I said."

Flustered, I grabbed my coffee as a distraction and tried like hell to change the subject.

CHAPTER 7

Dylan

I WATCHED AS KYLIE executed a graceful dive into the swimming pool, still wondering how even a small part of her still believed what her departed husband had said about her appearance.

And it was quite obvious that somewhere inside her, she *was* still listening to that bastard's words, even long after he was dead.

She'd been so young and so impressionable that it wasn't surprising some of what he'd said had stuck with her, even though those statements had been absolutely false.

She was so far removed from *average* that the idea that she *wasn't* gorgeous was preposterous.

Everything about Kylie Hart was extraordinary, yet she didn't seem to recognize how beautiful and unique she was, even when a man tried to let her know the truth.

Yes, she could be annoyingly positive, but even that attribute was part of her charm. Even a prick like me could eventually be swayed by her enthusiasm for life. Over the last three weeks, I'd begun to find her upbeat demeanor less and less irritating, and ultimately, I'd started to gravitate toward her warmth.

God, I actually *wanted* to be close to her now, even though I knew the way I felt was fucking dangerous.

It was too damn hard to be miserable when she was around, and I'd made it a habit to be as despondent as humanly possible.

I'd known she was trouble from the moment she'd barged through my door three weeks ago. I just hadn't realized that I'd become addicted to disruption.

Every time I turned around, if she wasn't there, I wished she would bother me with her presence.

I wasn't sure exactly when it had happened, but at some point in the last three weeks, I'd begun to like being around the smart-mouthed, intelligent, and utterly gorgeous female.

At first, I'd thought that I was just tired of being alone with my gloomy thoughts, but I soon realized I didn't just want some company.

I wanted *her*.

Just *her.*

Any other woman would have probably left after a day or two of putting up with my surly behavior.

Kylie Hart took it all in stride, and had slowly drawn me to her with her unshakeable optimism and cock-hardening smile.

She was like a mystery I wanted to solve, and my fascination with this woman increased every damn day.

She didn't talk much about her childhood, but she obviously hadn't had an easy life since she had no memories of her mother, who had died when Kylie was very young. It didn't sound like she was very close to her father, either, or that he'd given her much support.

Her dreams of being a pro tennis player had been completely shattered.

Her husband had been a bastard who had tried to crush her.

So, how in the hell was it possible for her to still be so damn...happy?

I wanted to understand this contrary female, but I simply...didn't.

I'd never met someone who could practice yoga and meditate for close to an hour in the morning for peace and serenity, and then went out on a tennis court a little later and competed fiercely like a champion.

I found it utterly captivating that there were so many sides to Kylie, and still so many more details about her that I wanted to discover.

What I *didn't* like was the fact that my dick seemed just as intrigued with by her as my brain.

My previously dormant libido had suddenly sprung to life the second I'd seen this gorgeous redhead, and I wasn't quite certain whether to curse her for that or be grateful that my cock could still get this damn hard.

Every. Single. Moment. She. Was. Nearby.

Fuck! I hadn't wanted a woman this much in...well, it had been a long time.

Yet she questions her ability to turn the head of every man who sees her?

Granted, in all other ways, she did seem totally confident and completely secure in her abilities. The only thing she seemed unsure of was her capability to captivate a man until he was half out of his mind with lust, which I could easily assure her that she bloody well had in abundance.

I wasn't sure why it bothered me that Kylie had any self-doubt at all, but for some damn reason, I wanted to protect her from *any* vulnerability. Especially since I knew someone had once hurt her so badly.

Really, like I was her knight in shining armor? *Hardly.* But there was something about Kylie that made me *want* to be that man she came to when she needed someone. And yes, I wished she'd start looking at me with lust in those beautiful eyes instead of just compassion.

What in the bloody hell is wrong with me? Have I completely lost my mind?

It's not like I'd done a brilliant job of taking care of myself for the last two years, much less been worthy of the job of protector for anyone else.

I frowned as I felt something wet on the back of my hand. I looked down to see Kylie's dog with his nose against my skin, nudging against it as a physical prompt.

"Worthless hound," I grumbled as I reached down and pulled Jake up and onto my lounger.

I might as well get *that* over with since the hound wouldn't be happy until he was sprawled out on the cushion beside me.

In the dog's defense, it was the most comfortable spot to be since the entire pool area was nothing but cement.

"At least you aren't worthless *and* an idiot," I muttered as he found his place beside my leg and dropped his head onto my thigh. "Although, you do realize that there's a completely empty chair about a meter away from this one, right?"

The canine simply looked up at me with a pair of adoring brown eyes that made me reach out and pet his head absently.

Jake didn't seem to care whether or not I *wanted* to be his human friend. For some unknown reason, he was apparently fond of me, even though I'd certainly never encouraged that affection.

The irritating mongrel had never really given me a choice as to whether or not I *wanted* to fully embrace his canine devotion. He gave it, and simply expected me to accept it.

"Are you having a one-sided conversation with Jake again?" Kylie teased as she surfaced at the side of the pool closest to my lounger.

I watched as she swiped the fiery hair from her eyes and rested her arms on the cement.

Her beautiful hazel eyes were dancing with amusement as she looked up at me, and my cock responded with unabashed enthusiasm to the only female who'd stirred its interest in a very long time.

"It's not exactly one-sided," I argued. "He always looks like he understands me perfectly."

She shot me a knowing smile that made my gut ache as she said, "Admit it. You like him, and he likes you. You're actually lucky. Jake is very picky about who he chooses to trust."

"Lucky me," I drawled sarcastically, even though I was willingly giving the hound the affection he'd demanded.

"Aren't you going to come in?" she asked curiously.

My eyes devoured her slick, wet form. She was wearing a very modest one-piece turquoise swimsuit, but it didn't matter. It wasn't difficult to look at the light, creamy skin that was exposed and imagine the rest.

Fuck! I'd been doing that exact thing for three weeks straight now.

Kylie was athletically fit, but she had curves in all the right places, and I was well aware of every single one of them.

Maybe I had teased her about her flame-colored hair in the beginning, but there wasn't a single second when I didn't want to bury my hands in those glorious locks and see if they were as soft and sensual as they looked.

After that, I wanted to bury my cock inside her shapely body because I already *knew* that shagging this woman would be a far better distraction than anything else I'd tried in the past.

Yes, I did usually join her in the pool in the evening, but it was probably safer and easier to fantasize from a place where I could see her and not be within groping distance.

Christ! I respected Kylie, and I liked her, but our budding friendship didn't stop me from wanting her naked, coming, and screaming my name while it was happening.

I was fairly certain that *nothing* was going to kill that particular recurrent fantasy anytime soon.

In fact, the need to touch her grew every single day until I now felt half mad because of that obsession.

"I don't think so," I finally answered. "I'm knackered."

Yes, that *was* a complete falsehood, but I could hardly tell her that if I got any closer to her, I wasn't going to be able to stop myself from reaching out and taking what I wanted.

Would that really be a bad thing? Kylie did say she had a dry spell, too. What if we could both get something out of a good shag or two...or a dozen?

If she was any other woman I was attracted to, I might be tempted, but she was Kylie, and unfortunately for me, I wanted her to trust me just as much as I wanted her in my bed.

Currently, those two desires were at war with each other, but in the end, I knew it was more important to prove that I wasn't a worthless tosser.

I had no fucking idea *why* that mattered so much. Possibly because it had been a long time since anyone had looked at me like she did.

Kylie had given me the benefit of the doubt when no one else had, and it made me want to be a better man.

Because she treated me like a man who was worthy of respect until I proved otherwise.

Because she wanted to know more about me when no one else gave a damn.

Because she actually seemed to like me, even though I could be a major prick.

Because she hadn't given up on me, even when I'd tried to chase her away.

I didn't know exactly what I wanted from Kylie Hart, but I did know I wanted more than just a fuck.

"You're tired?" she asked, sounding concerned. "Are you okay, Dylan?"

And just like that, she was suddenly worried about *me*, even though I didn't really deserve her kindness.

I realized that I wasn't worthy of her tenderness, but damned if I didn't want to completely drown in her warmth.

I almost craved it like a drug because I'd been cold and numb for so damn long.

Staying detached is far safer.

I hesitated, but for once, I ignored that dire warning voice in my head.

"I'm fine. Really," I assured her. "Too much rich food tonight at the restaurant. I'm feeling rather lazy."

She studied me with those expressive eyes beneath her long lashes. "Okay, but I ate a lot more than you did. If something is wrong, and you want to talk, I'm here, Dylan."

It was almost like I could feel one more of my defensive walls that guarded my emotions come tumbling down.

Her offer was completely guileless and heartfelt. Kylie was offering to be there for me without wanting a single thing back for doing it. *That* was exactly the kind of thing she did that really got to me.

That I really didn't understand.

I'd never had a female reach out to me like that and not want *something.*

Remember the past.

Remember that things aren't always as they seem.

Regardless of that warning voice in my brain, it took everything I had not to take her up on her offer and just let her in.

CHAPTER 8

Kylie

"I REALLY MISS OUR Friday night dates," my friend Macy said with a sigh as we FaceTimed a week later. "I got a coffee a few days ago and went down to the beach, but it wasn't the same without you and Nic."

I smiled at her image as I sat cross-legged on my enormous bed. "I miss those days when we were all together, too," I confessed. "I'm excited that we'll be together again in just a few weeks for the wedding, though. I've always wanted to go to England."

"I was there when I was younger, but I can't wait to be there with both you and Nic," she murmured. "I just wish I could stay longer and that we could fly over there together, but things are crazy at the sanctuary right now. I have to leave a few days after you. I don't think Karma is going to last much longer."

My heart squeezed as I looked at the sadness in Macy's eyes.

As an exotic animal veterinarian, my friend had lost more than one animal she'd become attached to, but she and Karma, an aging Bengal tiger, had a strange affinity for each other that most people would probably never understand.

I ached for her because I knew losing Karma was going to be particularly devastating.

"I'm so sorry," I said softly. "You've done everything you possibly can for her, Macy. You know that, right?"

She nodded. "I know. She's twenty years old, and the cancer is starting to cause her pain. If it gets to be too much, she'll have to be euthanized, so she doesn't suffer. It's not like I can expect her to live forever, but the sanctuary won't be the same without her."

Macy wouldn't be the same without her feline friend, either, but she'd get through it. Nic and I would make sure she did.

"So tell me how things are going with Dylan Lancaster," Macy insisted in a lighter tone. "Have you mentioned to Nic that you're actually living with her future brother-in-law?"

It was obvious that Macy didn't want to dwell on her sorrow, so I let that subject go. "Not yet," I confessed. "I'm actually hoping to surprise her by bringing Dylan home for the wedding. I think that would mean a lot to both Damian and Nic, especially if Dylan is ready to make amends."

Macy raised a brow. "Is he ready?"

"I think so," I said without much certainty. "I know he hates what he's done to Damian. I'm just not sure I can get him to confront his fear of being rejected."

I knew damn well that his worry about an unwelcome reception to his presence at Nic and Damian's wedding was the only thing stopping Dylan from going.

In some ways, I was convinced that he was actually trying to make sure he didn't do anything to upset the happy couple.

After spending a month with Dylan, I couldn't say he was exactly candid, but he'd said enough to make me believe that he didn't want to miss his identical twin's wedding. However, he didn't want to screw up the blissful occasion, either.

"Not going isn't going to make them happy," Macy said adamantly. "I've talked to Nic. She wants Dylan to show up. Damian is insisting it doesn't matter whether Dylan comes to the wedding or not, but Nic said it's all bravado."

I nodded. "I agree. Damian and Dylan were really close. For an event as important as his wedding, I know Damian wants his twin brother there."

"Can you convince him to go, Kylie? Do you think he's wised-up enough not to make a scene if he does?"

"He won't," I said firmly. "Dylan has come a long way from where he was when he upset Nic in England. He knows he was an asshole. He doesn't drink until he's intoxicated anymore. I just don't think he knows exactly how to face Damian or how to make things better with his family."

Although I told Macy everything about myself, Dylan's counseling was private, so I wasn't comfortable sharing something that personal about him with someone he'd never met.

Macy's eyes widened a little as she stared at me. "You almost sound like you're actually starting to like him."

"Guilty," I replied. "Dylan Lancaster is arrogant, obscenely wealthy, and probably one of the most stubborn men I've ever met. But he's also a hard guy not to like now that he's done being a jerk. He can be really nice when he wants to be, and he was only slightly a sore loser after I won every single tennis match we've played so far. The man is wicked intelligent, and he's helped me a lot whenever I go to him for business advice. Being a partner is a lot different than being the director at ACM, and he's making that transition easier for me. I wanted to hate him because of what he did to Nic, but I just...can't."

Macy wiggled her eyebrows. "I'm sure it doesn't hurt to look at somebody as scorching hot as he is every single day. Even though I've never met him, I have seen his half-naked photo. Plus, he looks just like Damian, right?"

I thought about that for a moment before I answered. "Yes, they are identical twins, but they're also...different. I can see how they probably complemented each other in business. Damian is very controlled and methodical, and steady is important in business. Dylan is slick when it comes to handling people, and he's more of a visionary. I think he likes the challenge of newer and riskier projects that could very well pay off much bigger than some of their usual acquisitions."

"So if the two of them don't kill each other over their differences, they're a pretty dynamic team," Macy observed.

"Exactly," I replied. "Each of them has their own strengths. Personality-wise, Dylan seems...edgier, more stubborn, and more cynical. Inside, I think they're both very decent men. It's just a little more obvious in Damian than it is in Dylan."

Dylan Lancaster wasn't an easy man to know, and at times, I still had no idea what he was thinking. But I'd seen his inherent kindness, and I couldn't unsee it, even though he tried extremely hard to hide it.

"I'm glad he's not as bad as we thought he was," Macy said. "But you still haven't commented on what it's like to spend every day with a guy that hot. If you're playing tennis together, you must be on pretty good terms."

She was digging for information in her typical Macy sort of way, but we'd been friends for so long that I knew what she was really asking. "He's ridiculously hot," I admitted. "And yes, I'm attracted to him. How could I *not* be? The guy is physical perfection, and that damn British accent does something to my hormones that I can't explain. Even worse, I actually can't help but like him."

Even more beguiling was the fact that the haunted, dead look in Dylan's eyes had slowly faded and had been replaced with amusement, intelligence, and animation.

It wasn't like I couldn't see or sense that Dylan was still in pain, but at least it wasn't as intense as it had been when I'd first arrived.

"You do realize that he's probably heartbreak waiting to happen, right?" Macy warned. "Maybe he is nice, but we also know he's a player."

I often reminded myself that Dylan was no angel, but I had my doubts that he was really a heartless jerk with women, especially if he hadn't gotten laid in over two years. "No worries," I assured her. "I'm very well aware that he's not boyfriend material, but that doesn't mean I'd mind burning up the sheets with him."

"If you already know that, and he's been that nice to you, then have a fling with him," Macy suggested. "How often do women like us get the chance to get hot and heavy with a drop-dead handsome billionaire? If you're going in with your eyes wide open, and you like him, go for it. Isn't that what we encouraged Nicole to do with Damian?"

"That was different," I sputtered. "It was obvious that Damian was crazy about her. Dylan Lancaster doesn't want me that way. You're insane."

"Of course he's hot for you," Macy said matter-of-factly. "You're a gorgeous redhead with an amazing body, a kind heart, and a fantastic sense of humor. You're also talented and intelligent." In a softer voice, she added, "Kylie, please don't let the things Kevin did and said dictate the way you look at yourself. You're gorgeous, inside and out. If Dylan Lancaster doesn't want to fuck you, there's something wrong with *him,* but I have a feeling that you're mistaken. Look, I know there have been guys since Kevin. Even a few boyfriends have come and gone, but when was the last time that you've really felt completely wanted?"

Tears sprang to my eyes as I looked at Macy's worried expression. "Like you should talk about that?" I scolded her.

"We aren't talking about me right now," she reminded me. "We're talking about you."

If it hadn't been for her and Nicole, I wasn't sure how I would have survived all the things I'd gone through years ago.

We'd all stayed extremely close, even though we'd been separated by geography.

"I'm fine with who I am," I insisted.

"I know that," she conceded. "But that doesn't mean you aren't carrying just a little bit of baggage. Or maybe even a midsize suitcase. You deserve a guy who really sees you, Kylie, even if it doesn't last forever. Does Dylan treat you with respect? Has he been good to you while you've been there? It sounds like he's been there to help you with ACM when you needed it."

I nodded as I impatiently swiped a tear from my cheek. "The first few days were rocky, but after that, he's been amazing. He offers to take me out to dinner almost every night, so I don't feel like I have to cook for both of us, which is ridiculous. And he helps me a lot every time I have a business meltdown. He comes and hangs out with me every single night at the pool like he just enjoys being with me for no good reason at all. I've never heard an unkind word from him since those first few days when we were trying to figure each other out. The crazy man even tried to tell me I was beautiful. God, even Jake adores him and follows him around like a puppy. I can tell he still has his own baggage, Macy, but he doesn't take it out on me. I guess we've developed this bizarre kind of friendship that's hard to explain."

"Don't tell me that you don't think that there's chemistry there on both sides, Kylie," Macy insisted. "Any man who can't stay away from you like that definitely wants to do you. I think you should take a chance and see what it feels like to have a guy who really sees you, even if it doesn't last forever. It could change your whole perception of yourself. No offense, but I don't think one single guy in your life has ever seen your worth."

I took a deep breath and let it out slowly. She was probably right. No, I *knew* she was right. "I'm an asshole magnet," I agreed grimly.

I'd had a few hot one-nighters when I was younger, and I'd done the club scene after Kevin had died, but that was all they'd been since I hadn't been ready for anything else.

Once I'd been ready to date again seriously, I just hadn't connected with anyone who really gave a damn about me.

Eventually, I'd accepted the fact that I might end up alone, and I was okay with that—most of the time.

"No, you are *not* an asshole magnet," Macy said adamantly. "The problem is, you just don't feel like you deserve something better. Can you honestly say that you make any attempts to meet nicer guys anymore?"

I shook my head slowly. "I think I gave up."

"Because you didn't want to be hurt anymore. I get it," Macy said quietly. "Honestly, I don't think there's anything wrong with a woman being independent and single if that's what she wants. Lord knows I've been happier that way. But that doesn't mean you have to cut yourself off from any intimate relationships for the rest of your life, Kylie. I'm not saying to go out there, risk your heart, and fall for Dylan Lancaster. I just think it might not hurt to see what it feels like to spend some time with somebody who appreciates you."

"When he tries to tell me I'm beautiful, I think he's just being… nice," I protested.

Macy snorted. "Guys don't say that kind of thing just to be nice, Kylie. Maybe you should stop making your own assumptions and really listen to him next time. Be objective. You might be surprised by what you discover when he looks at you."

I changed the subject, and we started talking about Nicole's wedding, our dresses, and the arrangements we'd been making for Nic's bachelorette day.

"At least think about what I said," Macy requested right before we hung up.

"I will," I promised before we ended our call.

I tossed my cell on the bed, trying to figure out if a few of Dylan's heated looks that I'd written off as my imagination were actually...real.

I rose from the bed and shut that train of thought down in a hurry.

If I started getting too objective, I was afraid I might have to admit that the smoking hot chemistry I imagined between Dylan and I was a lot more than just a fantasy.

CHAPTER 9

Dylan

"DYLAN. WAKE UP! It's just a dream. Wake up!"

The sound of Kylie's voice, and the gentle way she was shaking my shoulder, caused my eyes to fly open right in the middle of a loud, raw shout.

I shot up into a sitting position, fighting for air, feeling like I was suffocating.

"What the fuck!" I groaned as I rubbed my hands over my face.

The nightmares always started and ended the same way, but it had been a while since I'd had one, so this one had felt pretty intense.

Real.

And just as horrifying as it had always been.

"I think you were having a nightmare," Kylie said softly. "I could hear you yelling from my room. Are you okay?"

My hands came away from my face damp with sweat, and my chest was heaving like I'd just run a marathon.

Kylie continued to stroke her fingers through my damp hair, trying to calm me.

The whole scene was familiar, yet it was different, too.

The nightmare was the same one I'd have over and over for two years, but I usually woke up in the darkness…alone.

It usually took me a while to separate the dream from reality, but I was completely aware of what happened almost right away this time.

Maybe because Kylie had been here to yank me back into the real world.

"Same dream every time," I rasped. "It always turns out the same, even though I try to save her in that dream. I can never get to her in time to stop her."

The room wasn't completely dark. I could see Kylie's form in the dim light from the moon that was filtering through the shutters.

Instinctively, I reached for her, pulled her into my lap, and cradled her warm body against mine, like I needed to protect her from…something.

Or possibly just to make sure she was…safe.

For some strange reason, holding her helped, especially when she wrapped her arms around my neck and clung to me like she wanted to keep on comforting me until she knew that I was going to be all right.

"I know it feels real," she crooned softly. "But it was only a really bad dream, Dylan."

"Actually, it wasn't," I told her. "It's what happened that day, except, in the end, I realize it's a dream. I try to save her, but never succeed. I can never make things right, Kylie. No matter how I try. I never realize I'm dreaming in time to keep her from dying."

My body shuddered as my breathing started to slow down, and the fear that had gripped me in that nightmare began to subside.

"I'm here, Dylan," she whispered. "I won't let you go."

I squeezed her tightly as the horror of that entire day, and the days after, started to race through my mind.

That brief period of time had changed my life irrevocably, and I'd never seen the man I'd been before that particular day ever again.

"I shouldn't have argued with her. If she hadn't taken off angry, it never would have happened," I confessed in a raw, tormented voice.

"Don't, Dylan," Kylie said. "Don't let guilt suck you dry."

"You don't understand," I growled and buried my face into her hair. "It *was* my fault. It should never have happened."

I should never have pushed so hard on Charlotte that day.

I should never have just given up and let her run away.

I *could* have saved her, but I could never have imagined the repercussions of my inaction until it was all over.

"Breathe," Kylie whispered as she stroked the hair at the nape of my neck. "Just breathe, Dylan. Everything will be okay."

Fuck! She had no idea how much I wanted to believe her.

I didn't want to have these dreams anymore.

I didn't want to remember.

I didn't want the guilt of knowing if things had gone differently, Charlotte wouldn't be dead.

I didn't want to keep reliving the same five or ten seconds that had happened over two years ago, over and over again.

I definitely didn't want to worry about closing my eyes again at night, because I didn't want to have this damn nightmare anymore.

"Everything was getting better because of my treatment," I told Kylie, my voice raspy and desperate. "I stopped seeing the same damn horror scene over and over, all day, every day. I haven't had that dream for several weeks. Why. Fucking. Now."

"Breathe," she said a little more firmly. "Slow and deep until you clear your head. Focus on just your breath."

She took my hand and put it on her belly, signaling that she wanted me to follow her own breaths as she kept on belly breathing deeply and melted into me.

For some strange reason, the pattern of how the air moved in and out of my body did start to mimic hers.

Like I needed something to hang on to, I pressed my hand gently into her abdomen and silently began breathing at the same tempo as the gentle rise and fall of her stomach.

In.

Out.

In.

Out.

All I focused on was the rhythm of those slow, deep breaths, and eventually, my mind cleared, and those images faded away.

All I felt was Kylie.

"Feeling better?" she questioned after a minute or two.

"Yes," I grumbled as I took my hand from her stomach and buried it into her hair. "But don't move."

The feel of her soft, warm body against mine was the only thing that was keeping me sane at the moment. I was drowning in the faint, alluring floral scent of her hair, and I wasn't about to give up the only thing I needed right now, which was this. *Her.* The rightness of the two of us in exactly this position.

"I'm not going anywhere," she said in a soothing voice. "You said you dream about the same day over and over. What happened? Why is one day so significant to you?"

My first instinct was to ignore her question because that was what I always did.

I didn't talk about that day unless I was in a therapy session.

Ever.

But tonight, things were different.

It was Kylie asking, and she was the one person I couldn't just brush off anymore.

She was here.

She was real.

She cared whether or not I was okay, and her worry was so intense that I could feel it.

She'd shared her own demons that she'd conquered.

And she was the only person I really trusted when I felt this damn raw.

She deserved to know the truth.

It was just a hellish story to tell, for me.

I took a deep breath, my mind perfectly clear as I made the decision to finally tell someone who wasn't involved in my current treatment the truth.

It was time, and once I'd told Kylie, maybe it would be easier to tell everyone else.

She was a soft place to fall for me, and I knew she wouldn't judge. I trusted her.

I cleared my throat. "It was the day I had a disagreement with my pregnant fiancée, causing her to flee in anger. She was hit by a bus not more than three or four meters away from me. I watched her die right in front of me, and there wasn't a damn thing I could do to save her."

CHAPTER 10

Kylie

I WASN'T EXACTLY SURE what I'd expected Dylan to say, but what he'd just uttered was way more horrific than I could have imagined.

I closed my eyes and took a deep breath. *Jesus!* No wonder he was carrying so much pain.

The only thing Damian or Nic knew was that Dylan had tragically lost a woman he was apparently dating.

So really, nobody had ever known the real depth of his loss.

Until...now.

He'd lost a woman he loved, *and* his unborn child in the blink of an eye.

Unfortunately, he also seemed willing to shoulder all the burden for what happened, even though it was an accident, and it wasn't his fault at all.

"I know this means nothing, but I'm so sorry, Dylan," I said as tears of sorrow for him flowed down my face. "It was an accident. It certainly wasn't your fault, but I can only imagine how hard it was to lose someone you loved and your child in a matter of seconds. So you kept seeing her death over and over again in your head?"

God, how horrific would that be? To witness something like that once, and then not be able to stop seeing it happen countless times every day.

"Yes. I couldn't seem to get it out of my brain that if she hadn't impulsively decided to cross that street because she was angry, the accident never would have happened. She would have still been talking to me at the curb, and that bus would have rounded that corner without killing her," he said grimly as he shifted positions.

Dylan fell back onto the pillow and wrapped his arms around me as I sprawled next to him, one leg still over his thigh and my head cradled on his shoulder.

He kept his hand buried in my unruly hair like he needed that connection, and I wasn't about to complain. If he was willing to relive the most painful moments of his life, I wanted nothing more than to give him any kind of support I could.

"You can't torture yourself with those kinds of thoughts, Dylan. It will drive you completely insane. All of the 'what ifs' are easy in hindsight, but they could go on forever and ever. What if the bus had left just a little sooner or seconds later? What if that impulsive move had happened ten seconds later? What if, what if, what if. It was out of your control. You couldn't have prevented it from happening any more than you could have controlled Charlotte's actions. Grieve your fiancée and your child for as long as you need to, but you have to let go of the guilt. It will eat you alive," I said solemnly.

"I think it already has, don't you?" he asked. "It's not just the guilt. It was a pretty gruesome scene, and I relived those five or ten seconds of watching her die. For a while, it was like a loop in my head that just kept playing over and over. The sound of her body hitting the bus, the blood, and the way her broken body flew through the air before she landed on top of another vehicle. She was unrecognizable, Kylie. And I wish I could have just grieved, but it was a little more complicated than that."

My heart was breaking, and I couldn't imagine being that close to someone I loved and watching them die in front of my eyes. Even worse, Dylan had been seeing his child die right along with Charlotte.

I have to focus on him right now. I can't get distracted. He needs me to be the rational one while he's telling this story.

"What do you mean?" I asked, trying to keep my voice calm.

"Her death left a lot of unanswered questions that I'll never know the answers to, and that was probably one of the hardest things to accept," he said in raspy baritone. "Long story."

"I have nothing but time," I replied, knowing that Dylan really needed to tell someone what really happened. "Tell me the whole story," I coaxed gently.

"It's not pretty," he warned.

"It doesn't matter. Just talk."

"Charlotte's family and mine have known each other for a long time. We were acquainted as children, and we ran in the same circles. I was four years older than she was, so we lost touch when I went to university, and we didn't reconnect until a few months before her accident. I was attracted to her, but I never intended to have sex with her right after that charity event. It just…happened. She seemed determined to seduce me, and as you've pointed out before, I'm no innocent. We started dating after that. Two months later, she told me she was pregnant."

"So you were in love, and you asked her to marry you," I surmised.

"I was shocked at first," he explained. "I never had unprotected sex, even with Charlotte, but I wasn't naïve enough to think it *couldn't* happen. I'm not convinced I was actually in love with her, but I cared about her, and I told myself that those feelings would eventually grow over time. After the initial surprise wore off, I was honestly excited about being a father. The whole idea grew on me until I was determined to make things work with Charlotte. She told me she wanted to get married as soon as possible, before she started to really show, and I agreed a few days after she told me she was expecting. Everything happened so fast that I didn't get a chance to tell my family before Charlotte died. Mum knew that Charlotte and I had reconnected and that we'd gone out a few times, but that's all she knew. Damian and Leo were out of the country, so I was waiting until they came back so I could share the news with all of them together and in person. Leo and Damian were both coming back that week, and Mum already had a family dinner planned."

"So no one knew she was pregnant except you? Or that you were engaged?" I asked.

"Only her parents, and I told Charlotte to ask them not to share the information until I could tell my own family. I was planning on taking Charlotte to that family dinner to break the news. I thought it was rather unusual that she wasn't in any hurry to actually get her engagement ring, even though I'd proposed that shopping trip several times. Once the decision to get married was made, and she told her parents, it was like she lost interest in any of the details."

"It's definitely odd," I mused.

"It gets even stranger," he said drily. "Charlotte moved in with me two days before her accident. Everything seemed to be going well until the night before her death, when I mentioned that I wanted to be with her for her first ultrasound. She was only ten weeks, so I knew I couldn't find out the sex, but she said they wanted to pin down her due date. I was anxious to get my first glimpse of my child and hear his or her heartbeat. By that time, I was a very enthusiastic future father. However, Charlotte made it very clear she didn't want me there, even when I told her I wanted to be with her the night before. That's what we were arguing about on the street the next day. She didn't want me there. She didn't want me to drive her. She didn't want a car or driver. All she wanted was to leave, and for me to go away. Nothing she was doing made any sense, but I followed her down the street, trying to reason with her."

"Oh, my God," I said, astonished. "Why wouldn't she want you there? It's a special moment most women would want to share with the father of their child."

"She was adamant. At first, I refused to take *no* for an answer. She got so upset that I finally decided to let her go. She was pregnant, and she was already angry because I'd been so insistent. Giving up was the biggest mistake I ever made," he said hoarsely. "She stepped right in front of that bus because she was so eager to get away from me."

I choked back a sob as I visualized how broken Dylan must have been, standing on the curb, as Charlotte died right in front of him, from an impulsive action. "It was not your fault," I repeated. "Did you eventually tell your family about the baby?"

"No. I couldn't talk about it. I could hardly put two words together. They didn't even know I was there when the accident happened. Mum went to the funeral because she was acquainted with the family, but all I could do was sit next to her and try to keep my sanity. I couldn't get my thoughts straight or my head together. A few days later, I told Damian I had to disappear for a while because I had to pull myself together, and he made that happen. I still couldn't talk about it. All I wanted to do was escape," he finished in a raw, husky voice.

"I think that's probably a normal reaction," I told him gently. "I'm sure you were still in shock."

"I was completely broken," he confessed. "I tried to find anything that would stop those same five or ten seconds from running over and over in my mind. I rarely slept because of the nightmares, and when I was awake, alcohol was the only thing that erased those memories for a short time. The doctors at the treatment center said it was post-traumatic stress, but I honestly thought I was a lunatic because I felt so detached from everything and everyone. I didn't care about anything. They said that was a coping mechanism, and all of the other symptoms, like feeling paralyzed by fear sometimes, and reliving the moment over and over, were classic symptoms."

"So because it was untreated, it just got worse?" I questioned.

"It became my own personal hell," he said. "But after almost a year of that, I wanted to tell Damian and the rest of my family. I wanted help. I wanted my fucking life back. That's when this probably should have ended and the point when I should have gotten help. I was having some moments of clarity. Instead, before I could reach out to my family, I found out some other things that sent me over the edge again."

A shiver ran down my spine, and I already knew whatever he was going to say wasn't good. "What?"

"I went back to my flat because I knew I had to pack up Charlotte's personal belongings and send them to her parents. While I was packing, I found her journals, and I decided to read the most recent one because I really wanted to know why she was so upset that day. I found out the child she was carrying wasn't mine. The results of a paternity test were tucked in her journal, and I wasn't the father. I also discovered that she was having a long-running affair with one of her professors that she met while she was at university. He was twenty years older than her, and he was never going to leave his wife and children. So she'd decided that marrying me would allow her to keep seeing him, and have a father for her child, too. She didn't want me at the ultrasound because she was further along than she told me. She conceived before we even met up again, so her due date wouldn't match. That journal solved the mystery of why she didn't want me with her that day but opened the door to questions I'll never get answered."

"Oh, my God," I said, my voice horrified. "How could she do something like that?"

"Looking back now, I'm sure she was desperate because she didn't want to be a single mother. Her parents definitely wouldn't have approved, and she was still dependent on them financially. She was obsessed with this guy. It was obvious when I read her journal. I don't think she cared how her actions affected anyone else, as long as she found a father for that child, and a husband. Our reunion was pretty damn convenient. The due date wouldn't be too far off. Only about three weeks or so different, so I guess she thought she could pull it off, and maybe she would have if I'd never asked many questions during her pregnancy. Me wanting to be completely involved in her pregnancy, and with the child I thought was mine, didn't suit her plans well at all," he said, his tone a little bitter.

I was speechless for a minute before I said, "That's completely insane and totally selfish."

How could any woman use a guy like that? God, Dylan had been embracing fatherhood, and she'd been lying to him the entire time.

Dylan had gone through hell not once, but twice.

"I have to admit that I felt like an idiot because I'd fallen for the whole story without asking very many questions in the beginning," he admitted. "Probably because she was an old family friend. It never occurred to me to even ask for a paternity test myself. I guess I wasn't as smart as the real father."

"Really, why would you?" I asked. "I know you're a great catch and all, but if she socialized in your same circles, her family obviously had money. There was no reason it ever would have crossed your mind that she might be trying to trap you into marriage and attempting to pass off another man's child as yours."

"I was confused. Fuck! I didn't want to tell anyone because she was already dead, and everyone was still grieving. The truth would have only hurt Charlotte's family, and it wasn't like the biological father was going to go and tell them the truth. I couldn't figure out how I was supposed to feel. How was it possible to be so devastated over someone's death and fucking hate them at the same time?" he rumbled, sounding disgusted with himself.

Tears streamed down my cheeks as I turned onto my side and stroked my fingers through his coarse hair. "For you, that child *was yours*, Dylan. Don't you understand? That loss was still there, even though you eventually found out the truth. I also think it's really hard to heal when your feelings are that conflicted. The extreme sorrow is there, but you wonder if you ever really knew that person you cared about the way you should have."

God, and didn't I know what that felt like?

The pain of betrayal.

The confusion.

The grief.

The way something like that screwed up a person's head.

Dylan reached for my hand and threaded our fingers together like he needed something or someone to ground him. "All I wanted was to disappear again after that, but I found myself escaping into more alcohol and distractions instead. I wasn't coping. I was a fucking coward."

"No, you weren't," I said, needing to defend his brokenness. "You were lost, Dylan, and I completely understand. Jesus! That had to be like living in a nightmare all the time. And just when you were finally brave enough to face what had happened by trying to find professional help, closure, and by reaching out to your family so you could get through it, you got kicked down again."

"I completely detached at that point," he confessed. "I didn't know how to feel, so I preferred to feel absolutely nothing. I couldn't tell my family what had happened. I was too far down that rabbit hole by then. It was like I just drifted until what happened at the gala. When I really realized how much I'd hurt Damian, I knew I had to get help, or I'd lose my entire family."

I choked on a sob. I'd always sensed his pain, but I'd never known the depth of his despair and hopelessness. "God, you didn't deserve any of what happened to you, Dylan, and no one is going to blame you for not being able to cope. It would have completely crushed anyone."

"It changed me, Kylie. I'm not the man I was before," he admitted huskily. "I might never be that man again."

"You're still the same guy," I reassured him. "Maybe you're a little warier and not as trusting as you used to be, but you don't change a lifetime of being one person to become another from a tragic experience. You survived, Dylan, and you are getting your life back. Don't let this nightmare get to you. You've come too far for that."

"I doubt you'd let me get away with it if I did, sweetheart," he said in a lighter tone.

I smiled into the darkness. He sounded weary but not defeated. "Go back to sleep. It's late."

His arms tightened around my waist. "Don't move. Stay here with me, Kylie."

He was exhausted.

I was tired.

I saw no reason not to stay exactly where I was at the moment.

His breathing became deeper and slower as he finally slept.

I fell asleep moments later, lulled into slumber by the calming, reassuring, and steady beat of his heart.

CHAPTER 11

Dylan

"Y OU'RE BRITISH, AND you don't drink tea?" Kylie asked in a curious voice while I brewed myself a cup of coffee the next morning as she sat at the kitchen table. I'd been damn disappointed when I'd woken up alone this morning, but once I'd glanced at the clock, I'd known why.

Kylie was an early riser, and I'd slept way later than I usually did. I'd been surprised that after I'd kept her awake last night after my nightmare, she'd still rose early for yoga and meditation.

I shot her an amused look. "Bite your tongue, woman. It's almost impossible to be British and not drink tea. We Brits believe a good cup of tea solves almost any problem. I think we assume it has some kind of magical properties."

She smiled, and something inside my chest twisted when she did.

I'd been a little afraid that after spilling my guts the night before, that Kylie might look at me differently.

She didn't.

Her smile was exactly the same as it had been the day before, and those full, plump lips were still begging me to kiss her.

Well, they were in *my mind*, anyway.

"But I've only seen you drink coffee," she observed.

I shrugged. "I'm not a tea maximalist. I like coffee, too, and there isn't a decent brew in the house right now."

"Why didn't you say something," she scolded. "I could have picked some up from the grocery store while I was shopping."

"I'm not overly fond of grocery store tea in America," I replied as I picked up my coffee and wandered over to the table.

"So you're a tea snob, just like Damian," she said teasingly.

"No one is pickier about their tea than Damian," I informed her. "I'm perfectly happy with any decent quality black tea that doesn't taste like piss water. Can I ask what in the world you're doing?"

I leaned against the island and watched as she tied off strips of material dangling from a larger piece spread out on the table.

She paused and looked up at me. "I'm just putting together some no-sew comfort blankets for the dogs and cats at the animal shelter. My friend, Macy, is a veterinarian, and she volunteers there. Jake had one that somebody else made when I brought him home after adopting him, and it really seemed to lessen his anxiety. Since the shelter never seems to get enough, I try to make some of them every month to donate. I don't sew, but these are easy enough for me to handle."

I watched her as she went back to work, deftly tying off knots as she explained how the entire blanket was basically just two pieces of back-to-back fleece, bound together by artful cuts and tied strips of material.

"Wouldn't it be easier just to buy them?" I asked.

"These are special," she answered. "The big fringes make it a combination of a toy, and a blanket, too. Jake never took to any other blanket the way he did this one. He carried it everywhere for a while."

I looked at the hound that was spread out on the tile, his snout close to Kylie's foot.

Obviously, that canine and I had one thing in common: we both liked to be close enough to Kylie to drink in her alluring scent.

"I can help," I offered. "It looks easy enough."

It was Saturday morning. I didn't want Kylie to spend her entire day making blankets, even if it was for a good cause.

It was highly possible that my motives were a little bit selfish, too. If I helped, I'd be able to stay in the kitchen without looking like I was stalking her.

"You'd really sit here and do that?" she asked with a surprised expression.

I shrugged. "Why not?"

"Because you're Dylan Lancaster. No offense intended at all, but I doubt most billionaire moguls make dog blankets."

I grinned. "Probably because we're all rich enough to buy an unlimited number of blankets or hire somebody else to make them. But I am available, my morning is currently free, and there's nowhere else I'd rather be right now."

She sighed. "That's so sweet, but I'm on my last one. I'm out of material until I order some or get to a fabric store."

Sweet? I balked a little at the idea that Kylie thought I was *sweet*.

If she only knew what I was thinking most of the time when I looked at her, I doubted she'd feel the same way.

"So, what are your plans for the day?" I asked, hoping she had none.

I wanted to spend the day with her, do something to thank her for being there for me last night.

She nibbled on her bottom lip for a moment before she answered, "I should probably head back to Newport and check on my place.

There isn't much I can't do remotely for work now that I'm a partner. Someone is in the office doing my old job, but I haven't been back home for a month." Kylie paused before adding, "Honestly, I don't think there's really any reason I need to be here anymore, Dylan. You don't need a babysitter. I trust you."

I wasn't sure how those words could be devastating and transcendent at the same time, but she'd managed it.

Yes, I'd wanted to hear her say that she trusted me. In fact, gaining her trust had been my obsession for a month now. However, the *leaving* part of her conversation nearly gutted me. "I definitely don't need a babysitter," I agreed. "So stay just because you want to then. It's only two weeks until you leave for England."

"Why?" she asked. "There's no reason for me to be here, and if I don't have to work remotely, I could be in the office every day. There really is no reason for me to be living here with you."

"There's *every* reason," I said, hating the slightly needy note in my gruff tone. "I *want* you here, Kylie. Every damn moment you've been here with me has been an enormous reprieve from being alone with my own thoughts. I don't think you understand how much your presence here has helped me. I've even gotten somewhat fond of that beast spread out on the kitchen floor." I nodded at Jake. "Don't go. Not...yet."

Damn. It wasn't like I didn't know that I sounded pathetic and that needing Kylie went against everything I'd thought I wanted for the last two years, but right now, none of that mattered.

She stood, folded the blanket, and put it in a vacant chair with several others. "I can stay if you think it helps to have someone around," she agreed. "I just don't want you to feel like you have to put up with me being here all the time. It's not like we couldn't still meet up and talk on the phone. Everything I said when I first got here about this not being your home was complete bullshit. Damian would never do anything to hurt you, and this *is* your home. I respect everything you're doing to get your life back."

"Technically, the place belongs to Lancaster International," I clarified. "And Damian can threaten to cut me off because I gave him power of attorney all he wants. It would never stand if I legally challenged him, but I don't think it will ever come to that. If Damian decided he never wanted to nullify that power of attorney, I'd give up my share of Lancaster before I'd drag my own brother through a lawsuit. I already lost track of how important my family is to me. I don't plan on doing it again. Damian stood by me, even when he probably should have given up on me. I could hardly blame him for finally dumping me after what happened with Nicole."

Kylie moved closer to me as she said, "No guilt, remember? Damian and Nic aren't the types to hold a grudge, and they have no clue what you went through. Give *yourself* a second chance. You deserve it, Dylan."

Without thinking about my actions, I reached out, wrapped my arm around her waist, and pulled her closer, until her ass was against the island. I pinned her in as I put my hands on the counter on each side of her body. "How can you be so bloody certain that I'm actually worthy of starting all over again? I think you're perfectly aware of every asinine thing I've ever done."

My damn heart nearly stopped as she wrapped her arms around my neck, and she answered, "Aside from the orgy photo, I think accusing the prime minister of being a communist was probably one of the most original things you did."

"Bloody hell! How did you find out about that?"

She smirked. "Nic told me. You were drunk. What else can you do but laugh it off? I drank too much tequila once and danced on a table in the middle of a crowded bar. Once I got over the mortification when I was sober, it was kind of amusing. Lord knows that Nicole and Macy never let me forget about it, even though it happened a long time ago."

"Interesting," I said as I wrapped my arms around her waist. "So you have a wild side?"

"I can't party like that anymore. It didn't take me long to realize that tequila and I couldn't be friends."

I hated the thought of Kylie being that lost, at any point in her life, or that she'd ever been in so much pain that she'd tried to drink it away as I had.

I threaded my hand through her hair and tilted her head up. "I wish I'd been there for you back then, sweetheart."

She blinked as those beautiful eyes continued to stay trained on my face, and she stroked a gentle palm over my jaw. "I think I like things exactly the way they are right now."

"Did I ever thank you for what you did last night?" I asked her.

She shook her head. "Not necessary."

My entire being was focused on her and exactly how I was going to let her go without taking exactly what I wanted right now. "I think you're the most beautiful, incredible woman I've ever met," I told her honestly. "Do you have any idea how much I want to kiss you right now? But it's your move this time since I took way too many liberties the first day we met, and I happen to really like my balls intact."

"I have absolutely no desire to knee you in the balls again," she said breathlessly. "But I do want you to kiss me, Dylan."

I didn't hesitate for a single second in case she decided to change her mind.

The second my lips locked with hers, I felt like I'd never get enough.

Yes, I'd wanted her the first time I'd kissed her, but my desire for this woman had amplified to a fevered pitch since that day.

I wanted *her.*

I wanted *Kylie.*

Not just a gorgeous, redheaded stranger who had barged through my front door.

There was nothing mild or tepid about this kind of chemistry, and it had been slowly simmering since the first time I'd laid eyes on her.

Today, it had definitely reached the boiling point.

I explored her mouth with a desperation I'd never experienced before, going back for more every time I told myself to let her breathe.

She was so damn hot and so responsive that I felt like I was losing my damn mind.

"Dylan," she moaned as I finally forced myself to let her catch her breath.

I gripped her hair and pulled her head back so I could taste the soft skin of her neck.

I gripped her ass with my other hand and pulled her hips against my rock-hard erection so there would be no doubt in her mind what she did to me.

Christ! I knew I was losing it, but the second she'd moaned my name like that, I wanted...more.

I wanted her hot, wet, and naked.

I wanted her screaming my name while she came over and over.

"Bloody hell!" I cursed as I raised my head. "You're going to end up making me lose my mind, woman."

There was no angst in my words, and I pulled her body flush with mine, with her head against my chest.

Somehow, I need to slow the fuck down before I scared the hell out of her.

I'd gotten temporarily lost in the feel of her lips, her soft skin, her cock-hardening scent, and her passionate response.

"I guess you actually do find me attractive," she mumbled into my shirt, sounding stunned.

"Jesus! Did you ever doubt that?" I rasped. "It should have been rather obvious from day one."

She pulled back until she could shoot me a sheepish grin. "I guess it's been a while since any guy has found me irresistible or fuckable."

I chuckled. "Then America is full of wankers. You're much better off with an adoring Brit," I assured her. "You've had my cock hard since the first time I saw you, sweetheart."

She raised a brow. "I think there's something seriously wrong with you, Dylan Lancaster."

"Right now, nothing feels wrong to me at all," I bantered as I finally released her.

"You're twisted," she said with a delighted laugh that made my damn chest ache. "Do you want to come with me to Newport?"

"I have a better idea," I told her as a plan formed in my mind. A woman like Kylie deserved a lot more than a fuck on a kitchen counter. I wanted to see her happy, hear her laugh more often. "Would you fancy a weekend on the beach?"

CHAPTER 12

Kylie

"TELL ME YOU'RE joking," Nicole begged as we chatted on the phone. "You're not really with Dylan at that amazing house in Newport Beach that's owned by a Mediterranean prince. I was there once, but only to meet up with Damian, and he didn't tell me exactly who owned that beach house until later."

I'd finally decided it was best to come clean with Nic instead of trying to convince Dylan to come to the wedding as a surprise.

Now that he was doing so much better, I didn't want Damian to agonize over his twin brother any longer than needed.

I also thought it would be more helpful if Dylan could talk to Damian and set things straight, so he wasn't worried about showing up at a wedding where he wasn't wanted.

Maybe if Damian knew that Dylan was starting to become the brother he knew again, he'd be willing to reach out more readily.

"I really am," I assured her. "I'm staying here with Dylan for the weekend. He said his friend is delighted that someone is using it. I have a confession to make, Nic. I've actually been with Dylan for the last month. I was hoping I could keep Dylan out of trouble so you and Damian could have some quiet time together to plan the wedding. It was a longshot, but one of my objectives was also to try to get him to come to the wedding as the brother that Damian loved."

I filled her in on everything that had happened since I'd insisted on staying at the Beverly Hills mansion.

She was quiet until I finished.

Nic's voice was excited as she said, "Oh, my God, Kylie. If Dylan really is recovering, I know it would mean the world to Damian. He can deny that it doesn't matter if his twin brother doesn't come to our wedding all he wants, but he loves Dylan fiercely. He misses him. I can tell. If Dylan isn't here, I think he'll still feel like someone is missing. I just hope Dylan doesn't backslide."

"He won't. I honestly think he'll be doing even better by the time he gets to England. I know what he did to you was horrible, but he isn't that man anymore," I explained. "I've been where he was, and I know what it's like to slide down that rabbit hole. But now that he's finally climbed out of that madness, I know he won't go back. He's a good man, Nic. He's made mistakes, but he didn't fall down that hole in the first place without good reason."

"Did he actually tell you the whole story?" she asked in an astonished voice.

"He did, and it's horrific, Nic, but it's not my story to tell. Just know that there's more to the story than anyone knows, and he's spent a lot of time blaming himself when he shouldn't have. That guilt and grief ate him alive," I said.

I had told Nic about Dylan being in treatment because I thought it was important, but it was up to him how and when he told his family everything.

"Then I certainly understand why you two seem to get each other," Nic mused. "I have a feeling you helped him, too."

"Not really," I denied. "I think I was just an understanding listener when he needed a friend."

Nic snorted. "I doubt very much if that's true. I know your heart, Kylie. You do more than just listen. So what's my future brother-in-law really like when he's sober? I've always wondered. It seems so incredible that he and Damian look so much alike."

"Almost like identical twins?" I teased. "Seriously, they look even more alike physically now that Dylan is more animated, and his eyes have lost that walking dead look. But they're unique in enough ways that I don't think it would be hard to tell them apart if you saw them together."

"I really, really hope I get that chance at the wedding. Did Dylan say that he'd come?" Nic asked.

"I think he *wants* to," I replied. "But I think he's afraid he won't be welcome or that he's not worthy. He really hates himself for some of the things he's done, especially for hurting you and Damian. I'm afraid that he feels like you'd be happier if he wasn't there."

"That's so not true!" Nic exclaimed. "Yes, Damian was angry, but if he thought that Dylan had changed, he'd be ecstatic to have his twin brother back, even though he put him through hell and back for two years. He's even told me that he knew if their positions were reversed, the old Dylan would have never given up on him."

"I'm not sure he's exactly the same as he used to be. Psychological trauma changes a person, but he's not the asshole you saw in England that night," I said.

"I'm not sure what to say," Nic said solemnly. "You made a huge sacrifice for Damian and me, and you still have two more weeks that you're planning to spend with Dylan. How do I thank you for that?"

I snorted. "Please, Nic. You gave me a partnership in ACM that you haven't gotten a dime for yet. That's a lot bigger deal than spending some time with a hot, decent guy. Dylan had already crawled out of that hole before I got there. He started treatment the day he got back here after the gala. It hasn't exactly been a hardship to hang out with Dylan. In fact, he spoils me rotten sometimes. Look where I'm staying. I'm actually sitting on the sofa here, looking out the huge floor-to-ceiling windows at the water. Woe is me."

Nic laughed. "Are you attracted to him, Kylie? I mean, he does look like Damian, who is the hottest man in the world, in my opinion."

I answered truthfully. "I'm not sure what it is about Dylan, but I was drawn to him from the first day we met. Maybe it sounds weird, but I could sense his pain, and there's some weird connection between us that seems to get stronger the longer we're together. And yeah, he is pretty hot, too, so it would be hard not to be physically attracted to him."

"Well, I *have* found *my* Mr. Orgasm," Nic teased. "Maybe it's time for you to find yours. Just be careful with a Lancaster male. They can either make you ecstatically happy or demolish your heart. I'm not sure there's any in-between with them. They're way too intense."

I rolled my eyes. "I like him, Nic. I'm not sleeping with him."

"Yet," she chirped.

She was right, and if I had my way, Dylan and I would be burning up the sheets, but I wasn't sure that complicating our relationship would be good for either one of us.

He'd come a long way since he'd started treatment, but some of his issues were going to linger. Dylan needed time just to live a normal life again.

Now that I knew our attraction went both ways, it was really going to be hard to try to ignore it, but I had to try.

"How do you do it, Nic? How do you love a man as rich and powerful as Damian? And I won't even mention that he just so happens to be a duke, too."

"Because at the end of the day," Nicole said thoughtfully. "Damian is just a man. Granted, he's an extraordinary guy who has a hell of a lot of money, but he's never seen himself as superior to any other guy walking around London just because of his wealth and social status. And he'd give away the dukedom if he could get away with it. Don't get me wrong, I *was* overwhelmed in the beginning, but none of those other things matter if you have the right guy."

"I suppose," I said, still unconvinced. "But I'm still prepared to be intimidated when I get to England."

"You won't be," she insisted. "You'll love Damian's mother, Bella, and his brother Leo. And you obviously aren't intimidated by Dylan, even though he's just as rich and just as powerful as Damian."

"He's not a duke," I reminded her jokingly.

"No, but he's still Lord Dylan Lancaster. He's the son of a duke," she told me.

I groaned. "Oh, God. He never told me that."

"He doesn't use that title unless he's at formal events where he can't avoid it. Just like Leo doesn't use his, and Damian avoids his title as often as possible."

"I have no idea how to address any of the people coming to your wedding," I said, feeling a little panicked.

Nic laughed. "You don't need to know any of that stuff. If someone is stuffy enough to introduce themselves with their title, you'll know what to call them. It's a wedding, Kylie, and titles aren't important to this bride and groom."

"It's a good thing you aren't," I joked. "I'm not versed on the British aristocracy."

"No worries," Nic said. "I can't wait until you get here. This party won't get started until you and Macy are here in person."

"Is there anything else I can do to help?"

"Everything is under control. You two have been a big help, even from across the pond. Now all I want is to share the experience with you guys. I miss you both," Nic said. "I'm not surprised by what you're doing for Dylan, but I'm more grateful than you'll ever know."

"I can't make him attend the wedding, but I'll do my best," I promised.

"Something tells me just the fact that you'll be leaving him in two weeks if he doesn't come might be a big motivator," she said playfully.

"Honestly, I think I'd miss him, too. I've gotten used to having some intelligent company. No offense intended to Jake, of course, but it's kind of nice to have a companion that actually speaks," I confided.

"Especially when that *friend* is incredibly hot and outrageously handsome," she quipped.

"That part *isn't* always comfortable," I muttered.

"Just have fun," Nic advised. "You're going to be hanging out in a home that we could have only dreamed about staying in just a few months ago. God, I'm almost jealous because I only got an hour or so there."

"Please. You've told me about Damian's high-tech mansion."

"It's amazing," she agreed. "But it isn't waterfront."

"I feel kind of bad because I'm not in the office every day," I said.

Nic snorted. "You're a partner. You can do whatever you want, and please don't tell me you haven't been working every day."

"I have," I assured her. "Video conferencing mostly, and the home office I made for myself works fine. But you were the owner, and you were always there."

"Because I needed to learn the business from the ground up," she reminded me. "You don't need that experience, Kylie. You can run the business from any location."

"I'll be there more after the wedding," I informed her. "There won't be any reason not to be in the office once I'm back in my apartment."

"Right now, just focus on relaxing a little. It's sweltering hot there right now in the middle of summer. Enjoy the beach." She hesitated before she said tentatively, "Are you absolutely sure you're safe with Dylan?"

"If you're asking about my physical safety, hell yes, I'm safe with him. He's not violent, Nic. I guess I can see *why* you'd ask that, but that man would never lay a hand on a woman, drunk or sober. He might act like an ass, but it's not in his DNA to intentionally harm any woman. If you're asking if my virtue is safe, I doubt it," I said flatly. "There's rarely a moment when he's around that I don't want to get him naked. I guess hot, nice guys with British accents are just too much temptation for me."

"God, I can't wait to meet him and start over again," Nic said wistfully.

"So you think you can forgive him?"

"He was drinking," she mused. "And from what you've said, he obviously went through a lot. He does deserve another chance. Besides, I already adore Leo and Bella. I wouldn't complain about having one more family member of Damian's to love."

We chatted for a while about the wedding plans, and Nic and I hung up.

I put my phone on the coffee table and headed for the kitchen.

Once Dylan finished the call he was making, I was ready to embrace this opportunity of a lifetime by hitting the beach.

CHAPTER 13

Dylan

"I'M SORRY I missed your call a few days ago," I told my mum as I chatted with her from the master bedroom of the beach house.

It had taken me a few days just to get up the nerve to call my own mother, even though I'd been relieved that she'd finally reached out to me at all.

I wasn't sure what to say to her or how to apologize for the idiotic things I'd done over the last two years.

All I knew was that I'd missed her and that I needed to man up to be the son she'd raised me to be.

"I'm not going to pretend I wasn't disappointed in you, Dylan, but you're still my son," Isabella Lancaster said warily. "I have to know that you're all right."

Bloody hell! I would prefer that she slapped me silly than to tell me she was disappointed in me, but I deserved her censure.

"I've really done it this time, haven't I, Mum?" I asked, not expecting an answer. "Damian and Leo hate me, and I'm sure you're not overly fond of the son you raised right at this moment, either. Saying that I'm sorry doesn't feel like it's good enough, but I regret everything. All of it. I'm afraid I went too far this time to make things right again."

I sat down on the bed, feeling desperate to make my mother understand how much I wished I could take back every stupid thing I'd done.

"Oh, Dylan," Mum said in a more sympathetic voice. "You can't change what happened in the past. All you can do is move on and do better. Isn't that what your father and I always told you? When you hurt, I hurt for you," she explained. "If you're truly ready to be part of this family again, you must know that all any of us want is to have you back. I'll admit, you pushed Damian to his limits, but he's your twin, Dylan. He's been worried about you for two years, and so has Leo, but you've never stopped being a brother to either one of them. They understood that you were hurting. They just didn't approve of your recovery methods."

I raked a frustrated hand through my hair. "I know," I answered huskily. "I'm not proud of the way I checked out myself. It was selfish, and I never gave a thought to my family. For a while, all I wanted to do was escape from everything—even the Lancaster name."

I had no doubt that Charlotte had targeted me because marrying a Lancaster would make her family happy and much more willing to embrace the child she'd been carrying. Had I been anyone else, she may not have been as eager to trap me into a hasty marriage.

"And now?" my mother queried softly.

"Now, I've remembered how damn lucky I am to have a family like mine," I confessed. "No more heavy drinking. No more antics. No more escape. I'm done neglecting the people I should have appreciated and should have let help support me when I wasn't coping well on my own."

"Why do I think there's something you weren't telling all of us about why you had a difficult time?" she asked in a probing, motherly voice.

At that point, I broke down and stammered through the whole story of what had happened between Charlotte and me.

I stumbled over my words at first, but because I'd already done this once before with Kylie, it was a little easier this time.

I also told her about Kylie simply because it was impossible *not* to talk about her. Whether she knew it or not, she'd played an important role in helping me start to feel normal again.

"I blamed myself for Charlotte's death. Sometimes, I still do," I finished. "Even though she was no innocent, she didn't deserve to die. I wasn't sure how to feel when I found out the child she was carrying wasn't mine. I grieved, but I was angry at her, too. How is a man supposed to understand why she did the things she did?"

"None of that was your fault, Dylan," she reassured in a soothing voice. "You were just trying to do the right thing, and no one can fault you for being man enough to step up. Charlotte had…issues. Her mother and I talked sometimes. Charlotte's psychological difficulties were nothing you could have fixed or could have recognized without dating her longer. There are really no rational answers for what she did, Dylan. Her mind didn't work in the usual ways. There were many times her mother thought she was getting better, only to find out that Charlotte was just hiding her disorder better. Had I known you were contemplating a serious relationship with her, I would have told you. Now I wish I would have said something from the moment you told me you were seeing her. I guess I thought it was a passing attraction and would just fizzle out quickly because you two had nothing else in common. I also wasn't sure if she was even having issues anymore. She was diagnosed with a personality disorder before she went to university. Her mother helped her get into several treatment programs, but nothing seemed to help Charlotte permanently turn things around back then. Her fixation with her married, older professor obviously became an obsession, Dylan. A very unhealthy one."

"Everything just happened too fast," I replied in a raspy voice. "I was going to tell all of you about her and the baby at the family dinner that week. Well, the baby I *thought* was mine."

"Oh, my poor boy," Mum crooned. "You were heartbroken about the baby, weren't you?"

I let out a self-mocking laugh. "Ridiculous, right? I was mourning a child who wasn't even mine."

"You didn't know that. It was yours in your mind," she said defensively. "And I know you, Dylan. It's understandable now why you were so distraught that you didn't want to talk about it. It was too horrific to even comprehend, much less put into words."

"It's been two years, and it's still hard for me to get the words out, as I'm sure you noticed. Please don't mention the truth to her family if you speak to Charlotte's mother," I requested. "Charlotte was her only child, and I'd rather they didn't know. I disposed of those journals, so they'd never have to know."

"I won't," she agreed. "I haven't spoken with Charlotte's mother since her daughter's death. I don't think she's gotten over losing her only child. You're right, Dylan. It's much kinder not to reveal the real story, but I'm glad you told *me*. It's incredible that even though you were suffering, you still did everything you could to protect her family. I feel so horrible that I wasn't there for you, son."

"Don't, Mum," I requested firmly. "I didn't *allow* anyone to be there for me, and I was so detached that I wouldn't haven't listened to anyone."

"When it comes to emotional pain, it rarely works to ignore it. Had I known just how bad things were for you, I probably would have followed you everywhere until you were ready to talk," she informed me.

I smiled. Likely, she would have done exactly that. "Which is one of the reasons I didn't tell anyone," I explained. "I didn't want to draw attention of any kind. I just wanted to be alone and not talk about it."

"Are you truly all right, now?" she questioned in a tearful voice.

"Yes, I think that I am. I'm certain there will still be times I wish Charlotte and I hadn't argued. I doubt my nightmares are gone forever, but at least they're not as frequent as they used to be. The guilt hasn't gone away completely, either, but it's a work in progress. I guess I have to learn to admit that there are some things I can't control," I joked weakly.

Mum replied in a lighter voice, "Which is a very hard thing for any Lancaster male to admit. All of you think you can arrange things to your liking. I hope Kylie isn't letting you get away with too much bossiness."

"That would never happen, believe me," I said wryly. "She's a redhead with a stubborn streak. If I get too cocky, she's always happy to bring me down off my high horse. She's been good for me, too. She's kind but doesn't always tell me what I want to hear."

"At least you know when she's telling you the truth. I think she is good for you," my mother agreed. "I'm looking forward to meeting her when you two come for the wedding. You are coming, right?"

"That really depends on Damian," I told her. "If he can't get over what happened with Nicole, I'm not going to blame him for that. It sounds like he really loves her, and I put him through a lot."

"He does love her," she disclosed. "Very much."

"Then I'm happy for him," I said honestly.

"I don't think that happiness will be complete if you're not here, Dylan," she mused. "I'd like to share the whole story about Charlotte with him if you'll allow it."

I was done running away from what happened in the past. "Of course. Feel free to tell Damian, Nicole, and Leo if you want. It's not an easy story for me to tell. It still won't justify my behavior, but they deserve to know. If Damian and Nicole are comfortable with me being at their wedding, I'll go. I'd never willingly miss it. We've always been together for every important event, good or bad, that's happened in our family."

"Yes, we have," she said firmly. "And this one will be no different. I love you, Dylan, and so do your brothers. We've all missed you terribly."

"I've missed all of you, too," I said hoarsely, acknowledging how painful it had been to push my own family away. "So, are you willing to forgive me for being such an idiot for so long?"

"There's nothing to forgive," she said softly. "I understand why you reacted the way you did now. I knew that whatever happened, you'd work through it. You might be the most stubborn of all my sons, but your responsibilities have always weighed heavily on your shoulders, too. I didn't doubt that your love of family would win out in the end. It isn't your fault that you moved away from all of us for a while. You were in so much pain, and you had to do whatever you thought was necessary to survive first."

"I doubt my brothers have that much faith in me," I commented wryly. "Not that I blame them. Don't think that I don't realize how many of my responsibilities I dumped on Damian. I put him in a difficult situation in so many ways, and what I did to Nicole might be unforgivable for him."

"Did you know who Nicole was and that Damian was in love with her?" she asked gently.

"No. Even drunk, I don't think I would have crossed that line if I had known," I replied. "However, we both know that wasn't my only offense."

"Damian managed," she said. "It was actually good for him to learn how to make that expensive upper management do their jobs, and his reputation never suffered for the things you did in the end. The press is too involved in the fairy tale love story of the duke and his American bride. Really, I'm sure I saw a few female reporters ready to swoon at the last event Nicole and Damian attended. He's definitely in their good graces for being so in love with his fiancée."

I shook my head. "I guess it's hard for me to imagine my twin brother falling that hard for someone. He's never been into public displays of affection."

"He wasn't," Mum said. "I think he was saving all that for the right woman. I don't think he can help himself with Nicole. She's special, Dylan. I think you'll see for yourself that they're perfect for each other. She doesn't put up with his nonsense, but she obviously adores him."

"I think I'd like to see that," I confessed. "I've already missed the entire courtship."

"It's not as if it lasted very long," Mum said with humor in her tone. "His behavior was much like your father's when he swept me off my feet. I think once a Lancaster male finds the right woman; they think it's totally unnecessary to waste any time."

She was absolutely right about my father. His adoration for my mother was there for all to see until the day he died. "You still miss him, don't you?" I questioned.

Even though it had been years since my father's death, my mum still talked about him every day.

"I will until the day I die," she said firmly. "He was an exceptional man, just like his sons."

"I miss him, too," I shared. "All I ever wanted was to make both of you proud, but I haven't done a very good job of that over the last two years."

"Dylan," she said in a fond tone. "Do you really think the last two years have erased all of the good things you've done? And considering the circumstances, a few scandals that have already been forgotten, and an ill-advised comment to Nicole doesn't seem important anymore. Not to mention the fact that Damian had some culpability for what happened during the gala, too. If he'd told Nicole the truth in the first place, I think she would have known that you weren't Damian. Your father and I were always proud of all three of you, and nothing you can do will change that. I know your heart, my sweet boy, and that tender heart was the very reason you've been suffering for the last two years. If you didn't feel things so deeply, you wouldn't have struggled so much over what happened."

I grimaced. What guy really wanted their mother to tell them that they wore their heart on their sleeve or something similar?

"I'll do better," I said, repeating the words I'd said since I was a child when I'd managed to screw something up.

"I know you will," Mum said, giving me her usual response. "Try not to be too hard on yourself, even though I know that won't be an easy task for you. Stop being so willing to take the blame for all of the bad things that happened to you."

We spoke for a little while longer about lighter topics, and then I insisted on letting her go since it was getting late in England.

I rose and put my mobile down on one of the side tables, wishing Damian could welcome me back into the family as willingly as my mum just had.

CHAPTER 14

Kylie

"I'M REALLY GLAD that you spoke to your mom," I told Dylan later that evening as we relaxed side by side in a double lounger on the patio of the beach house. "I'm sure it wasn't an easy conversation if you told her everything. Did it surprise you when she told you about Charlotte's issues?"

"A bit," he replied. "But it did explain some things and her odd behavior the day she died. It also made some of her rants in her journal make more sense. If things didn't go her way, it set her off, and she got completely irrational. She didn't like the fact that I backed her into a corner that day."

"Manipulators usually don't like getting caught," I agreed with a sigh. My body was exhausted, but my mind was a lot lighter now that Dylan had taken that step to talk to his family.

We'd spent most of the afternoon swimming and wandering on the beach looking for shells.

Okay, it was mostly *me* who was looking for seashells. Oddly, Dylan seemed completely satisfied to simply walk down the beach with me until I was done.

Even though groceries had been delivered to the beach house, he'd refused to let me cook, so we'd ordered delivery from one of my favorite restaurants.

When we'd finished eating, we'd gravitated out to the patio area.

God, how could I not watch the sunset over the water while I listened to the waves hitting the shore? In the most incredible place, with the most amazing man I'd ever met?

We hadn't said much as we'd watch the sun slowly creep down until it was completely dark.

Our legs and shoulders were touching, and Dylan had reached for my hand, twined our fingers together, and rested our hands on his thigh as we'd silently watched the sun slip down until darkness had fallen.

It may not appear to be the most intimate way to watch a sunset together, yet I'd never felt more connected to a guy in my entire life.

Maybe it was the way he stroked his thumb tenderly over my wrist like he wanted me to know that he was always aware that I was there, right next to him, even when we weren't talking.

It was a tender closeness that squeezed at my heart and made my entire being ache with longing.

I felt like I'd fallen into some kind of fantasy that I never wanted to escape.

"To be honest, it wasn't all that difficult once I made the call," he said thoughtfully. "We were always close. Once I started talking, I couldn't stop. I think she was always there for me and just waiting for me to talk. Mum is scary like that sometimes. She might not always speak up, but she just *knows* what's going on in all of our heads."

I laughed and took a sip from my bottle of water before I commented. "I've heard some mothers can be that way. Nicole's mom was like that sometimes. Even though I wasn't her daughter, she treated me like one. I was devastated when she died."

"What about your own family? Siblings?" he asked.

I shook my head. "None. Like I told you, my dad lives in Florida now, so I don't see him very often. He's remarried and has pretty much adopted my stepmother's family. He is and always has been an alcoholic, so he calls me once in a while when he's sober and thinks about me. Those occurrences have gotten less and less often over the years."

Dylan frowned. "So you've never really had much of a family?"

"Not true," I denied. "Nicole and Macy are like sisters to me, and Nicole's mom was like the mother I never had."

He squeezed my hand. "How do you do that?" he asked, sounding genuinely puzzled. "How is it possible to always find the positive in any situation? Is there ever a day that you feel sorry for yourself? Even if it's only for a little while?"

I snorted. "All the time. It's not really my natural disposition to constantly be a glass-half-full person. I had to learn to redirect myself out of self-pity and into a more grateful state of mind. Once my mind was trained that way, I guess it became more normal for me, but it's not like I don't go there sometimes. I just prefer not to if I can help it. I spent too long being sad, anxious, and depressed."

"I'm not criticizing, Kylie. It's an amazing way to view life. But even before the accident changed my life, I was never completely content, even though I was happy," he said. "And I probably had more reason than most to be a glass-half-full kind of guy. I have a great, supportive family, more money than most people in the world, and the ability to do anything I want, go anywhere I want. Working with Damian on maintaining our legacy with Lancaster International is what I was meant to do. But I was still restless sometimes. Like something was missing, but I wasn't quite sure what that something might be."

I sighed. "I feel that way occasionally," I admitted. "Maybe it's just human nature to want more, even when we have more than enough."

In my case, I knew what that *something* was, and it was actually *someone*. Once in a while, I did get lonely, but just dating anyone had never helped. That was probably why I'd given up and focused on other things for the last few years.

"I guess I could try getting a worthless hound from a shelter that sleeps fifteen hours a day and is seeking food, a walk, or attention during the other six hours," he mused.

I snorted. "You adore my worthless hound, and you know it, Dylan Lancaster. Do you really think I don't see you sneaking him treats or hear you having those one-sided conversations with him?"

He rolled, pinning my body beneath his. "He is a good listener," he answered huskily. "But I think I adore his owner even more. She's a beautiful, brilliant redhead with the most incredible pair of hazel eyes I've ever seen."

We hadn't bothered to turn on the patio light. There was only enough illumination coming from inside to see his form, but I couldn't make out the expression on his face. I wrapped my arms around his neck because the action was so instinctual. "I'm not sure I know her," I teased.

"I'm absolutely positive that you do," he answered, his head so close to mine that I could feel his warm breath on my lips.

I shivered with need. He was close, but not close enough.

I craved that connection, even though I knew it was dangerous.

"Then allow me to remind you just how fucking gorgeous you are," he growled before his mouth came down on mine.

The second he started to kiss me, I was lost.

Dylan owned my lips, my entire mouth, and his demanding exploration wiped nearly every thought from my mind.

I opened to him, and his tongue sought and found mine, both coaxing and insisting on my full capitulation.

I moaned against his lips, just as hungry for this frantic, crazy contact as he was.

I submerged myself in Dylan.

His scent.

His touch.

His urgency.

I was surrendering to the red-hot chemistry that continually flowed between the two of us.

"Dylan," I whimpered as he pulled back and nipped at my bottom lip.

I threaded my hands through his coarse hair, my entire body quivering with desire.

He buried his face in my neck and ran his lips and tongue along the sensitive skin there, making me crave more.

Liquid heat flooded between my thighs, and I fisted his hair, pressing my body up until I could rub against him so I could try to sate the unrelenting lust coursing through me.

His hand grasped my ass and yanked my hips up. He pressed his hard erection against my core as he rasped against my ear, "This is what you do to me, Kylie. I'm so fucking hard every time I look at you. All I can think about is burying my cock inside you until it makes me nearly insane. So don't ever deny that you're the most stunning woman on the planet ever again."

"Dylan," I said in a desperate voice.

"Do. You. Understand?" He growled the question.

"Yes," I panted. "Yes."

Jesus! He made me feel like a sexual goddess, so I wasn't about to argue.

He nipped my earlobe. "Good," he said hoarsely. "Glad we straightened that out."

"I want you so much that it hurts," I confessed without a qualm.

"I can make it go away," he told me, his baritone low and sensual.

He reached between our bodies and easily slid his hand into the stretchy material of my shorts.

I would have shot out of the lounger if he hadn't been on top of me when his strong fingers slipped into my panties, and he slid between my folds.

"Jesus, Kylie. You're so damn wet." His voice was gruff and heated.

When his finger slid over my clit, I cried out. "Yes. So good, Dylan. Please."

"You're one woman who never has to beg for anything, Kylie, but it's hotter than hell when you do." He traced my bottom lip with his tongue while he put more pressure on my clit, circling, teasing, and then satisfying with bold, harder strokes.

"I'll do anything if you just make me come," I whimpered. "Please."

"I fucking wish I could see your face," he grumbled. "But I can wait until next time."

"Oh, God," I moaned as I felt my climax starting to build. "More."

"You mean like this?" he asked harshly as he gave me the hard pressure I needed.

"Yes!" I whimpered. "Just like that."

I felt one of his fingers slide inside my entrance, and Dylan groaned. "Fuck! You're so hot and so damn tight. Come for me, love."

I arched my back, the pleasure so sharp that I could hardly breathe. "Yes. Dylan. Oh, God, that feels so good."

He slammed his mouth down on mine as my orgasm rocked my body, kissing me breathless as his fingers brought me to release.

When he lifted his head, I was panting, and my heart was racing so fast I felt like it was going to explode.

He moved onto his back and cradled my head against his chest for a few minutes before he asked, "Feeling better?"

"Yes," I said, my breath still heavy. "But that probably shouldn't have happened."

My pulse was slowing, but my head was still spinning.

I'd known Dylan was hot, but the way he'd gotten me off so easily like that was mind-blowing.

The man had assaulted my senses until I was mindless—without even breaking a sweat.

"Why not?" he asked huskily.

Calmer now, I reached up and stroked his stubbled jaw. "I want you more than I've ever wanted anyone, Dylan Lancaster, but we can't possibly make this relationship complicated. We have a few weeks left, and then I'll come back to my life in Newport Beach. You'll be in England where you belong. I don't want something so wonderful messing with either of heads after it's over. And I don't want either one of us to end up hurt."

He wrapped his arms around me tightly. "Kylie, the last thing in the world I want is to hurt you, but do you really think we're going to walk away from each other after the wedding and never see each other again?"

"No," I assured him in a rush. "We'll talk on the phone. Stay in touch. This has never been about just our crazy physical attraction."

"I've never wanted anyone as much as I want you, sweetheart, but I'm not going to push you for something you don't want. You're too damn important to me. This has to be your move, even if it kills me. I'd never regret anything that happens between the two of us, but know this…I'm not planning on walking away from us."

My pulse raced, and he'd never know how much I wanted to believe those words. I wanted to think he wouldn't forget me once he rejoined his family and his normal life back in England, but I found that possibility highly unlikely. He might be saying that now, but once he'd completely healed emotionally and met some gorgeous woman in England, he'd feel differently. I doubted that we'd end up friends after he was involved with someone across the pond.

"My bedroom door will never be locked," he said huskily. "Not here. Not in Beverly Hills, and not in England if I go to Damian's wedding. It's always going to be open for you if you change your mind, Kylie."

My heart skittered as he stroked his hand through my hair and placed a short but devastating kiss on my lips.

After that admission, I wasn't sure how in the hell I was going to stay away.

CHAPTER 15

Dylan

L ATER THAT NIGHT, I opened the large linen closet in the hallway and started collecting some supplies for the master bathroom.

The beach house had been extremely clean, but it had obviously been a while since anyone had been here.

I'd just used the last bath towel after my shower, so I grabbed a few more and a couple of floor mats.

Without Anita and Clarence around in the Beverly Hills house, I'd gotten pretty good at fending for myself, with the exception of cooking my own meals. I'd also realized to appreciate just how many little things the couple did around that home simply to ensure my comfort and convenience.

I wished I could say I felt better after the long shower, but I didn't. I'd gotten myself off to fantasies of burying myself inside Kylie's tight, hot, gorgeous body, but that had barely taken the edge off.

After hearing and feeling her climax beneath me, sexual imagery while I stroked my own cock until I watched the results of that empty orgasm disappearing down the shower drain felt nearly useless.

I wanted the real thing.

My cock buried inside her while I lost myself in her scent and her needy little moans as she begged me to fuck her.

"Jesus!" I muttered as I loaded the linens and supplies on my arm.

I *had* to accept that cock-hardening scenario was never going to play out in real life.

Kylie had made that perfectly clear.

Even though the white-hot chemistry was there for both of us, she didn't want to take a chance on us.

Could I really blame her? Hell, no, I couldn't.

I understood why I didn't seem like the kind of guy a woman could trust, given my past actions.

But that didn't mean I liked the fact that she thought I could fuck her and just walk away.

I couldn't. And it was much more likely that *I'd* end up being the injured party if our relationship was just a few nights of casual sex.

That wasn't the way I felt about Kylie, and whether we got down and dirty over the next few weeks or not, I would prove to her that I was worth taking a gamble on.

Maybe it had taken me a while to admit it to myself, but Kylie Hart was meant to be mine.

I knew that with a clarity of mind I hadn't experienced in a long time.

I'd never been the possessive type, but just the thought of any other guy except me touching her made me completely and insanely demented.

Not. Going. To. Happen.

No matter how long it took, she'd eventually realize that she had me by the balls and that my days of seeking out distractions were over.

I didn't need to be diverted anymore.

All I needed was to see her smile, and my whole fucking day was complete.

I'd just closed the closet when I heard the sound of breaking glass.

"Dammit!" Kylie cried out, her voice distressed.

Her bedroom door was right next to the linen closet.

I dropped the supplies on the floor.

"Kylie," I rasped, my heart hammering inside my chest.

I stormed into her room, and when I didn't see her, I pushed open the door of the en suite bathroom.

I froze as I saw her on her hands and knees, dressed in sleep shorts and a matching tank top, her red hair falling in a curtain around her face.

"Kylie," I said in a harsh whisper.

She pushed her hair back to look up at me, but my eyes were riveted on the mess in front of her.

"Blood. So much blood. Broken glass. Fuck!" I cursed, paralyzed as the scene I was witnessing was overlaid with what had happened two years ago.

"Dylan?" a female voice said, her tone full of concern.

"Too much blood," I rasped.

Kylie rose and stood in front of me, pushed me back, and pulled the bathroom door closed behind her.

"It's not blood, Dylan," she said softly as she took my hand. It's just a broken candle. I lit it while I was taking a bath. I knocked it off the bathtub ledge when I went to blow out the flame. It's just bright red, liquid candle wax."

I shook my head, trying to reason out what was real and what wasn't as I reached out for her, tugged her into my arms, and held her so tightly that she squeaked.

"You have to be all right, Kylie. Please fucking tell me you're not hurt," I said, my voice half pleading and half demanding.

She felt warm, soft, and…alive.

Kylie was speaking.

She was standing on her own two feet, but I still couldn't shake off my disabling fear.

She wrapped her arms around my body protectively as she crooned, "Breathe, Dylan. It wasn't blood. I wasn't injured. I was clumsy, that's all."

I suddenly realized that my breathing was heavy, and my heart was pounding in my ears.

I threaded my hand into her hair and pulled her head against my chest, trying to make sure she was protected as I rocked her smaller body in my arms.

"Breathe, Dylan. Just breathe," she said in a calm, gentle voice. "It was just a flashback. I'm okay. You're okay. Trust me."

"I don't give a fuck about me," I said in a graveled voice. "I care about you. Nothing can happen to you, Kylie. Nothing."

My irrational terror had subsided, but I still couldn't let her go.

"I'm fine, Dylan," she said as she pulled her head back and put a palm on each side of my head. "Just look at me."

I did, and my relief at seeing her smiling face nearly floored me. "Thank fuck!"

"Flashback gone?" she asked in a serene voice.

I shook my head as I told her, "It wasn't exactly a flashback. Nothing has triggered a reaction like that in a long time. It was like my past and my present got confused for a minute. I thought you were hurt. Bleeding."

"It makes sense," she assured me. "It was red candle wax that looked just like blood, and the glass shattered. I was just wiping it up."

"Don't," I said gruffly as I kissed her forehead and then pulled her toward the bed. "Sit. I'll clean it up. There's too much broken glass. You could cut yourself."

She sat down next to her sleeping miniature beagle with a small smile on her face. "And you can't cut yourself?"

"Better me than you," I replied as I moved to the bedroom door and retrieved the towels I'd dropped on the floor. I could handle watching myself bleed profusely, but I wasn't sure my heart could take seeing even a drop of Kylie's.

"Are you okay to be doing that?" she asked, sounding worried.

I opened the bathroom door, my mind perfectly capable of seeing the mess as glass and liquid candle wax…now. "I'm good. As long as you and this accident aren't together in the same place."

I dropped a towel over the liquid, letting it absorb into the thick cotton material before I swept most of it up.

"I'm really sorry," Kylie said remorsefully. "I should have been more careful. I probably never should have lit the candle, but it smelled so good that I couldn't resist."

"What was it?" I asked as I wrapped the towels up, the floor now dry, without a single drop of the red substance remaining.

I started to search the floor for any glass fragments that might have escaped cleanup.

"Apple spice," she replied. "The smell was just too tempting not to light."

I made a mental note to make sure Kylie had a good supply of them to use in Beverly Hills if she'd enjoyed it that much.

"Don't be sorry. It was an accident." I said as I did another sweep for glass further away from where the candle had broken. If Kylie was going to be walking around in this bathroom, I wanted to make sure every piece was gone.

"Has that ever happened to you before?" she asked.

"Not quite like that," I confided to her. "I've had flashbacks, but it's been a while. Nothing has triggered one."

"I'm sorry this incident did," she replied in a melancholy tone.

"Stop," I demanded. "I consider it a win that it's been a long time since I've had any kind of flashback. Where's my glass-half-full girl?"

"She's over here feeling like shit because she upset you," she answered.

I tied off a trash bag with the towels inside and strode back into the bedroom. "I'll toss these. And stop feeling like shit. I don't like it."

She looked up at me with a heart-stopping smile. "So you think you can just make feelings you don't like just go away?"

"Yes, I like to think so, no matter how arrogant that sounds. I'm a Lancaster. We like to believe we can make any kind of problem go away. What will it take to make you *not* feel like shit? There aren't very many wishes I can't make a reality."

She got to her feet and smacked me playfully on the shoulder. "Silly man. The only thing I want is for you to feel good."

I shot her a grin. "I can think of any number of ways you could accomplish that," I said. "Not all of them require both of us to be naked, but most of them do."

She rolled her eyes adorably. "You know that's not what I meant, Dylan."

I lifted a brow. "I realize that, but those enjoyable activities happen to be on my mind a lot lately."

I wasn't sure how I could avoid my lurid thoughts when my cock was hard one hundred percent of the time when she was close to me.

I continued more seriously, "I feel better than I have for two years, sweetheart, but I don't expect every symptom I have to magically disappear. I can handle these occasional bumps in the road."

She put her palm to my cheek as she answered, "I don't think there's much of anything you can't deal with, Dylan. That's one of the things that makes you so extraordinary."

"No, love," I replied. "*You* are one of the things that makes *me* seem extraordinary. I think some of your awe-inspiring qualities may have rubbed off on me over the last four weeks."

She smacked my shoulder again. "Your strengths have nothing to do with me."

I drew her hand from my face and kissed her palm.

Didn't this woman realize that most of the mental fortitude I'd gained had *everything* to do with her? That just being so close to her light and warmth had torched a million of the dark places inside me.

I frowned as I looked at her guileless expression and fell into the depths of her gentle, affectionate gaze.

No, maybe she *still* didn't understand just how special and unique she was, so maybe she needed a little pampering, Lancaster style.

CHAPTER 16

Kylie

"GOD," I SAID with a moan of appreciation. "This is the most decadent hot tub I've even seen. It's more like a small pool."

I leaned back in the comfortable seat as the powerful, plentiful jets soothed away all of my tension.

The luxurious spa had all kinds of LED light selections, but we'd settled on a simple, muted, white light that was more relaxing than the crazy colors.

Before Dylan had taken the towels out to the trash in the garage, he'd told me to put on my swimsuit and meet him downstairs.

I hadn't been sure what to expect, but it certainly hadn't been the enormous sunken hot tub just off the outdoor patio. I hadn't really noticed it because it had an automatic cover that matched the outdoor pavers.

I'd almost squealed with delight as Dylan had activated the switch that exposed the enormous, jetted tub, and pulled me down the steps.

"This is so much better than the possible *Jaws* scenario," I told him with a sigh.

"Sorry? What did you say?" he asked, sounding puzzled.

I stretched my arms out, knowing I could actually swim in this particular hot tub, but I was too lazy to bother.

"I thought you might be suggesting a midnight swim in the ocean," I explained. "Don't get me wrong, I would have been game, but it would have reminded me of that scene in the original *Jaws* movie where the first female victim takes a late-night swim alone and gets attacked by the monster great white shark. Have you seen it? It's an older, seventies movie."

"I think we need a bigger boat," Dylan said, quoting the iconic line from the movie in an American accent.

I grinned at him as he relaxed in another seat only about a foot or so away. "Exactly."

"Did you really think I was going to drag you to your death?" he asked in an amused voice.

"Of course not, but I've never done a late-night swim, especially after seeing that movie."

Dylan chuckled. "I saw it a long time ago. My younger brother, Leo, is a wildlife biologist, and he likes to poke fun at all of the horror and thriller movies with outrageous depictions of giant or killer animals. Honestly, I think he secretly enjoys them."

My chest ached as I thought about how normal Dylan's family life had been before the last two years. From what he'd said about his brothers, he'd had a really close relationship with both Damian and Leo.

Obviously, they'd spent a lot of time together doing the normal sibling stuff.

"Nicole, Macy, and I used to get together for movie nights all the time. It's going to be so strange not to have Nic close by anymore," I said in a whimsical voice.

"I think she'll come across the pond often enough," Dylan mused. "She'll have a private jet at her disposal whenever she needs it."

"I know," I agreed. "And I'm glad she found Damian. I just wish she wasn't going to be so far away. She hasn't been back in Newport Beach for that long, but I got so used to seeing her every day."

"It won't be long before you, Macy, and Nicole are spending some time together," Dylan pointed out.

"I know. I'm really excited. I've always wanted to go to England. There's so much I want to see in London."

"Where are you planning on staying?" Dylan asked in a curious tone.

"With Nic and Damian in his high-tech mansion," I said jokingly. "His home sounds extraordinary."

"I'm sure it is," Dylan agreed. "I'm familiar with the plans for his place."

I tilted my head and studied him. "You mentioned that you had a flat, better known as a condo or apartment to Americans. How long has it been since you've been there?"

"I sold it after I went back to pack up Charlotte's things to send to her parents."

"So you're homeless?" I teased.

"Hardly," he drawled. "Lancaster International owns homes all over the world."

"I'm sure. But no personal home?"

He shot me a sexy grin. "I had a new one built. I just haven't been there yet. It was just completed two weeks ago. It was planned, engineered, and built by the same dream team that constructed Damian's home."

"Oh, God," I groaned. "Not another home that's a technical and architectural marvel."

He chuckled. "I'm afraid so. It's not a carbon copy, but the same premise. It was genius. Damian and I actually planned those homes out right before Charlotte was killed. He's the one who made sure mine was built, too."

"So you'll be seeing it for the first time when you go home for the wedding?" I asked excitedly.

"*If* I go," he corrected.

"Dylan, you have to be there," I coaxed.

"Are you inferring that you'll miss me if I'm not?" he asked in that sexy, fuck-me-baritone-with-a-British-accent that made me crazy.

"I will," I said honestly. "Who will be there to tell me how I should act and what I should say to all of those high society guests? It's going to be rather intimidating, even for a woman who does PR for a living. God, will I have to call you Lord Dylan in public? I don't want to say or do anything that might embarrass Nic or Damian."

He held up a hand to stop me. "First of all, it's a wedding, not a royal coronation. Is it taking place at Hollingsworth House?"

"Yes. Your mom's estate in Surrey. Nic has sent me pictures. It looks like a castle."

"It's actually our childhood home, too," Dylan informed me. "I'm sure the wedding will be very elegant because Nicole and my mother probably planned it together, and Mum is an expert at arranging formal affairs. But there's no snobbery in our family, Kylie, and Damian would never expect you to act like one. We grew up in a mixed culture environment. Our mother is Spanish, and she didn't grow up wealthy. Even though she tried to mold herself into the perfect duchess in public, my father refused to let her lose her entire culture just because she married a Brit. I'm sure there will be family there from our maternal side, and Damian will get his thirteen gold coins to present to his bride, which is a Spanish tradition. Damian isn't going to invite anyone he doesn't like to something this important to him. All the British women will put on their best fascinators, and everyone will have a great time."

"Fascinators?" I asked. "Translation, please."

It was a term I hadn't heard before.

"Simply put, they're hats in all colors and shapes. And you do realize we speak the same language, right?" he asked with a smirk.

I ignored his smart-ass comment. "So are your weddings the same as ours here?"

"For the most part," he said, looking like he was thinking. "I'm sure Nicole and Damian will have a mix of traditions. Thank God Damian hates fruitcake with a passion, so he'll be ecstatic if Nicole suggests something different from the traditional wedding cake."

"Actually, they are having a fruitcake because Nicole likes it, and she wanted to incorporate some English traditions, but the main cake is coming from a London bakery. I think they decided on chocolate," I told Dylan with a smile. "I take it you don't care for fruitcake, either?"

He shook his head. "No. Nasty stuff."

I laughed at his exaggerated expression. "Okay, so I won't have to worry about royalty at this wedding."

"I won't guarantee that," Dylan answered carefully. "I'm not sure how far out Damian is extending the guest list. It's even possible that the owner of this beach house, Crown Prince Niklaos of Lania, will be there if he's able. He was raised in England, and Damian and I went to school with him. He's been a mate of mine and Damian's for a long time. But he's far from being a snob, and please don't tell me you're intimidated by titles or wealth. You're American."

I let out an audible breath. "It's not so much the money or the titles. I guess I just don't want to feel out of place at my best friend's wedding, and I don't want to say or do anything that isn't appropriate. I am her maid of honor."

Maybe I didn't want to admit it, but the guest list was bound to be daunting for me, even if I was American.

"You've certainly never been worried about speaking your mind with me," he grumbled.

I thought about that before I answered, "If we hadn't met the way we did, or if the circumstances were different, I doubt I would have been this comfortable around you. I don't know if we would have had much in common. Maybe I forget who you are sometimes, but you are the son of a duke and one of the wealthiest men on the planet. We've lived very different lives."

"Take my word on it, gorgeous; I would have talked to you, no matter what the circumstances. If you don't know what to say to a Brit at the wedding, just talk about the weather. We're obsessed with the topic. You can either grumble about it or speculate about it. Either one of those is perfectly normal since our climate is so unpredictable. It's a favorite topic of conversation for two people who don't know what else to say. You'll endear yourself to any true Brit if you just discuss a possible incoming storm," he finished with amusement in his tone.

I tried to read his face. "You're joking, right?"

He shook his head firmly. "Absolutely not. Just wait and see. I still feel the compulsive instinct to check the weather first thing every morning, even though it's much the same here every day in the summer."

I snorted. "Hot and dry, really hot and dry, or unbearably hot and dry."

Usually, I was much more likely to check the fire danger level than the actual forecast every day.

"But the weather will be good for the wedding, right?" I asked nervously. "It is being held outdoors."

He chuckled. "Now you're starting to sound British. Don't worry. I'm sure Mum has a backup plan in case it rains, but it's usually quite nice this time of year. Longer days, warmer weather."

"I've checked out the average temperatures there," I said. "It would be ungodly hot for an outdoor wedding here, but I think your summer temperatures are perfect."

"You'll love it," he assured me. "Hollingsworth has always been magical in the late spring and summer. Mum has a very colorful English garden, and there's a small lake on the property. It's the perfect venue for a wedding."

The slight melancholy note in his voice made my heart ache.

"Then it's a good thing I'll have you there to show me around Hollingsworth," I said firmly.

Dylan could act as nonchalantly as he wanted about going to the wedding.

I knew better.

This was a man who was missing his family and downhearted about possibly not attending one of the most important events in his twin brother's life.

It took everything I had not to reach out and wrap my arms around him and share his space.

Don't do it. You were the one who backed off from getting too physical with Dylan.

If I got too close, I knew I wasn't going to be able to stop touching him.

I craved his touch, the feel of his body, and the obvious affection he had for me.

I knew this wasn't a relationship that could ever go anywhere. As close as we'd become, he was still Lord Dylan Lancaster, British billionaire, and I was still Kylie Hart, an American who knew nothing about the sort of life he led.

We'd been drawn together by sharing similar experiences, but our lives were nothing alike.

When I'd told him that I didn't want either one of us to get hurt, I hadn't been talking about *him*.

I'd been referring to myself.

Dylan wasn't the kind of fling I'd be able to get over easily or walk away from without some kind of heartbreak.

We hadn't met and fallen madly in love like Damian and Nic.

We'd bonded through tragedy, and we'd become friends who just happened to share a physical attraction, too.

Maybe Dylan just felt like he needed me right now because I'd been there to listen and understand what he was going through.

I wasn't naïve enough to think he'd be attracted to me forever.

No guy ever had.

I'd managed to live through Kevin's dwindling interest, and after that, I'd generally bailed out of a relationship as soon as I saw the disinterest coming.

Okay, so Dylan wasn't showing any kind of indifference…yet, but I was going to be ready when that happened and guard my heart as much as possible.

It was much safer that way.

CHAPTER 17

Dylan

"WHY DIDN'T YOU tell me the whole story about what happened with Charlotte, Dylan?" Damian asked gruffly the second I answered his call.

Apparently, it hadn't taken Mum very long to get to my brothers with what I'd told her yesterday.

It was still early, and I'd already heard from Leo. Our call had been relatively brief since he was in the field, but we'd managed to get back on good terms during our call.

I'd barely had time to put my mobile back on the kitchen counter before Damian's number had popped up on my caller ID.

"Good morning to you, too," I said, trying to make light of his greeting and his rather abrupt question.

Damian hadn't even bothered to say *hello*, which wasn't really unusual. My brother was a get-right-to-the-point type of person.

"It's afternoon here," he reminded me in an irritable tone. "And don't even try to brush off what I just asked you."

I let out a deep breath as I reached for the cup of coffee I'd brewed while I'd been talking to Leo.

It wasn't as if I hadn't planned on calling Damian later today anyway, but if *I'd* called *him*, I would have had a little more time to prepare for this confrontation.

"You've obliviously spoken with Mum," I said. "So, you know what happened."

"I did," he said brusquely. "What I don't really understand is why you didn't explain sooner. Bloody hell, Dylan. Did you really think I wouldn't have sympathized? All I knew is that someone you were apparently dating for a short period of time died a tragic death. You didn't share anything else. You didn't tell me you thought you'd lost a child or that you were right there when it happened. Or that you blamed yourself for everything."

I tried to ignore the sinking feeling in my gut because Damian sounded wounded that I hadn't confided in him, but I couldn't just shrug it off.

We'd always been close.

And I should have told him the truth.

"I'm sorry," I said in a hoarse apology that was long overdue. "I couldn't talk about it, Damian, not even to you. Maybe having someone to talk to after I found out the child wasn't mine would have mitigated some of my anger and confusion, but I wasn't in my right mind after that happened, either. I was a complete idiot, but I'm not sure I could have changed the way I reacted at the time."

"You weren't and never will be an idiot, Dylan," Damian said in a milder tone. "It's not like I don't understand why you reacted that way or that your responses later were due to a disorder you couldn't control. Charlotte's death turned your life upside down, and I respect the fact that you did everything you could to preserve

Charlotte's memory for her family. I'm not sure if I could have done the same thing. That definitely would have fucked with my head."

"It did," I confessed. "But what else could I have done, really? To be honest, there was a part of me that *was* grieving, even after I knew about all the lies. Maybe I was mourning what could have been, or the woman I thought she was, but it was...painful."

"It was completely fucked up," Damian rumbled. "You'd already based your entire world on your future wife and that child, which doesn't surprise me. All you wanted was to do the right thing. No one should be punished for that like you were."

I thought for a moment before I responded. "Maybe I should have insisted on proof like the real father of that child did. For some reason, it just never occurred to me that she wasn't telling the truth. The Charlotte I remembered was a sweet kid."

"Charlotte was a family friend," he noted. "Maybe they aren't as wealthy as we are, but you knew she wasn't after your money. She already had a highly respected family name, too. So why would you even suspect she wasn't telling you the truth? She wasn't diagnosed with her mental illness when we knew her years ago. Honestly, I would have reacted the same way."

"I doubt that," I said wryly. "You've always been more careful and rational than me."

"And you've always been more trusting and willing to find the best in people and situations than I ever did. That's always been one of your best assets, Dylan, and something I wished I could develop myself instead of being a cynical bastard all the time. Don't blame yourself for that."

"I'm not exactly trusting anymore," I informed him. "Everything that happened...changed me, Damian. I'm not the man I was before. I can't erase the things I've done or what I put you through. Being sorry isn't going to make it go away, and it isn't going to change the fact that I hurt the woman you love. I can't use the excuse that

I was pissed most of the time, either. Ultimately, I was responsible for getting that way in the first place. The only thing I can do is move forward and hope you forgive me someday for everything I've done for the last two years."

There were a few seconds of silence before Damian answered. "I'm not even going to try to pretend that I wasn't angry enough to hurt you after what happened with Nicole, but I had no idea what was going on with you. I'm not angry anymore, and Nicole forgave you right after it happened. She said you never attempted to touch her and that it was just a few silly words."

"I never touched her," I confirmed. "I just couldn't keep my mouth shut when she walked into that bedroom. I had no fucking idea she was yours, Damian, or that you even knew her. I certainly didn't know that she was in love with you and that she had no idea that you had an identical twin. If I had known those things, even though I was thoroughly pissed, I couldn't see myself crossing that line. Neither one of us ever did."

It had always been an unspoken rule between the two of us that if one of us expressed interest in a woman, the other backed off immediately.

I'd always respected any woman my brothers were dating, and vice versa.

"A lot of it was my fault because I wasn't honest with Nicole," he admitted. "Maybe I didn't want to admit that in the beginning because I was frantic to get her back, and it was easier to put everything on you."

Damian went on to explain what had happened between him and Nicole from his point of view, and I was somewhat surprised by how frank he was about his insecurities and fears.

He'd obviously been half out of his mind at the thought of losing her, even before my idiotic stunt.

Honestly, I'd never seen my twin brother get anxious about anything. He was the one who always had everything under control.

In fact, he'd always been fastidious about following a pre-planned schedule and never deviated from his normal habits.

"You actually backed yourself into a corner," I said, astonished.

"You have no idea," Damian said in a self-mocking tone. "Nicole is the only woman who has ever been capable of making me throw the rulebook out the window. Thank fuck she's in love with me, too, or I'd be in sad shape right now."

"I'm glad she makes you happy, Damian," I told him earnestly. "I think that you actually needed a woman like her. She has to be special if she pulled your attention away from Lancaster International long enough to get you to notice her."

He chuckled. "I more than just noticed her, and she's beyond special. I'm looking forward to you two meeting under different circumstances." In a more serious tone, he said, "I want you at the wedding, Dylan. You're my brother, and it will be the most monumental event of my life. I'd also appreciate it if you stood up for me along with Leo since my fiancée decided she needed two maids of honor. She's close to both Kylie and Macy, so she couldn't decide between them. It would be ideal if I could have a second best man."

I swallowed the large lump in my throat. This was way more than I'd expected and probably something I didn't deserve. "You know I will, but the wedding day is getting close. Didn't you already choose a second one?"

"I thought about it," he answered in a hoarse voice. "Couldn't do it when I knew the other guy standing up for me should be you. You may have acted like an idiot, but you're still my twin. We've been best mates since we were born."

I swallowed again. For some reason, that damn lump in my throat hadn't quite disappeared. "I'll be there, Damian, and I guarantee that I'll be on my best behavior. My days of running away from my problems are over."

"Fuck! Are you really all right, Dylan?" Damian asked. "Have you stopped blaming yourself for what happened when you shouldn't be? Has the memory of that day faded, and has it really stopped playing over and over in your mind? It's not like I don't understand why that drove you half crazy. If I were put in your position, I'm not sure how I would have handled it."

"I dealt with it the only way I could, Damian, but I'm done running away from my issues. I am better. I swear. Some of the treatment I'm getting is faster acting than others. I'm well aware that everything won't go away overnight, but for the most part, I feel good. I do have an occasional flashback or nightmare, but I'm hopeful that even those will disappear over time."

Damian released what sounded like a relieved breath. "Speaking of not running away, it seems you've taken over a significant amount of work from the Los Angeles office. I wasn't sure if we'd ever get some of those projects off the ground because the negotiations would be complex, but you've actually managed to finalize some of them. How did you do it?"

We talked about some of the work I'd done in Los Angeles, and I explained where I was with each acquisition and merger before I finally told him, "I think I needed the challenge. I'd stopped drinking until I was numb, and I'd started talking about my feelings with a counselor until I was nauseous, but my mind was still too idle. It helped to have complicated problems to solve. I know I said that I didn't care about Lancaster International, but that was bullshit. I just temporarily hated anything that made me Dylan Lancaster. My name and status was the only reason Charlotte targeted me in the first place. If I wasn't Lord Dylan Lancaster, she would have moved on and found someone else with a prestigious name that would impress her family. Maybe that doesn't make sense—"

"It makes total sense," Damian interrupted. "We're incredibly privileged, and I think we know how lucky we are, but there are some negatives to being a Lancaster. We make enemies, and there are very few people who don't see our money, title, or family name before they recognize anything else about us."

"Exactly," I agreed. "But I am proud of who we are, our family history, and what our father achieved. Lancaster International is our legacy, Damian, and I hate the fact that I dumped all the responsibilities on you for a while. I'm doing what I can to make up for that now."

"You're doing a brilliant job, Dylan," he replied. "I appreciate having my partner back, but I think I'm even more grateful to have my twin brother back. I know you think that what happened has changed you, and maybe it has—to an extent. But you survived, and I don't think it's going to change the important things. By the way, I'm sending you the papers to sign to nullify the power of attorney you gave me. Even though I think we both know my threat to enforce it was a bluff."

I opened my mouth to thank him, but my expression of gratitude was interrupted as I bumped one of the metal bowls I'd taken out, and it hit the floor with a very loud *crash!*

"What in the bloody hell was that?" Damian asked. "Dylan, are you all right? What in the world are you doing?"

I put the bowl back on the counter as I replied, "I'm trying to make pancakes for Kylie. She always ends up cooking. I thought I'd try something that might be edible...for once."

"Mum told me all about the situation with Kylie, and then my wife admitted she already knew that you and Kylie were staying together. Why was I the last one to know?" he grumbled. "You do realize that Mum is already hoping that you'll fall madly in love with her," Damian warned. "Now you've got *me* wondering how you feel about her if you're actually in the kitchen trying to cook.

I have to admit that I make Nicole pancakes occasionally. Usually as an apology on the rare occasion that we argue. It does generally get me out of trouble."

"Kylie isn't angry with me," I informed him. "I just want to do something nice for her since she always cooks. Maybe I should have just ordered out."

"Absolutely not," Damian advised. "Women only find it incredibly thoughtful if you make something yourself. Add plenty of maple syrup. She's American, and Americans do love their syrup on pancakes, although I have no idea why."

"Noted," I said. "And Mum will just have to keep on wishing. Kylie isn't interested in anything serious," I confided. "Fuck! I didn't plan on this happening, but I'm already obsessed with making her happy for some damn reason I don't understand. I have no idea what's gotten into me, Damian, but here I am, up in the morning making pancakes just because I thought she might think it was romantic...or something. When have I ever been a man who cared whether or not something was romantic? It would have been easier to make a phone call and have something delivered. It's like I've suddenly lost all of my common sense, and it's been replaced by... sentimentality."

"I think you're probably fucked," Damian said calmly. "If you start getting addicted to doing things that make her smile, then you'll know it's all over."

Bloody hell! I wasn't about to admit it quite yet, but I was well on my way to that fixation, too.

"She's the most incredible woman I've ever met, Damian," I said.

"You don't sound very happy about that," he observed. "And just so you know, Kylie is like a sister to Nicole, and I'm extremely fond of her as well. If you hurt her, twin brother or not, I'll kill you. If you aren't serious, don't get involved with her, Dylan. After what she's been through, she deserves a man who really cares about her."

Obviously, Nicole had already told Damian about Kylie's history. "I'm mad about her," I said solemnly. "But she talks about us like we're a limited-time deal only."

"Given the fact that she's seen your naked orgy picture, can you really blame her?" Damian questioned.

"I suppose not," I agreed reluctantly. "If I were her, I'd probably set a limit to how involved I wanted to be with me, too. In her eyes, I doubt I'm a very good candidate for anything long-term. Given my past behavior, I guess I'll take whatever I can get."

"Maybe you should just take things slow and be consistent so she has time to realize she can trust you. It's not like you're ready to make a commitment, either."

"I'm making pancakes here, remember?" I grumbled. "Even though I have an obscene amount of money and could have very easily ordered a spectacular meal for her."

"I have to admit, that's definitely a warning sign," Damian told me, his voice ripe with amusement.

"Why do I feel like you're enjoying the fact that I'm suffering?" I asked.

"I'm not, really," he said. "I'm just happy that I'm not in your position anymore. It isn't as though I don't sympathize."

I wasn't completely sure that was true. He sounded too damn happy to be capable of empathizing, but there was nobody who deserved a fantastic woman who adored him more than Damian.

"No worries," I said. "As you said, I'm not as anxious as you are to make any kind of commitment. Maybe it's better if we just stay...friends."

I wasn't sure if those words were meant to convince my brother or if I was trying to reassure myself that I could stick to Kylie's terms without wanting more.

Honestly, I had a feeling that the only reason I'd be able to walk away was the fact that Kylie Hart deserved a man without a history of being a total wanker.

And that guy definitely wasn't *me*.

CHAPTER 18

Kylie

A S SOON AS I read Macy's long text message, I wandered out of the bedroom to look for Dylan.

Surprisingly, I found him in the kitchen, my miniature beagle watching Dylan intently from the floor in the hopes that he might score an unexpected treat.

Dylan looked up from whatever he was doing and shot me a grin that immediately made my panties melt.

I'd rolled out of bed, and I'd gone in search of Dylan without bothering to get dressed like I usually did before I sought him out.

It wasn't like my sleeping attire was exactly sexy, but it was summer, so I was wearing a pair of skimpy sleep shorts and a matching cutoff tank that exposed my midriff.

"Nice pajamas," he said huskily as his eyes swept over me.

I was a little horrified when I actually blushed like a teenage girl.

Hell, no guy had ever said anything that turned my cheeks this hot, even when I *was* a teenager.

"Sorry. I wanted to talk to you," I said softly.

"Please, don't apologize," he answered. "Feel free to wear as little as you like."

I coughed uncomfortably, having already noticed that he was bare-chested and only wearing a pair of black pajama bottoms.

Once I stopped drooling, I remembered exactly why I'd been looking for him in the first place.

"Dylan?" I started. "Did you really send hundreds of handmade comfort blankets to Macy's animal shelter? She said you made a ridiculously large monetary donation, too."

He shrugged. "It wasn't like I made them myself. The work was given to a few families who were thrilled to make some extra money. And I donate to good causes all the time. It wasn't something I don't ordinarily do."

I rolled my eyes. Dylan hadn't just made a small donation. What he'd given would support the shelter for quite some time. Because of Damian's generosity, and now Dylan's, the animal charity would be able to take on a lot more abandoned dogs and cats than it ever had before.

"Don't act like what you did was nothing," I said as I approached the kitchen island. "It was a big deal for those animals and for Macy. I'm not sure how to thank you, but it means a lot to Macy and to me."

I wasn't exactly sure how he'd known what the name of the animal shelter was, so it had taken some time and effort for him to figure it out and to arrange for someone to make a boatload of those comfort blankets, too.

It made my heart ache that he didn't seem to expect any recognition for doing something so thoughtful.

"If you really must thank me, I can think of a few different ways that would be more than acceptable," he said huskily.

The mischievous look in his eyes told me exactly what he was thinking, and *all* of those possibilities probably included the two of us getting naked.

"You're so twisted," I accused him.

I knew his sexual innuendo was his way of blowing off what he'd done because he didn't appear to be comfortable with a normal expression of gratitude.

I was certain that Lancaster International, and the Lancaster brothers themselves, gave generously to charity. Had the recipients of those donations gotten so used to receiving those funds that they didn't thank them personally?

Most likely, checks were sent, and there was no personal interaction in the whole process.

I walked around the island, stepping over my hopeful canine as I moved closer to Dylan and kissed his cheek.

He snaked a powerful arm around my waist. "I doubt there's any man who would let you get away with just an innocent kiss like that, gorgeous," he said in a low baritone right before he lowered his mouth to mine.

I closed my eyes and savored the intimate embrace.

It was a slow, sizzling kiss that I felt from my mouth all the way to my toes, and every intimate location in between.

When he finally lifted his head, he said, "Now that just made my whole fucking day, sweetheart, so don't tell me it's better if I keep my distance."

Dammit! I couldn't tell him that, even though I knew I should.

My heart tripped at the sincerity in his sexy eyes. "Mine, too," I murmured as I walked over to the coffee maker to brew myself a cup of coffee. "What are you doing at that stove?"

"Feeding you," he said as he lifted the pan and slid something onto a plate.

I turned as I waited for my cup to fill and raised a brow. "You're… cooking? I thought that wasn't in your wheelhouse of skills."

"Don't get too excited," he said as he lifted a bottle of syrup. "Pancakes are the only thing I can make that might be edible. Pancake Sunday was a tradition in our household growing up. My parents, Damian, Leo, and I made them ourselves every Sunday morning. Occasionally, if all three of her sons are around at the same time, we still do that with Mum. Unfortunately, it's something we haven't done in a long time. Sit," he instructed, waving at the chairs on the island.

I added creamer and sugar to my coffee, still feeling stunned.

I turned and blinked as he put the plate in front of one of the seats.

Dylan Lancaster, billionaire, and co-CEO of one of the most powerful corporations in the world, was actually spending his time making pancakes…for me.

God, no guy in my past had ever made me anything, so it touched me to the point of tears that a man like Dylan had tried to cook for me instead of just ordering out.

I moved to the chair and sat my coffee beside the plate. "This is the sweetest thing anyone has ever done for me," I said, my heart squeezing inside my chest. "Thank you."

"You better try them *before* you thank me," he said drily. "They might not be edible."

I didn't give a damn if they tasted like sawdust. It didn't change the thoughtfulness of the gesture.

I smiled when I saw how much syrup he'd added to the British pancakes, that looked more like crepes than pancakes to me.

Were they supposed to look that way?

I took a bite and savored the mouthful as I chewed and then swallowed. "They're amazing," I told him honestly. "Even better than our typical American pancakes."

Even with a half-gallon of syrup, the edges were still a little crispy, and they weren't soggy.

I watched as Dylan added lemon juice and sugar on his and folded them.

"That's it?" I asked as he took a seat next to me. "No syrup on yours?"

"Never," he answered adamantly. "We Brits use a variety of toppings, but rarely do we drench our pancakes in syrup. That's an American tradition that I just don't understand."

I smiled as I continued to shovel the pancakes into my mouth.

When I finally took a break and reached for my coffee, I informed him, "I can't imagine breakfast pancakes without syrup, and there's something wrong with that whole lemon thing you have going on there."

He grinned, filled his fork, and held it out to me. "Don't criticize until you've tried it."

I gave the utensil a dubious glance, but I opened my mouth and let him put the fork between my lips.

I chewed slowly and then swallowed, shaking my head at the same time. "Nope," I decided. "It's not *inedible*, but it's missing something. The sugar is okay, but the lemon just doesn't do it for me. I'll stick to syrup. Do you want to try mine?"

"I'll pass," he answered hastily. "I guess I'm somewhat of a traditionalist when it comes to British pancakes. I've tried the American version. They're extremely…soggy. If I wanted sticky toffee pudding, I would have ordered it."

I laughed. "What is that?"

"You've never had it?" he asked, sounding appalled. "Who hasn't tried sticky toffee pudding?"

"I love food, and I've never tried it," I said. "I'd have to guess that some other Americans never have either."

"We'll wait until we get to England, and I'll find you some of the best you'll ever have. It's a dessert made with a very moist sponge cake, dates, and a very sweet sauce. We usually top it with vanilla ice cream or custard," he explained. "Absolutely worthy of one of your foodgasms."

"Will I see you in England?" I asked hesitantly.

He frowned. "I guess I haven't told you yet. I've already spoken with Damian and Leo. Not only am I going, but I'm standing up for Damian as well. You and I can go together and take my jet."

I was so happy that I had a very hard time not doing a fist pump. This is what I'd wanted so much for Dylan and for his family.

I let out a sigh. "I'm so glad you're all communicating again. But I already have a plane ticket, Dylan. Macy is going to have to fly over a little later than me, so I told her to take Damian's offer of his jet. I'm the one who wanted to go earlier, so I just bought a ticket."

"So, cancel it and get a refund," he said.

"I'm not sure I can cancel it this late," I replied. "But I can still go over with you if you want."

"Who were you going to fly with?" he asked.

"Transatlantic Airlines. Who else? They have the best rates to the UK."

He grinned as he put his empty plate on top of mine. "It's rather convenient that I just so happen to own the airline, so a refund on your ticket won't be an issue."

I smiled back at him. "I guess I'm extremely lucky to know such a powerful man."

Knowing Dylan the way that I did, sometimes it was hard to remember that all he had to do was send a one-line email, and the gigantic airline would be falling all over themselves to do whatever he wanted.

"I just wish you wanted to know me a lot more...intimately," he said in a disgruntled tone. "How would you feel about hanging around here a few more days? You could show me around Newport Beach."

I was silent for a moment, not sure what to say, before I finally answered, "I'd love that," I admitted honestly. "But neither one of us has an office set up here."

"I think we'll manage for a few days," he said. "I doubt ACM or Lancaster International is going to go belly up if we just check in by email for the next two days."

I chewed on my bottom lip.

He was right, but that also meant we'd spend two more days constantly in each other's company, which was probably dangerous.

On the other hand, when in the hell would I ever have the chance to spend two uninterrupted days with a guy like Dylan Lancaster? In a beachfront home like this one?

Throwing caution to the wind, I asked, "What would you like to do first?"

He wrapped his arms around my waist and lifted me into his lap. "You have no idea the multitude of things I'm capable of doing, woman," he informed me in that fuck-me-baritone-with-a-British-accent that melted my damn panties.

I looked down at him, and my heart skittered when I saw the heated look in his eyes.

"Right now, I think I'd better get dressed before I decide to explore one of those things I think you're probably *very* good at doing," I said breathlessly.

"Fuck!" he cursed. "I hope your mind is thinking just as dirty as mine, and it's my ability to make you come until you beg for mercy."

"I've been thinking about that exact same thing since the moment I saw you standing here in the kitchen. There's nothing hotter than a shirtless guy with an amazing body who is making me breakfast."

"So are you saying that you'd have the same reaction to any man without a shirt who's trying to feed you?" he questioned.

My heart started to race as I saw his disappointed expression.

What I'd thought was a joke was actually a serious question.

Jesus! How could a guy like Dylan Lancaster have any insecurities *at all*?

And why, the moment I saw any of those uncertainties, did I feel the need to make sure he never had a single one of them ever again?

Maybe because he let me see them in the first place?

"Not at all, handsome," I reassured him. "It seems I prefer hot, brilliant, British men who send comfort blankets to animal shelters, whip up English pancakes, and make me feel like a sexual goddess."

He looked relieved as he said, "Thank fuck for that, gorgeous, because I'd really hate to become a jealous prick."

I sighed as he threaded his hands into my hair and pulled my head down to kiss me. Even though I knew he was joking, my heart stuttered just thinking about a scenario where Dylan never wanted to see me with anyone else.

It was a dangerous fantasy, so I brought my mind back to the real world, determined to enjoy every single second that he was temporarily all mine.

CHAPTER 19

Kylie

"**B**ETTER LATE THAN never, right?" I asked Dylan the following evening as I watched him try his black tea. I'd taken him on a whirlwind tour of the Newport Beach area over the last two days.

Yesterday, we'd taken the ferry to Balboa Island, and we'd walked around like tourists. I'd introduced Dylan to chocolate-covered frozen bananas and the joy of watching the pelicans like lazy bums for an hour or two after we were done seeing the island.

I'd driven around today, showing him some of my favorite places before we visited the nature preserve for a short hike with Jake.

This evening, we'd visited a coffee shop that had tea Dylan approved of and had taken our drinks to go so I could bring him to the place where Nic, Macy, and I usually spent our Friday nights together.

I'd tossed down a few beach towels, and we flopped onto them to enjoy our drinks.

"It's good," he said after he swallowed. "I think I'd forgotten how much I missed a really good cup of tea."

I took a sip of my latte and smiled at him. "I know we have the perfect beach spot at the house, but I love this place, too. I think Nic, Macy, and I have told every one of our current secrets and hashed out all of our problems right here over the last year. We always come at night because it's not as crowded."

There were other people around since it was summer, but most of them were couples trying to find a private spot of their own since it was getting close to sunset.

"I hope we've come here so you can tell me all your secrets," Dylan said hopefully.

I snorted as I looked at him sitting across from me. "I think you pretty much know them all by now. You're still more of a mystery to me than I am to you. You've seen where I live, how I live, and I've spilled my guts about my past."

"Not all of it," he protested. "Tell me why there isn't a man who's already snatched you up, spoiled you rotten, and made damn sure that you weren't available to be with a man like me."

My breath caught as I saw the serious look in his gorgeous green eyes. "Maybe that guy doesn't exist. The one who's so interested that he spoils me rotten and wants my spare time."

He shook his head. "Not believable, gorgeous. You're beautiful, successful, intelligent, and any man would be crazy not to want to monopolize all of your time. Try again."

I let out an exasperated breath. "I'm serious," I said, deciding to just be upfront with him. If nothing else, we *were* friends. "I've never found a decent guy who was all that into me. I'm a jerk magnet. My husband started to stray not long after we were married, and the few boyfriends I've had haven't been able to keep their dicks in their pants, either. They got bored really quickly. I'm not into the club scene, and I work a lot. If I do have free time, I like to spend it with my dog somewhere outdoors. I'm perfectly happy doing a movie night or going to the theater, museums, or art galleries. I'm usually happier reading a book than watching reality television, and I do yoga and meditation every morning to keep myself grounded. There's nothing mysterious about me. I'm very…predictable."

"You're also very loyal to the people you care about," Dylan said. "What in the hell is wrong with knowing that the person you're dating is always going to have your back? Or that they care about you so much that they aren't looking for anyone else? Who wants to feel like they have to entertain their partner all the time? That would get utterly exhausting. Do you have any idea just how fantastic it is to be with you, even if we're just quietly watching the sunset or hanging out with Jake? I like it because you don't expect me to be the Dylan Lancaster people expect to see all the damn time, the billionaire who they think should be living a glamorous life every minute of his day. Do you have any idea how nice it is just to be treated like a normal person?"

I opened my mouth and then closed it again, not quite sure what to say.

To me, Dylan was an extraordinary guy, but not because he was wealthy or powerful.

He was just…Dylan.

"Most of the time, I forget that you're that wealthy and that powerful," I finally said. "I just see you as a very intelligent man with incredible business skills who's been strong enough to overcome a horrible tragedy that might have destroyed someone else completely. I guess I don't understand why no one would think that there isn't a very human side of you, too."

"Most people never want to see that," he grumbled. "What woman would want to look for that guy who makes a mess in the kitchen because he can't cook. Or the one who's happy sometimes with a good burger instead of a meal prepared by a chef. Or the one who would rather read a good book than go out to the latest hot spot at night. Or even worse, the man who nearly lost his mind because he watched his future wife and supposed child die right in front of his eyes. No one has ever wanted that man, Kylie. And I couldn't blame them for not wanting all of that craziness, but I'm pretty fucking grateful that I found someone who just…accepted it as being part of me, part of my history, and doesn't judge me for it."

My heart squeezed as I saw the vulnerable look in Dylan's eyes. "There are plenty of people who aren't going to define you because of the crazy things that happened during those two years of your life. A woman like me is going to admire the strength it took to overcome what happened."

"Well, that's a problem, sweetheart, because I've never met a woman like you. Most of them would prefer that there's nothing more to me than the billionaire CEO, the son of a duke, and my family name. Look at Charlotte. The only reason she wanted me was because I was the perfect cover for her inappropriate love affair. A man her parents would thoroughly approve of and welcome as a son-in-law and the father of her child. She didn't give a damn what I was thinking or how I'd feel if I knew the truth. Before that, I'd never had a girlfriend long-term because once they really got to know me, they didn't find me very exciting, either. So we have that in common."

"Not believable," I said, repeating his words.

"It's true," he confided. "Sometimes I'd come home from the office exhausted after a twelve-hour day, and if I wasn't in the mood to go out on the town, they were disappointed. Dating a guy like me came with a lot of expectations, and having a quiet dinner and an early evening wasn't one of them. Ever. So don't try to tell me that every man in the world wants a woman who craves excitement all the time. We don't. I don't. If I'd ever found a woman like you, I would have stuck to her gorgeous ass like glue."

I blinked back the tears that were forming in my eyes as I tried to imagine exactly how Dylan had felt.

Probably…much like I did most of the time.

"Then there's something wrong with those British women you dated," I said. "Maybe you needed to meet an American nobody with a demanding job that doesn't expect you to be anyone but who you are. No man is superhuman, Dylan. Your Dylan Lancaster, billionaire, and powerful CEO switch, can't *always* be in the *on* position—because you are human, too. God, I'd hate it if I *always* had to be a dynamic public relations crisis manager. Having downtime away from your professional image or persona is absolutely necessary."

He shot me a grin. "Tell that to people who think that just because I'm rich, that my life is always perfect and exciting."

I wrinkled my nose. "That's a little unrealistic, isn't it?"

"Very," he agreed.

"I'm not sure what kind of woman would *want* a perfect guy. It would be a little scary. I mean, you're already drop-dead gorgeous, incredibly sexy, off the charts intelligent, ridiculously accomplished, with a wicked sense of humor. If you didn't have a few flaws, you'd be terrifying, and needing some downtime isn't exactly a flaw. Okay, the kitchen mess was *definitely* a flaw, and you do tend to be a little bossy sometimes, but seriously, what woman wants a flawless man?"

He folded his arms across his chest, and I got a little distracted as I watched his T-shirt stretch over his powerful biceps. "What about the orgy thing?" he asked as he raised a brow.

"You said it was a setup."

"It was, but I put myself into that situation, and all the other ones where I made an idiot out of myself, too."

I shrugged. "None of us will go through life without some embarrassing things in our past. Not an issue. Especially since you have a very fine ass that was on display in that photo. It's almost a shame that Damian found a way to make most of the online copies disappear."

I was trying to make him take the situation a little lighter, but unfortunately, that backfired on me when he said, "Why bother with the picture when you can have the real thing, gorgeous?"

"I guess I have some voyeuristic tendencies," I said breathlessly, trying to blow his comment off.

"I think I could give you something better than a photo of my drugged and drunken self, showing my bare ass to the entire world," he said drily. "Is there anything I could have done that would have shocked you?"

"No," I said firmly. "You weren't the real Dylan Lancaster back then. You were a guy in so much pain that he didn't know how to handle it. Knowing you're embarrassed about it simply tells me that none of the things you did were part of your true character."

He shook his head. "And if I hadn't been in pain?" he asked.

"Then you would have been a major jerk," I affirmed. "Luckily, you aren't."

He fixed me with an intense gaze as he said, "What would I have done if you hadn't stormed into my life, Kylie Hart?"

"Healed peacefully in private," I quipped. "Without me, my worthless hound, or my presence in your beautiful Beverly Hills mansion. You would have been just fine without all that."

"I adore you, your worthless hound, and everything about being with you," he argued. "And if you think for even a second that I'm going to let you walk away when you come back here after the wedding, then you're absolutely mad. Maybe you can't trust me yet, and I understand why you can't after all the things I've done, but I'll wait, Kylie. It took me a very long time to find you, so I'm not about to go anywhere unless you tell me to piss off. You aren't boring. It's impossible for a man with any sense to lose interest in you. Luckily, I'm not witless, and I don't exactly feel sorry for all those other tossers."

My pulse started to race as I saw the earnest expression on his face.

It wasn't that I didn't trust *him*.

Maybe it was *me* I really didn't trust.

"Dylan, I—"

"Don't," he growled as he held up a hand. "At least let me think I might have a chance someday. In the meantime, I'll do everything possible to make you see I'm that man worth trusting. Fuck knows I'm never even going to try looking anywhere else because the only woman I see anymore is you."

I took a few deep breaths, trying to calm my heart rate down.

I watched Dylan as he took a large gulp of his tea and stayed silent.

As I took a sip of my coffee, I realized that my hand was shaking just a little.

What exactly had he been trying to say?

It was clear that he wanted more than just friendship and sexual gratification, but I wasn't sure *how much more*.

Honestly, I wasn't quite sure if the answer to that question even mattered anymore.

Whether he realized it or not, he *was* that guy I could trust.

He was that guy who actually accepted me and didn't want me to be anything other than…*me*.

I crawled a little closer to him, and he pulled my body between his powerful thighs, settling me so my back was against his front, both of us facing the water so we could enjoy the sunset.

As he wrapped his arms around my waist, I leaned my head back on his shoulder, wishing I could ask him all of the questions dancing through my mind right now.

CHAPTER 20

Dylan

"I JUST FUCKING CUT her off," I told Damian later that night as we talked on the phone. "She was trying to say something, probably trying to tell me to sod off, and I just didn't want to hear it. What kind of prick does that make me if I wouldn't even listen to what she had to say?"

It was midnight in California, but I'd known that Damian would be up since it was morning for him and a workday.

He was trying to catch up as much as possible at Lancaster International headquarters before the wedding because he and Nicole were taking a long honeymoon to tour a couple of different European countries.

"You poured your heart out," Damian commiserated. "It makes sense that you didn't want to hear her brush you off. But how do you know that was her plan?"

"I don't know that," I said, feeling miserable. "I think I just got concerned that she would. Fuck, Damian! How did you live with uncertainty every day when Nicole had your balls in her hands?"

Damian chuckled. "I didn't handle it well, I can tell you that, but at least Kylie knows everything about you, and you aren't lying to her."

"She knows too damn much," I grumbled. "Nothing seems to dissuade her from thinking I'm a decent person, even though she knows the very worst."

"You *are* a good person, Dylan," Damian affirmed. "I take it you decided to dump the plan to take it slow?"

"I didn't. Not really. I wanted to take things slowly, but she makes it absolutely impossible. I want her way too much, Damian. I want to shake this friendship up and complicate the hell out of it—if that means she'll end up being mine. I can't lose her now that I've found her, but I can't have her unless she wants me the way I want her. I know it's going to take time, and she deserves a man who isn't going to rush things, but with Kylie, holding anything back is almost impossible. I want her to know she's the most incredible woman I've ever known. All. The. Fucking. Time."

"I'm not sure that's a bad thing," Damian mused. "Maybe she needs to be convinced that you're serious, Dylan. I think she's had a lot of idiots in her life. I have no idea what's wrong with American men, but their loss is our gain."

"Exactly," I agreed enthusiastically. "I'm not about to let some American bastards get their hands on Kylie. Not now. They had their bloody chance."

"You really are mad about her," Damian said, sounding slightly surprised.

"I told you I was," I reminded him. "But it's more than that. This isn't just an infatuation that's going to go away, eventually. She belongs in my life, Damian. I can't shake the sense that she was always supposed to be mine. I know that sounds crazy—"

"It doesn't," Damian interrupted flatly. "I get it, but now I know you're fucked. I feel the same way about Nicole."

"Like she's the one woman who really knows you, and not the Damian Lancaster that most other people see?" I questioned.

"Yes."

"How can I let that go?" I asked him.

"You don't," he replied. "Treat her right, Dylan. You need her."

"Like I don't already know that?" I asked. "What do I do if she doesn't need me?"

Fuck! I was starting to sound pathetic, but I was getting to the point of desperation, so I really didn't care.

"You stay patient until she does," Damian answered. "I have no doubt that Kylie needs a man she can trust and who adores her. After the tossers she's had in her life, you can hardly blame her for being afraid to try anymore."

"I don't. I haven't exactly acted like a man worthy of her faith."

"I don't believe it's that, Dylan. I think she knows that you aren't the man you've appeared to be over the last two years. I think it's her hesitance to trust *any* man or to believe that she's more than worthy of one who will stay and not stray."

I tossed a pillow behind my back and leaned against the headboard of the bed. "Her father left her the moment she turned eighteen," I told him. "Do you think that's where it started?"

Damian released an audible breath. "The question is, was he ever really there for her in the first place?"

"I don't think so," I told him. "Physically, maybe, but he was an alcoholic, so I doubt he ever had anything to give. I find it more likely that she took care of him and not the other way around."

I'd never really thought about the fact that Kylie's lack of trust toward men may have started even earlier than her dead husband, but it made sense that it had really started with her father.

I gripped my mobile a little harder, hating the thought that nobody had ever been there for Kylie when she was so willing to give to everyone else.

Yes, she'd had Nicole's mother and her friends, but regardless of her glass-half-full attitude, it must have hurt when her father had never made time to be with his own daughter.

"You and I have no idea what it's like to deal with that kind of rejection," Damian said thoughtfully. "We had two loving, supportive parents. Essentially, Kylie had nobody as a child and was probably put into more of a caretaker role than a daughterly one."

I explained to Damian what I knew about her childhood, her aspirations to be a pro tennis player, and how those dreams had ended.

"I know she did most of it on her own," I finished. "Raised the money and found a sponsor for the Junior Grand Slams by herself. So now that I think about it, I don't think she had much parental guidance."

"For all that Kylie has been through in her life, she's turned out to be an extraordinary woman," Damian commented. "She never gave up."

"No, she didn't," I agreed.

At any point, Kylie could have just accepted that her life was always going to be hard and wallowed in her own misery.

Instead, she found a way to change it.

My chest was tight as I thought about the day she'd considered ending it all and had gotten back up through her sheer strength of will.

Knowing Kylie and what had happened to her, I wasn't surprised that she'd thought about it, but there was no doubt in my mind that she wouldn't have given in under any circumstances.

Hell, I'd considered it myself a few times when the guilt had become overwhelming, but I was too stubborn to go that route.

And so was she.

Throughout the last two years, there was always some small piece of me that wanted to believe I could get my life back someday, even if I hadn't admitted to myself that I wanted that.

"I do think patience will pay off, Dylan," Damian said. "I don't think it's a lack of trust or interest on her part. I think it's fear. No matter how together she may seem, if her own father is disinterested in her, that has to hurt."

"Undoubtedly so," I replied. "Then I think it's my job to show her what it's like to be wanted."

"Because you know what that's like," Damian pointed out. "We had parents who loved us unconditionally and gave us nothing but support. Kylie wasn't nearly as lucky."

"I guess it's easy to forget to be grateful when that's all we've ever really known," I mused.

Kylie needed someone to wrap her up in affection and never let go.

And that someone *was* going to be *me*.

"She's wearing some pretty heavy armor," Damian said. "No one would ever know that there's still a little girl inside her who wants to be loved."

"I can't fix that little girl," I said huskily. "But I can love the woman in the hopes that it will eventually help her inner child, too. I should have listened to her, Damian. My reaction was purely selfish. I started off well by letting her know how much she meant to me, but then I stopped her from telling me how *she* felt. From now on, I'm going to have to learn to listen, even if I don't like what she has to say. I can listen and still not let go until she seriously tells me to sod off."

"Even if she did, I'm still not sure you'd walk away," Damian said with a hint of amusement in his voice. "You've always been incredibly stubborn."

"No doubt you're right," I said. "I'm more likely to try to change her mind if I think she's just trying to push me away."

"I think you'll know if you listen to your heart and not your insecurities," Damian said. "You deserve her, Dylan, and if you don't believe that, try to remember that no one will ever care about her more than you do. Do you ever want to leave her available for some other idiot who won't appreciate her?"

"Fuck, no!" I answered, the very thought making me edgy.

"Then let her talk, and try to understand what she's really saying, not just with her words, but with her actions as well. She might say she doesn't want anything serious, but is she saying that because it's the truth or because she thinks you're going to end up leaving?"

I ran a frustrated hand through my hair. "I would hope not. After tonight, I would think there would be no doubt in her mind as to what I want."

"Don't count on that," Damian warned. "You'd be surprised how easily a woman can discount something that we think is perfectly obvious. Dylan, you can charm the birds out of the trees when you really try. I find it very hard to believe that you can't win Kylie over if that's what you really want."

"As I said, I'm not the same man anymore, Damian. I've become a cynical prick."

"I don't believe that," he answered adamantly. "If you were, you wouldn't give a damn about Kylie. So use some of that old Dylan Lancaster charm that could always sway anyone in your direction."

"She's not the type to fall for it," I said gruffly.

"Then make sure you mean everything you say," he suggested. "It is possible to be charming *and* sincere at the same time. It's not a skill that I've ever mastered personally, but I'm sure you can do it."

"I always tell her the truth, and I'm not sure if I can be as slick as I used to be. Not with her, anyway. My instinct is to just blurt out whatever I'm feeling," I said unhappily. "I doubt that will change anytime soon."

"I know it doesn't seem like it," Damian answered solemnly. "But everything will work out the way it's supposed to be. If you know she's the one, you'll hang on like your life depends on it because it will. I would have hounded Nicole until she finally took pity on me and forgave me because I knew I'd never survive if she didn't. And because I knew she loved me too, even though she didn't want to admit it. I think you realize at some point that it isn't possible to be feeling the way you do alone. There's a connection there that you know isn't one-sided."

"It gets stronger every day," I told him, still astonished to hear Damian talking about his own emotions so readily.

We'd always been close, but I'd never seen him fall for a woman like he had Nicole. I wasn't used to seeing Damian wear his heart on his sleeve so readily.

"The paperwork to nullify the power of attorney is done," Damian informed me. "You should be getting a copy of the legal document any day now."

"Thanks," I said. "It's nice to know that you've decided not to threaten me with poverty."

"Dylan, I'm so—"

"Don't," I insisted. "For fuck's sake, don't apologize. I was joking. You've been a damn good brother to me, Damian. Nobody would have stuck with me the way you have, regardless of the circumstances. You never gave up until I pushed you too far."

"Honestly," Damian said hoarsely. "I'm not sure that I wouldn't have gotten over my anger at some point and kept trying. You were a brother worth fighting for, Dylan. I just wasn't sure how to reach you or if that was ever going to be possible. You have no idea how glad I am that's over."

"Me, too," I said, knowing exactly how lucky I was that Damian had been persistent, even though I'd pushed him away many times. "I'm not going anywhere, and I had to reach myself before anyone else could. I just really wish it hadn't taken so long."

"You've always been annoyingly stubborn about doing things in your own time," Damian joked. "Oh, and by the way, I stopped by your place today. If I didn't like my own home so much, I might be jealous."

"It wouldn't exist if it wasn't for you, so I'm not the only stubborn Lancaster brother," I said drily.

"I knew what you wanted," he answered mildly. "It wasn't like we didn't work together to find a team who could build the homes we envisioned."

"I certainly didn't give you any encouragement to continue with mine when you talked about it," I reminded him.

Damian and I had planned out our homes together. We'd been trying to figure out how we could engineer a house to get everything we wanted without taking up an enormous amount of land.

We'd also searched for the best technology available, and we'd finally found that, too.

Unfortunately, I'd never made it to the groundbreaking stage, which had been scheduled within days of Damian's return from his long business trip to Canada.

And not long after Charlotte's death.

Damian had built his home, but mine had been postponed because he hadn't wanted to continue without my input, and I hadn't been in the frame of mind to think about building a new home.

I wasn't exactly sure why Damian had decided to go forward on mine after I told him I didn't care about the house.

"I guess I thought you might take interest after it got started," Damian said. "You didn't, but I had your plans, so it's everything you hoped for, Dylan. You'll be surprised by how the engineering came together. I was a little stunned by the technology myself, but you'll get used to it. Mum helped with the décor, and you can change anything you don't like. I'm sending the keys by courier."

"I appreciate everything you've already done," I told him, trying to swallow that obnoxious lump in my throat…again. "Thanks to you, I'll actually be coming home to a place I could only imagine two years ago. I'm anxious to see your place as well."

"Should I assume that Kylie won't be staying with us?" Damian asked curiously.

"If I have my way, she won't be," I replied. "It's a good thing we aren't too far away from each other. She's going to want to spend as much time with Nicole as possible."

"That can be arranged," Damian said lightly. "Just make sure she gets back to me safely every evening."

I grinned as I told him, "Considering your reaction when she left the gala without telling you, I wouldn't dare to do it any other way."

CHAPTER 21

Kylie

"HE SAID HE couldn't see any other woman except me," I muttered as I slapped some moisturizer on my face after taking a shower. "Do you really think that's true?"

I eyed Jake like he was actually going to answer, but he just continued to look at me with what I wanted to perceive as sympathy from his spot on the bathroom rug.

"You really do listen well, but you're absolutely no help," I told the canine. "You adore the man as much as I do, so I suppose you're not unbiased, either."

I fluffed my still-damp hair and flipped the bathroom light off as I exited, still not exactly sure what to do.

I'd turned the words that Dylan had said over and over in my mind, and my brain was still reeling.

We'd watched the sunset in silence, but I'd felt the tension in his body as I'd leaned back against him, and the quiet between the two of us hadn't been as easy as it usually was.

I'd wanted to ask questions, but I'd been too afraid that I was reading more into his words than he'd actually said.

But how can that be true?

What else could he have possibly meant?

I took a sip of the bottled water on the nightstand and then flopped onto the bed.

The truth was, I knew that Dylan had feelings for me.

He'd made that perfectly clear.

The question was…did I dare explore this relationship the way I really wanted to delve into it?

I was crazy about Dylan in a way I'd never experienced before.

Not with my husband.

Not with a boyfriend.

Not with *any* man I'd ever known.

The two of us were connected in a way I didn't understand and wasn't comfortable with, either.

But God, I *wanted* that kind of bond, even though it was terrifying.

I wanted to be close to him with a desperation that was almost physically painful, but Dylan Lancaster was such an unknown to me.

If and when he lost interest in me, would I even be able to survive it?

Shit! Shit! Shit!

When had I become this frightened female who was obsessed with tomorrow? Or the next day? Or next week?

What had happened to the Kylie who tried to stay in the present?

Dammit! I hadn't been the same since I'd met Dylan Lancaster.

That *other* Kylie flew the coop the moment I realized that Dylan was like no man I'd ever known, and that he was capable of destroying my heart.

I let out a sigh as I rested against the headboard.

Wasn't I the one who had told Nicole that she might regret it if she didn't take a chance on Damian?

And I'd meant it.

It had made sense…for her.

But isn't Dylan trying to tell me that he's crazy about me, too?

"I'm not sure that this whole thing is just a relationship born out of tragedy anymore, Jake," I told the beagle as he hopped onto the bed.

It didn't sound like Dylan was uncertain about how he felt or that he only cared about me because I'd been around to listen as a friend.

Honestly, he'd poured his heart out to me, told me about how he'd felt in other relationships, and explained how *we* were different.

"I'm just…scared," I told Jake as he put his head on my thigh, and I reached out to pet him.

I wanted to give Dylan what he was asking for, but giving him a chance was high stakes for me.

If I made myself completely vulnerable, he could leave me devastated.

Or…he could make me the happiest woman on the planet.

"Have I been living, or just…existing?" I questioned out loud.

For the most part, I *was* happy with my life, but wasn't there a part of me that really wanted…more?

A few months ago, maybe I'd been willing to settle for what I had, but that was before I'd met Dylan.

Before I'd realized it was actually possible to have these kinds of feelings for a guy, this kind of connection.

Did it really matter how long that happiness lasted?

If I wasn't willing to try, I might not experience it at all.

It isn't like there are more men like Dylan Lancaster out there who actually want to be with me as much as I want to be with him.

Sometimes, that thought terrified me more than anything else.

It had taken me thirty-two years to meet a man who made me feel like this.

Was I really willing to piss away the chance to be with him because I was too afraid to reach out and grab what I wanted?

Wouldn't it be better to try than to regret not giving this thing with Dylan a chance just because I was afraid?

Do I want Dylan Lancaster to be my one regret for the rest of my life?

No. No, I didn't. I knew myself. I knew I'd always wonder...

Maybe it wouldn't last forever, but was I going to be any less miserable when I came back to Newport Beach after the wedding if I didn't throw my heart into this relationship?

No. Probably not.

I couldn't feel less for Dylan by trying to push him away.

I'd tried.

So didn't it make more sense to let him care about me and for me to let my guard down and show him how I felt?

With Dylan Lancaster, there was really no middle ground for me.

I was either fully in, or...nothing.

I cared about him too damn much for it to be any other way.

Maybe if he hadn't put himself out there earlier this evening, it might have been easier to pretend that I was protecting myself because he'd eventually...leave.

But I wasn't so sure that he would get bored and walk away anymore. I wasn't certain we were simply drawn to each other because we'd both experienced a period in our lives when we were in a dark place.

Hell, there was more to this relationship than just that.

We'd share much more of ourselves than just that.

If we hadn't, I wouldn't be sitting here talking to my dog and trying to find the courage to really show Dylan how much I wanted him.

If he'd really meant everything he'd said tonight, he deserved that.

I just wasn't sure how to explain why spilling my guts was so damn difficult for me or why letting my guard down was almost impossible.

Dylan was the only man who had ever tempted me to throw caution to the wind and just see how and where things landed.

Probably because it killed me to see him put himself out there and not get the similar response he deserved.

I knew Dylan.

He wasn't saying anything he didn't believe.

It was *me* who couldn't accept that every word he said was genuine because I was ridiculously insecure when it came to him.

The sad thing was, he'd never given me a single reason to feel that way.

I was almost certain that he was *the* guy, the one I'd always hoped to find but never had.

Which was the reason I hadn't been able to stop myself from falling head over heels in love with Dylan.

That's why I was terrified.

"I love him, Jake," I whispered. "What in the hell am I supposed to do now?"

Let him walk away without knowing how I felt about him?

Nope. That wasn't an option.

He probably wasn't head over heels in love with me, but I knew he had feelings for me.

Whether it lasted forever or not, I *was* going to experience what it felt like to be with someone who cared about me.

Dammit! I deserved that, and I desperately wanted it, even if I had picked the hottest man on the planet to have that unknown adventure with.

My decision made; I glanced at the bedside clock and realized it was close to one a.m.

"He did say his door would always be open to me," I muttered nervously.

Did that include really late at night?

I rose from the bed, disgusted with myself.

If I really wanted Dylan, I wasn't going after what I wanted halfheartedly.

For the first time in my life, I was going all-in because Dylan Lancaster was worth it.

"Wish me luck, Jake," I said as I gave the dog one last pat.

If Dylan didn't want me to crawl into his bed in the middle of the night, he should have never put an offer that tempting out there in the first place.

CHAPTER 22

Dylan

I WASN'T QUITE ASLEEP when I heard the faint creak of my bedroom door opening.

I rolled onto my side, glad I'd left on the small bedside lamp that afforded enough light to allow me to watch as the gap in the door got a little wider.

My heart started to pound against my chest wall, and I swore that the door was opening at a bloody snail's pace.

A little more…

And then it stopped.

Slightly wider…

And then…nothing.

"Are you planning on coming in, or are you just here to torture me," I said drily.

She pushed the door open and popped her head inside. "I wasn't sure if you were still awake."

And…she completely leveled me with a slightly timid smile.

When in the hell had Kylie ever been shy or hesitant?

"As you can see, I'm awake," I said, stating the obvious.

"Can we…talk?" she asked as she opened the door wider.

Could we…talk?

Fuck! Did she really think she could sashay into my bedroom, and I'd still have the ability to put two coherent thoughts together?

"Is it urgent?" I asked hoarsely. "Are you all right? Is Jake sick? Is someone dying?"

She shook her head. "None of those things. I just wanted to tell you something."

"Then, by all means, come in, but before you do, I think I should warn you that if you walk through that door, there won't be a very long discussion before I get you naked and into this bed," I said bluntly.

I saw absolutely no reason not to be truthful with her.

She simply nodded, opened the door completely, walked inside, and closed the door behind her.

Kylie was dressed in pajamas that were similar to the ones she'd been wearing the morning I'd made her pancakes.

Her hair was down and starting to curl on the ends like she'd showered, and it was still damp.

I doubted very much that she was *trying* to seduce me, but I'd never seen anything sexier than her right now in my entire life.

I sat up and leaned against the headboard, my cock so hard that it was almost painful.

I'd warned her, right?

She knew exactly what she was getting herself into, but she'd walked into the lion's den anyway.

I clenched my fists and told myself to slow down.

Hadn't I just told my brother that I needed to *listen* to her?

Yes, I had, but I hadn't counted on doing it in my bedroom, knowing that she'd just silently agreed to let me get her naked.

"Talk," I said, forcing myself to be patient as I watched her lean back against the door.

Obviously, she wasn't ready to saunter over here quite yet.

"You said some things earlier that took me a while to digest," she said softly. "I feel the same way, Dylan, but I have to be honest; it scares the hell out of me."

The tension in my body started to fade away because her fear was a lot more important than my lust. "Why?"

"I'm not used to this," she answered, her voice a little more certain. "I'm not able to accept that a guy like you really cares about me, and only me. Maybe that sounds pathetic, but it's the truth. I wasn't kidding when I told you that men get bored, and they leave, or they're unfaithful. It's the only kind of relationship I've ever known. In every relationship I've ever had, I felt like I was always just waiting for it to happen, and it always did, or I'd run like hell when I thought it was coming, even if it hadn't happened yet. I never seem to find that guy who just wants me and wants to…stay."

My chest ached as I recognized how difficult this admission was for her. "Has it ever occurred to you that maybe you sought that out on purpose because if someone gave you what you wanted, you wouldn't know how to handle it?"

She nodded slowly. "I don't think I realized that until tonight. I don't know how to handle *you*. I don't know how to handle *us*. I didn't realize that I wanted you so much that I was willing to piss away a chance at something really special just to avoid getting hurt. I don't want to do that anymore. I want to let you care about me, and I want you to let me care about you, too."

It took everything I had not to get out of bed and snatch her away from that door until I knew for sure she couldn't just suddenly bolt. "Sweetheart, I have absolutely no problem letting you show me how much you care. I want that, Kylie. I always have. Maybe I don't deserve a woman like you, but that doesn't keep me from wanting you anyway."

"No!" she said adamantly. "You do deserve someone who really cares about you, Dylan. That's why I'm here. I want to try this whole mutual affection thing, but I had to tell you that I'm not good at it, in case I screw it up."

Fuck! Like I cared if she made a few mistakes? I didn't. As long as she didn't leave, I'd be ecstatic.

"I'm not going anywhere, Kylie, so I guess we just keep trying until we get it right. If you try to run, I'll find you. As long as you end up being mine at the end, I don't give a damn how long it takes," I grumbled.

"Have I told you what an incredible guy you are, Dylan Lancaster?" she murmured.

"Maybe," I replied. "But it never hurts to hear it again."

Hell, she could probably utter those words a million times, and I'd never get tired of hearing them.

Honestly, what I really wanted was for her to move her gorgeous self a whole lot closer than she was at the moment.

Yes, I'd told her what was going to happen, but it was still her choice to make.

And she was way too close to that damn door.

"Okay, so if we've gotten all that out of the way, I'm ready to get naked now," she said as she moved forward, pulled that barely-there top she was wearing over her head, and tossed it on the floor.

I watched, stunned, as she tossed that glorious flame-colored hair, and it flowed down to frame the most perfect pair of breasts I'd ever seen.

Kylie was fair, and her nipples were a luscious shade of pink that made my mouth water.

My dick twitched as she shot me a sultry smile that I'd never seen before.

"I hope you realize how close you are to getting hauled into this bed and landing flat on your back," I growled.

"God, I really hope so," she said in a fuck-me voice that made me come very close to losing it. "I feel like I've been lusting after you forever, Dylan."

"Right. That's it. There's only so much a man can take," I rumbled as I rose, wrapped my arms around her, and tossed her onto the bed.

I pinned her arms over her head and just drank in her startled expression.

"Do you have any idea how long I've wanted to see you just like this?" I asked her, my voice desperate. "In my bed, and telling me that you want me?"

Seeing her this way, the need in her eyes telling me everything I wanted to know without words was heart-stopping.

"I do want you," she said softly. "I need you, Dylan. Make love to me. Fuck me. Make the ache I can't seem to get rid of go away."

Fuck! I knew that gut-wrenching hunger, and I was about to sate it for both of us. "We can't go back after this," I warned her.

She shook her head. "I don't care. All I want is you."

Didn't she know that she already *had* me?

That she'd become an obsession that wasn't ever going to go away for me?

"You've got me," I said, my voice graveled as I lowered my head and kissed her.

I took her mouth like a madman, and once I'd tasted that naked desire I'd seen in her eyes, I couldn't get enough.

I wanted everything from her, and I wasn't going to be satisfied until I got it.

As soon as she tugged her wrists free and wrapped her arms around my neck, I knew any semblance of control I might have had earlier had completely vanished, and it wasn't about to reappear anytime soon.

CHAPTER 23

Kylie

I LET GO OF my insecurities the moment his mouth started to devour mine.

His urgency.

His voracious need.

His hunger to possess my body.

All of those emotions were so thick in this passionate kiss that I couldn't doubt that he wanted me as much as I wanted him.

"Dylan," I panted as he released my mouth and trailed his tongue down my neck, not stopping until he'd worked his way down to my breasts.

I gasped when his heated mouth closed around my nipple, sucking, nipping, and then laving over the painfully hard peak.

I speared my hands into his hair, not sure if I wanted to bring him closer or push him away because the pleasure was so intense.

"Oh, God, yes," I hissed as he moved to the other breast and kept tormenting the first with his fingers.

I fisted my hands in his hair and arched my back, my entire body vibrating with a desperate need that was almost unbearable.

"Please," I whimpered, the ache I'd been feeling moments ago turning into an agonizing longing that was completely relentless.

"You're so fucking beautiful, Kylie," Dylan rasped against my skin as his mouth trailed down my stomach, setting fire to every area he touched.

Relief flooded over me as he lowered my shorts and panties down my legs and tossed them aside.

He stood and yanked off his boxer briefs like he was impatient to free himself of anything that he saw as an encumbrance.

My eyes roamed over his incredible body, my core clenching as my gaze locked onto his large and very erect cock.

I opened my legs, panting, needing him inside me, but I was startled when he didn't come down on top of me.

Instead, he buried his head between my open thighs, and I moaned as his tongue made its first electrifying connection with my swollen clit.

"Yes," I panted, my body trembling as Dylan devoured my pussy like it was the sweetest thing he'd ever tasted.

Like making me come was an obsession.

And the way he boldly took what he wanted was the hottest thing I'd ever experienced.

I squirmed, but he wrapped his powerful arms around my thighs, holding me in place, while he tasted, teased, and devoured until I was overwhelmed with sensation.

"Dylan," I moaned. "Please."

I couldn't take anymore, and my body was on overload.

I fisted my hands in his hair and pulled, but that just seemed to urge him on.

I could feel my climax building, and when Dylan finally took that tiny bundle of nerves between his teeth and gave me the pressure and stimulation I needed to come apart, my body rocked with the force of my release.

"Dylan," I screamed, riding the wave of intense pleasure because it was the only thing I could do. "So good, so damn good."

He didn't come up for air as he wrang every ounce of pleasure he could get from me, stretching out the carnal satisfaction for as long as possible.

He finally crawled up my body, and I shivered with anticipation as I saw the wild look in his molten green eyes.

God, he was breathtaking when he was this primal and completely lost to his desire...for me.

I wrapped my arms around his neck, and I moaned against his lips as he kissed me.

Tasting myself on his tongue just made me even more frantic to feel him inside me.

Connected to me.

Claiming me.

Satisfying the voracious need we had for each other.

"Fuck me, Dylan," I demanded the moment he ended the erotic embrace. "Now. Right now."

I couldn't wait another second.

I wrapped my legs around his waist, and I watched the tense expression on his face as he rasped impatiently, "Condom."

"I'm on birth control, and I'm clean, Dylan. Are you?" I asked, air sawing in and out of my lungs so fast that I couldn't catch my breath.

"Yes," he answered huskily. "Are you sure?"

I threaded my hands in his hair. "I trust you if you trust me. I've never let a guy have sex with me without a condom except for my husband, so maybe we—"

"Should do it," Dylan said as he found my entrance with the tip of his cock.

All thoughts of backing down on my suggestion flew out of my head.

After what he'd been through, it had suddenly occurred to me that Dylan might not want to leave himself open for an unwanted pregnancy.

Obviously, I'd thought…wrong. Apparently, he trusted me, which was pretty miraculous considering his history.

"Yes," I murmured as Dylan buried himself to his balls inside me. "Oh God, you're so…big."

The way he stretched my inner muscles didn't hurt. It was a quick discomfort that faded away fairly quickly.

"Is that good or bad?" he asked, his voice strained but not moving a muscle. "Fuck! You're so damn tight, sweetheart, and not using a condom is intense."

"First time?" I asked.

"Yes," he affirmed tersely, his body tight.

"It's good, Dylan. So. Damn. Good. Fuck me," I demanded.

The moment he knew I was okay, he began to move, and the two of us got lost in a frenzied rhythm that neither one of us could slow down.

I lifted my hips, meeting every surge of his hips to take him deeper.

Harder.

Faster.

The way he took me was primitive.

Primal.

Sensual.

Wanton.

And the way we came together couldn't have happened any other way.

We'd waited way too long, had craved each other too desperately.

I was completely shameless about satisfying my relentless hunger for him.

"Yes. Dylan," I moaned, my body shaking with emotions I couldn't suppress anymore. "I need you. Please."

"Come for me, gorgeous. I want to watch you," he growled.

This man's overwhelming desire to satisfy me, and see proof that he had, was surprisingly erotic.

I wanted his eyes on me.

Watching me.

Seeing what he did to me.

Our gazes locked, and I fell into the ferocious, possessive, covetous emotions those breathtaking eyes were revealing.

Maybe I should have been terrified, but I wasn't.

I wanted every animalistic desire he had because they matched the way I felt.

He moved without breaking his pace, adjusting until every thrust stimulated my clit.

"Shit! Too much." I moaned. "I'm-not-sure-I-can-handle -this-much."

I could feel my impending orgasm, and my body was so fraught that I wasn't sure I'd survive it.

"Just let go," Dylan rasped against my ear. "I'll be here to catch you."

"Too-damn-intense-and-way-too-strong," I babbled.

I dug my fingernails into his back, trying to ground myself as he pounded into me, wrapped himself around me, pleasuring me and making me crazy at the same time.

"Dylan!" I screamed. "Dylan!"

My climax rolled over me like a runaway train, and as I lost control, his eyes never left my face.

The elemental satisfaction in his gaze as he watched me come was the hottest thing I'd ever seen.

My core pulsated around Dylan's cock, squeezing him, milking him.

"Fuck!" he roared. "Kylie. Fuck!"

Fighting for breath, I watched as Dylan went over the edge, mesmerized by the way his powerful body strained as he found his own release.

His mouth came down on mine in a fierce, passionate embrace that left me even more breathless.

He rolled as we both tried to catch our breath, pulling me on top of him, our bodies still connected.

"I think you just completely wrecked me," I muttered as my heart rate started to slow down. "I'm not sure I can get off you, much less out of this bed."

"Perfect," he said, his deep baritone infused with a touch of humor. "Then I have you exactly where I want you."

"Sweaty and draped over your body like a wet noodle?" I asked.

Dylan threaded his hand through my damp hair. "I think sweaty and satiated is a very sexy look on you, sweetheart."

"You're so twisted," I murmured.

"Is that your way of telling me that you don't believe you're amazingly sexy?" he asked huskily.

I opened one eye to look at him. "Probably."

I squeaked as I found myself flat on my back, with Dylan's handsome face above me as he said, "Since you're definitely going to hear me tell you how attractive you are in some form or another every single day, maybe we could find an alternative response. I suppose you could say nothing at all, which is acceptable and preferable to the insults. You could also just say 'thank you, Dylan' and leave it at that. You could smile at me, but that would probably just lead to me telling you how beautiful you are all over again—"

I put a finger to his lips to stop him. "I told you I suck at this. How about I just tell you how amazingly handsome you are and ask you to fuck me?"

He grinned down at me. "I think that would probably be my favorite response, but you might get tired of being in the bedroom."

"I'm already here right now," I reminded him.

"Then let's think about better responses later," he suggested.

"Fuck me, Dylan," I whispered in a sultry voice that I didn't know I had.

"Much later," he said hastily, right before he lowered his head to kiss me.

CHAPTER 24

Dylan

"HAVE I THANKED you for this?" Kylie asked as she fastened her seat belt and turned her head to look at me. "I can't believe that you arranged everything so we could leave a week early to see the sights of London. And this jet is so magical."

I shook my head. I'd never heard anyone call my private jet "magical" and all I'd really had to do was make sure the flight crew was ready. But if she wanted to look at me like I'd pulled off something special, then who was I to argue?

"It's not like you'll have much time to sightsee when all the wedding excitement is happening," I said.

Really, my motivations had been somewhat selfish.

Yes, I wanted to show her London, but I wanted time to take her around from a tourist's perspective before she was submerged into my world as Dylan Lancaster.

They were two different things entirely.

After we'd returned to Beverly Hills, Kylie and I had gone back to our usual routine for several days before it had occurred to me that we could be in London, doing the same thing.

Since my nausea-inducing therapy sessions had been cut down significantly because I was done with some of the more time-intensive parts, I'd arranged to do my sessions by video conference.

It hadn't been difficult to get an office set up for Kylie at my home in London, although I didn't plan on letting her spend much time there.

She had a lot of places on her list of must-see attractions in London, so we'd have to do the whirlwind tour.

Nicole and Damian would be at Hollingsworth House this week to finish up last-minute arrangements for the wedding, so I'd get this one week with Kylie all to myself.

I didn't plan on wasting a moment of it.

Additional time wasn't necessary for me to discover that I couldn't live without her.

Honestly, that fact had probably been crystal clear to me for a while now.

I just wasn't so certain she was convinced that she couldn't live without…me.

Not that she hadn't embraced the whole mutual affection relationship.

Hell, if anything, she'd become so damn good at it that I spent most of my time walking around with a glass-half-full mentality myself these days.

Or maybe that glass was literally overflowing, which made me determined to make sure things stayed this way.

My damn heart couldn't take it if Kylie decided she was anything other than completely and irrevocably mine.

The sooner that commitment was made, the better in my mind.

If that didn't happen soon, I was afraid I'd lose my sanity…again. Only this time, I was afraid I'd never recover.

It was rather frightening that the gorgeous redhead sitting next to me had the power to make or break my happiness, but there it was, and there wasn't a damn thing I could do to change that.

"Oh, Dylan, look! I can see all the lights of Los Angeles," Kylie squealed as she looked out the window with an awed, happy expression on her face.

I'd seen it before, many times, but watching it through her eyes was so much more gratifying. "I see that," I answered with a grin. "I guess I don't look all that often anymore."

"How could you not look?" she asked. "It's beautiful."

No, *she* was beautiful, and I found myself watching *her* instead of the lights below.

Damian had warned me about getting to the point where I'd do anything just to see Kylie smile, and I'd reached that stage without ever realizing it had happened at first.

Now, it was a bloody obsession.

Once the LA lights were behind us, she took her eyes off the window and leaned back in the leather recliner with a sigh. "This has been such an unbelievable week. I'm on my way to London early with you…and that incredible beach house. That was a once-in-a-lifetime experience, too."

"Hopefully not," I told her. "Since I'll be finishing up the paperwork soon to become the new owner, we'll be staying there as often as you like."

Her gorgeous hazel eyes widened, and I was mesmerized by the way those irises seemed ever changing. They seemed to change color from green to light brown, to gold, in a matter of seconds.

Right now, they were more greenish-gold, the shade that occurred when she was inquisitive, which seemed to appear a lot.

"Are you serious?" she asked, like she wasn't quite sure that I wasn't joking.

"Of course," I informed her. "Something special happened there, love. I wasn't about to let a place with memories like that go to someone else. Nick told me he was planning on selling because he's so busy that he never gets to spend any time there anymore. So I purchased it. We can go there whenever you like."

"Just like that? You just…bought it?" she asked as her brow furrowed.

I shrugged. "It was a minor purchase. I don't have a personal home in the States. It seemed like a good choice. You don't approve?"

"It's not that," she assured me. "It's a spectacular home, but so expensive. I guess I've just never known anyone who can just casually buy a place like that with little more than a snap of their fingers."

"It's not exactly grand like the Beverly Hills house."

"It's not the size, and it's not exactly small," she said. "It's the location. And it's a lot more awe-inspiring than the place in Beverly Hills. To me, it is, anyway. The beach has always been like my sanctuary. It's so peaceful there."

"Then feel free to escape there any time you choose. Just don't forget to take me with you," I said, only half-joking.

If she thought the Newport Beach home was pricy, I wasn't even going to mention what the technological marvel had cost in London.

She smacked my shoulder. "Like I'd go without you?" she asked.

"I thought it would make you happy. It certainly has good memories, for me anyway," I told her, my mind returning to every place we'd had sex in that house before we'd taken off the next afternoon.

"I'm glad no one else bought it," she confessed with a sigh. "I guess maybe I *haven't* seen that granite in the kitchen for the last time."

I grinned as I remembered exactly what had occurred on that kitchen countertop. "I'd be happy to reenact that memory whenever you want."

"Would you?" she asked in that sexy, do-me tone of voice I'd gotten to know so well.

Fuck! As usual, my cock reacted immediately to the simple possibility of getting inside that gorgeous body of hers.

One come-fuck-me look from her was all it took.

I reached out and stroked the soft skin of her cheek. "Have I told you how beautiful you are today?" I asked, wondering how I'd neglected to say that if I hadn't.

"A few times," she answered as she took my hand and twined our fingers together. "It got us in trouble every time. You know I'm going to tell you how breathtakingly handsome you are, which is always true, and—"

"Don't say it," I said, my voice graveled and rough. "Food first. Dinner will be here shortly. I remember now. You already missed lunch when you said it last time."

"Do you hear me complaining?" she asked with a sensual laugh.

"No," I said stiffly. "But you should remind me that food comes first. I shouldn't just drag you off like a caveman every time you say that without making sure you've eaten first."

If I kept this up, she'd starve to death since I couldn't seem to keep my hands off her, with or without a blatant invitation.

She unbuckled her seat belt, raised the armrest, and slid closer to me.

I released my own belt impatiently, wrapped my arms around her warm, soft body, and hauled her into my lap.

Bloody hell! The seat belt sign *was* off, and I was never satisfied unless she was as close to me as possible.

"I don't know," she said softly. "The whole horny Neanderthal thing is pretty hot. I don't think I've ever inspired that much passion in any guy before you."

Yes, so that was another thing…how had she gotten through her adult life so far without a man *not* wanting to drag her off to his cave?

Over and over again.

"Then you were obviously in hiding," I grumbled.

"I think maybe I was just waiting for you," she mused.

"I bloody well hope so," I said as I tightened my arms around her waist.

Honestly, I was just fine with being the first guy who had noticed how irresistible she was. I just wasn't sure exactly how that had happened.

She threaded her hands in my hair, and I closed my eyes, savoring that tender touch as she said, "Maybe you're the first man I ever wanted to carry me off to his lair."

I'd also be the last one who did.

I'd already claimed Kylie Hart, and she was mine.

If that made me appear to be a cave dweller, I had no problem with that as long as she didn't.

"Does that bother you?" I asked.

She laughed, and my chest ached, just like it always did when I heard that sound.

"Like I said, it's pretty hot," she reminded me. "And it's always one very...posh cave."

I grinned, knowing she'd gotten the word "posh" from Nicole.

"And even if it wasn't," she continued. "There's nowhere I wouldn't go if I'm with you, handsome. Primitive or posh."

I opened my eyes and looked up at her, my heart in my throat as my eyes searched her face.

She'd braided that glorious red mane today, but some of the locks had escaped, and those wisps of bright red hair framed the silken, creamy skin of her face.

She'd concealed those adorable freckles with some makeup, but I knew they were there. I'd memorized the placement of every one of those adorable, tiny dots.

I reached up and toyed with the fat braid behind her head. "How did a man like me ever get lucky enough to have a woman like you walk through my door?"

She opened her mouth, but before she could speak, I pulled her head down and stole those sensuous lips.

It was definitely the most satisfying way I could think of to keep her from denying that I was the most fortunate bastard on the planet.

CHAPTER 25

Kylie

"T HIS IS SO amazing," I told Dylan as we strolled through Hyde Park two days later.

We'd started at Kensington Gardens, and meandered by the Italian Water Gardens, where people were relaxing on the lawn or lining benches near the fountains simply to enjoy the beautiful summer day. That area had been busy, but once we'd passed it, the path had gotten quieter, and Dylan had pulled me into a grassy area where we'd followed a less trodden path to the Serpentine Sackler Gallery.

Once we'd wandered through the exhibits, we'd started toward Hyde Park.

Dylan had seemed perfectly relaxed, but it hadn't escaped my notice that when we'd gone to cross a busy street, he'd wrapped a protective arm around my waist, his body tense until we'd gotten away from the traffic.

A casual observer probably wouldn't have noticed his reaction, but because I knew his history, I recognized why he'd experienced some discomfort.

It wasn't obvious, but his arm had been like a powerful band around me, as though he needed to make sure I didn't dart into oncoming traffic.

He'd simply gritted his teeth through the discomfort, and I marveled at how dogged his determination was to put his past behind him.

It would get easier with time, and there was no apparent flashback, but I hated to see him uncomfortable because he was usually a guy who rarely hesitated to do anything.

"It's crowded," Dylan observed as he held my hand and pulled me closer to him to avoid a crowd of tourists.

I could hear several different languages being spoken around me as we cautiously approached a swan swimming close to the edge of the Serpentine.

"I don't think it's *just* tourists," I told him, surprised by how disinterested the swan seemed in the crowds.

He grinned at me, his eyes obscured by a pair of dark shades. "We Brits learn to enjoy our short reprieve from the rainy, chillier weather. We don't get a lot of days like this, and our summers are short."

Dylan was dressed casually in a pair of jeans and a short-sleeve polo shirt, but the casual attire did nothing to take away from how devastatingly handsome he looked today.

I'd put on a pair of forest green capri pants and a matching floral shirt this morning—after checking the forecast, of course.

I smiled at an older woman who had come up next to me to look at the swan.

"It's quite warm today, isn't it?" she commented.

Dylan grinned and shot me an I-told-you-so look.

"It's a lovely day," I agreed with a nod.

She beamed at me and wandered away.

"You just made her entire day," he said as he leaned closer. "You see how easy that is, right? Agree with a Brit's perception of the weather, and you make a friend for life."

I burst out laughing. "Don't be a smart-ass."

I'd actually noticed that Brits did love to talk about the weather, and to my surprise, Dylan *hadn't* been pulling my leg about that.

He tugged on my hand gently. "I think we'd better move. You're getting a little pink. If we can find some shade, you should put on more sunscreen."

My fair skin was a complete pain in the ass for a woman who loved to be outside, but I'd learned to be generous with the tube of sunscreen I rarely went anywhere without.

"The birds are so tame," I said as we walked away from the water's edge.

"They're used to the crowds, and since they get fed by humans, they don't actually fear them."

We kept strolling, and I thought about the busy days we had ahead of us.

We'd already covered a lot of ground.

Since we'd slept on Dylan's jet on the way over, we'd hit The Tower of London yesterday and walked to the Tower Bridge.

Today, we'd taken a driving tour around the city in a sleek, black Rolls Royce Ghost—that I'd since learned was Dylan's new personal car and chauffeur—before we exited the vehicle at Kensington Gardens.

I couldn't say I was completely used to his new home. I was still awed every time I walked through the door of the spectacular mansion. The sheer size of it was overwhelming, but my astonishment was more about the way it was built in subterranean levels, with three levels underground and two above.

Because the house was so automated, I felt like I was in the middle of a sci-fi movie sometimes.

Not that it wasn't gorgeous, but it would probably be a while before I got used to staying in such an amazing place.

I sat at a picnic table in the shade to slather on more sunscreen while Dylan went inside the building and returned with a tray of food and some sodas.

"This is really good," I told him as I started to devour the fish and chips.

We'd both removed our sunglasses since we were sitting in the shade, so I could see the amusement in his eyes as he looked at me.

He shot me a grin as he started on his second piece of fish. "It's really hard for anyone in England to completely ruin fish and chips. I've had better, but you need to eat."

I smirked. "Like I ever miss a meal if I really want to eat?"

Dylan never seemed to stop feeding me, and his nonsense about me missing meals because he dragged me off to fuck me was totally ridiculous.

"What's this?" I asked as I took a small forkful of something in a small bowl.

"Mushy peas," he replied.

I lifted a brow and tasted them. "They're delicious. What's in them?"

"I can't tell you every single ingredient," he said thoughtfully. "But there's definitely cream and butter. We know how to make nasty vegetables palatable and much less healthy."

Since I wasn't especially fond of most green veggies except in salad, I wasn't about to complain because the mushy peas were tasty.

"Have I thanked you for today?" I asked, wanting to make sure that Dylan knew how much I appreciated everything he'd done to make this week special for me.

"It's not over yet," he pointed out. "And yes, you've thanked me. At least a half dozen times already today."

"Okay, I'll do it again later."

He shot me a don't-even-go-there look. "You don't have to thank me, Kylie. I'm enjoying this as much as you are. It feels good to be home."

He looked so relaxed that I believed him.

Dylan was obviously in his element here, and while we'd been in the US, it had been difficult to remember that he actually belonged somewhere else.

Other than the sexy British accent, he hadn't seemed out of place in the States, either.

"I'm surprised no one seems to recognize you," I mused. "I'd think you're a famous face here."

"A lot of these people are tourists, and before the whole scandalous photo debacle, we tried to keep our faces out of the media. Mum wanted us to try to have a normal childhood. We spent some of our vacation time in Spain as children, and once we were adults, none of us sought the limelight. Damian and I had a corporation to run, and Leo spent most of his time in the wilderness. We didn't wind up in the gossip rags because we didn't really attend social events unless we had to do it. For the most part, we lived pretty normal lives."

I snorted. "If you can call riding around in a Rolls Royce and owning homes that only a tiny fraction of the of the world's population can afford. You, Dylan Lancaster, are far from normal."

"It's normal for me," he said matter-of-factly, his expression a little defensive.

"Hey," I said in a softer voice. "I didn't mean that in a bad way. I know this is all ordinary for you. I'm just saying it's not for *most* people. To me, it's pretty extraordinary."

The last thing I'd meant to do was hurt him. Dylan had been born into his life, and who wouldn't want to live his lifestyle if they could?

He and Damian busted their asses for their corporation, rather than just doing the social rounds and events, living off their wealth without working for it.

That was the reason they *were* so outrageously wealthy.

"Being born a Lancaster isn't always easy," he grumbled. "There are very few people who see anything *except* our massive wealth. Damian and I make sure Lancaster International does good things for the entire world. We think it's our responsibility to contribute when it comes to solving world crisis situations. Not only with money but with innovation as well. Everything Leo does is to try to save endangered species after we've been idiotic enough to drive animal populations to the brink of extinction. It's never been about primarily making more money for any of us."

I looked at him, stunned because I'd never really thought about the downsides of being ultra-wealthy. "Lancaster is well-known for all of the innovation you do to solve world problems," I assured him. "And I have no doubt you donate heavily to charity every year, probably far more than you need to give. I don't know a lot about what Leo does, but it obviously isn't for the money since his sanctuary is nonprofit. If people don't see the substance behind your wealth and all of the good things you do, then they're idiots."

I suddenly felt extremely defensive about the fact that no matter what the Lancasters did to help humanity, they'd always be seen as simply billionaires with more money than God and a prominent family name that everyone recognized.

Did anyone look beneath the surface when they met the members of this amazing family?

From what Dylan had said in the past about his dating experiences, I assumed...not.

"I know I'm extremely privileged, Kylie," he said sheepishly. "You don't have to defend me."

I smiled at him, my heart tripping as I looked at his solemn expression. "Yeah, actually, I do. I know how hard you and Damian work, and judging by the fact that Leo is rarely home, I'm sure he does, too. If none of you are going to toot your own horns, maybe someone needs to do it for you. It pisses me off that no woman has ever seen the real Dylan Lancaster because I know what an incredible guy you really are."

His expression turned into a full-fledged grin. "You're the only female who actually matters to me."

My pulse raced as he winked at me boldly, but didn't say another word.

Holy shit! It might be a little mind-boggling to be the sole focus of Dylan Lancaster's romantic attention…

But it felt pretty damn magnificent.

CHAPTER 26

Dylan

I KNEW I WAS running out of time, but I still had no idea how to start the discussion I needed to have with Kylie.

We'd been in London for six days, but neither one of us had broached the topic of our future together.

We'd frolicked all over London together, locked in a bubble of happiness I hadn't wanted to pop.

It wasn't like I planned on letting her get away.

Kylie Hart was mine.

She'd stay mine.

We just needed to work out...the details.

"Oh, my God, this is heaven on a spoon," Kylie said with a sexy moan.

I couldn't help but smile when I watched her eyes close as she took another bite of her sticky toffee pudding.

We'd decided to stay in this evening because we were both knackered from running around London from morning until evening every day.

I'd had a chef cook our dinner, with a special request for dessert.

I'd just brought the pudding out to the dining room table a few minutes ago.

"I did promise you that I'd find you a good sticky toffee pudding," I reminded her.

"Why don't we have this stuff in the States?" she said, sounding unhappy because it wasn't routinely on every menu back home.

I'd devoured mine already, but Kylie was savoring hers in small bites, like we didn't have more in the kitchen.

I watched her from my seat in the chair across from her, taking in every nuance that crossed her beautiful face.

I loved the fact that even small things absolutely delighted her and that she nearly always found something to marvel over wherever we went.

There wasn't a single thing I did for her that she didn't notice or that she didn't thank me for profusely.

In some ways, I really hated that because it told me that very few people in her life had ever done anything for her or appreciated her.

By the time she was finished, she had leveled me with a glorious smile that felt like a sucker punch to my stomach.

Christ! Would there ever be a time when she smiled at me like that, and I wouldn't feel like someone had knocked the wind out of me?

Little by little, Kylie had managed to chase out most of the remaining darkness in my soul, leaving nothing but her luminous essence behind.

Whether we had the discussion about geography and those other details, she at least knew that we were going to be together and stay together, right?

Really, how could she think otherwise?

This woman was part of me.

I didn't want to sleep a single night without her warm, soft body cuddled up to mine.

I didn't want to spend a day in this house without her here.

I didn't want to eat a meal without her sitting at the table.

Certainly, she *must* know.

No, we hadn't *talked* about it, but she must be tossing around ideas in her head, suggestions she just hadn't mentioned yet.

She sighed as she pushed her plate back. "I suppose it's time for me to start thinking about the wedding. I'm looking forward to that, too, but this has been such a magical week."

Magical.

There was that word again.

Had it been magical because we were together, or because she thought London was enchanting?

"They delivered your dress today for the Monday night pre-wedding gala," I said casually.

She frowned. "What dress? I didn't order anything."

No, but I did.

I'd taken Kylie on the necessary tourist trip to Harrods, and while we'd been there, a beautiful evening gown had caught her eye.

Worried that the dress she'd brought wasn't formal enough for Mum's gala, she'd gotten her size and was ready to try it on...until she'd seen the price.

She'd hustled away from that Zuhair Murad gown like she couldn't get away from it fast enough.

So, I'd had it delivered today.

"It's in your master closet," I informed her.

"Dylan Lancaster," she said in a low, warning tone. "What did you order? God, please don't say it's that gown from Harrods."

"All right, I won't *say* that," I replied obligingly. "But I won't promise it's not in your closet."

"No," she groaned. "Dylan, that gown was nearly as much as my car."

"It's a gift," I told her.

"You've already given me this entire trip," she argued. "Please send it back. I don't buy dresses like that. I mean, it's stunning, but you've done enough for me."

"I'm not sending it back," I told her stubbornly. "Kylie, what's the point of me having money if I can't spend it on you? The price for the things I bought you is nothing to me. Small things. Your boyfriend is, in fact, a billionaire with more money than God, and in the future, you'll get more gifts that are even more expensive. This is who I am, love. Don't ask me not to give you anything your heart desires because I just can't do that."

She crossed her arms over her chest.

I watched as she opened her mouth and then closed it.

And then did it again.

"What am I going to do with you, Dylan Lancaster?" she finally asked, sounding completely exasperated.

I lifted a brow. "Keep me?"

She rolled her eyes. "I wouldn't change a single thing about you, but the gift-giving thing is *not* going to be easy for me. I've never had a man give me flowers, much less a five-figure dress and an all-expenses-paid luxury vacay in London. Including expensive dinners I never could have afforded. Oh, and let's not forget the private jet."

"Do you like flowers?" I asked her, realizing I hadn't bought her any yet.

"Of course," she huffed. "I mean, in general, yes. But we aren't talking about a bouquet of flowers here, Dylan."

I could start the delivery tomorrow, a different type of flower bouquet every day.

If I did that, I could see what she really liked by her reactions.

"Dylan!" she said sharply.

"Yes."

"God, are you even listening to me?"

She stood, grabbed our plates, and stomped toward the kitchen.

I followed her, of course, because that was just what I did and because I knew something wasn't right.

"Kylie," I said as I entered the kitchen. "What the hell is wrong?"

"Nothing," she said tersely. "Never mind."

I put the utensils into the dishwasher and closed it. "Talk to me," I demanded, stepping in front of her and blocking her exit. "Running away won't resolve this."

She looked up at me, her expression turbulent as she said, "What can I say? You're you, and I'm me. I was trying to explain that I'm uncomfortable with expensive gifts. You weren't hearing me. Right now, I think you're probably the most stubborn man on Earth."

"I heard you," I clarified, feeling my frustration level rising. "Every. Single. Word. But you know what stuck with me, Kylie?"

She shook her head.

"Fine. I'll tell you. All I could think about was the fact that you've never gotten flowers. Ever. Which I think is the saddest fucking thing I've ever heard since you had a husband and a few boyfriends. In comparison, it's cheaper for me to buy you the items I purchased for you than it is for a normal man to purchase your flowers. Yet you want to toss those gifts back in my face. My only intent was to make you happy and to let you know I appreciate you. I think you deserve to be treated like the most important woman in my life because you are. I'm not those other men, Kylie, because I *do* give a damn about making you happy and making sure you have everything you want or need. In fact, I feel privileged to be the man who can do that because I know you don't *need* me to take care of you. You choose to be with me because you want to. But I'd prefer you also let me give you gifts because it makes me feel useful, even though you don't need them or me."

She stared up at me with a quizzical expression. "Do you really think you need to do anything else to be useful to me?" she asked softly. "And you're right, they are inexpensive gifts to you, and I didn't mean to toss such a thoughtful gesture back in your face. I'm sorry, Dylan. Maybe I'm just not used to anyone caring about me that way."

"Someone should have," I grumbled.

She sent me a warm, adoring smile that made my cock even harder than it already was, which was almost an impossible feat.

"So if you do all those things, what can I do for you?" she asked. "I adore you, but my bank account doesn't stretch to designer clothes."

Stay with me.

Just breathe next to me.

Wrap your arms around me and let me happily drown in your affection.

I took her face in my hands as I said gruffly, "Just keep on adoring me, and I'll be the happiest man on Earth, love."

She put her hands under my shirt and stroked those soft palms up my torso in a sensual gesture that made any rational thoughts I had suddenly fly right out of my head.

CHAPTER 27

Kylie

THE WARMTH IN my chest spread throughout my entire body, finally landing straight between my thighs.

God, how I loved this man.

The way he cared about me.

The way he thought about my needs.

The way he gave so selflessly, without expecting anything back.

I savored the feel of his skin beneath my fingers as I whispered, "How did I get lucky enough to find you, Dylan Lancaster? It doesn't matter what happened before you because you more than make up for every crappy life experience I've ever had."

Being with him had taught me what it was like to be cherished and adored, and sometimes it felt so good that it was almost scary.

"That's my goal, baby," he answered huskily as he grasped my hips.

"Mission accomplished," I said with a sigh as I pulled his shirt over his head. "Let me just touch you, Dylan. I love your body."

I smoothed my hands over his broad shoulders, down his chest, and then traced every hard, solid muscle of his abdomen.

Dylan was breathtaking, with a body so drool worthy that I still marveled over the fact that every inch of him was mine.

I moved my hand lower and groped his hard cock, pressing my hand over the denim of his jeans.

"You've got a little problem here," I teased.

"Sweetheart, that's a *big* problem," he rasped.

"So it is," I agreed. "But I think I can help."

He sucked in an audible breath as I popped the top button of his jeans.

"You're the only one who can," he said in a graveled voice.

I loved how desperate he sounded for me. No matter how many times Dylan and I had sex, it was always just as fierce the next time.

Sometimes more so.

The better we got to know each other's bodies and what pleased each other, the hotter it got.

Dylan was insatiable, and I needed him just as much as he needed me.

I liberated his cock, and dropped to the floor, taking his jeans and boxer briefs to his ankles.

He kicked out of them impatiently.

I stroked my hand down his enormous cock. I never got tired of touching what felt like silk over very hard steel.

"Kylie? Baby," Dylan said in a choked voice.

I pushed his ass back against the counter, leaned forward, and swirled my tongue around his tip, tasting the bead of moisture that was waiting there for me.

"You're going to fucking kill me, woman," Dylan said as he tangled his hand in my hair.

The raw desire in his voice set my body on fire.

I opened my mouth and took as much of his shaft as possible, and then pulled back slowly, my lips wrapped around him with as much suction as I could create.

"Christ! Kylie!" He grunted, his fingers tightening on my scalp.

Every sound of pleasure that left his lips urged me on. I stroked his tight, firm ass as I devoured him, finally tightening my fingers until I grasped a cheek in both hands.

"Fuck!" he cursed, his hand guiding my head as I bobbed up and down. "So. Fucking. Good."

I moved one hand from his ass to his balls, stroking with just the right amount of pressure that I knew would set him off.

"Not. Fucking. Happening," Dylan growled and pulled me up.

"What's wrong?" I asked him in a sensual daze.

"Although I'd love to come with those beautiful lips wrapped around my cock, I need to be inside this sweet body of yours a lot more," he said in a low, fevered tone as he quickly got me naked.

He scooped me up and strode the short distance back to the dining room.

"Not going to make it to the bedroom," he rasped as he bent me over the table.

"Don't care," I whimpered. "Just fuck me."

He didn't.

He stroked his hands over my ass and then moved one of them between my thighs.

I almost hit the ceiling as his finger found my clit.

He stroked over the slick bundle of nerves, his other hand stroking over my back and then down to my ass.

I panted as my head dropped to the table, my body close to climax as Dylan stroked through my slick folds over and over again.

"Dammit, Dylan! Fuck me!" I demanded, my body primed and ready to explode.

I was needy and desperate to get his cock inside me.

He'd satisfy me when he thought I was just as hungry for his cock as he was to give it to me, and not a second before that.

Dylan always made sure I was right there with him, but right now, I might be *ahead* of him.

I almost wept with relief as I felt the tip of his cock at my entrance.

"Is this what you need, Kylie?" he asked roughly. "Tell me."

My heart was racing with anticipation, my body thrumming with need.

"Yes. You know it is," I whimpered.

"I'm always going to give you what you need," he said in a hoarse, raw tone as he surged forward and buried his cock inside me.

"Oh, God, yes!" I moaned. "You feel so good."

His hands gripped my hips as he began to move with steady strokes, each one deeper, harder than the one before.

I felt his hand start to stroke up and down my back, and then he leaned forward and buried his face in my neck, his tongue and mouth devouring every inch of sensitive skin he could find.

"Dylan," I choked out as my body burned white-hot.

This man consumed me, possessed me every single time he touched me, until I wasn't sure where one of us ended, and the other began.

"Wish I could make this last," Dylan rumbled, his chest against my back. "There's no slow speed with you, Kylie. You make me completely crazy. You're my sanity and my insanity."

"Me, too," I murmured, savoring the moment of intense closeness when our bodies became so entangled that I could feel Dylan inside my soul.

He straightened, his thrusts becoming more urgent, more frenzied as neither one of us could hold back any longer.

"Harder," I urged.

He gripped my hips, and every time he buried himself inside me, his cock was so deep that my body vibrated with satisfaction.

"Yes!" I cried out. "Dylan!"

My climax began to peak, the release so powerful that my body felt like it was imploding.

"Kylie," Dylan roared as he pounded into me, finally finding his own release.

My heart was hammering as Dylan leaned forward, his chest heaving, and buried his face into my neck.

I turned my head, and we shared a quick, breathless kiss as his body covered me like he had to protect me.

"You wreck me every single time," I told him as I reached behind me and stroked my hand through his hair.

He plopped his bare ass into a chair and pulled me onto his lap, his arms wrapped around me protectively.

I put my head on his shoulder and threaded my hand into his hair. "I'm sorry if I hurt you. That's something I never want to do," I muttered as I fingered the strands of hair at the back of his head.

"I shouldn't have pushed you. If you aren't comfortable, I should have listened," he said as he brushed a hand up and down my back.

"I don't think it was even the price of the gifts," I confessed. "It's not like I don't know you're obscenely wealthy. Maybe it's just because I'm so unused to anyone giving a damn enough to think about being thoughtful, my female friends excluded, of course. You make me feel special, Dylan, and that's just so foreign to me. I love it, but I'm not quite sure how to accept it like I really deserve it. Thank you for that incredible dress. I'll feel like a princess in it. It's a relief to know I won't feel underdressed. I can probably get through almost any event, nervous or not, since I am in public relations, but it's a confidence boost to know I'll be dressed appropriately."

I was going to have to learn to get past my insecurities. If I didn't, I'd end up hurting Dylan more. I didn't want to crush his generous nature.

"You'll be the most beautiful woman there, no matter what you wear. So, you'll keep it?" he asked hopefully.

I nuzzled his neck and dropped a kiss on his stubbled jaw. "Yes, you crazy, generous, thoughtful man. I'll keep it."

If it came to a choice between me being a little uncomfortable versus hurting him, I was going to choose to be a little ill at ease every single time.

"There are a few other things in your closet, too," he said cautiously.

"Like…anything I looked at when I was at Harrods and liked?" I asked.

"Maybe not everything," he hedged. "I may have missed something."

"Considering your attention to detail, I somehow doubt that," I said with a smile. "I'll thank you for those when I see them."

Since I didn't remember looking at anything pricier than that dress, I was probably safe.

"I have no idea why my mother decided she needed to hold another gala. Probably because the wedding and reception guest list didn't include anyone Damian isn't close to, so she didn't want acquaintances to feel slighted. She probably planned it on a weekday on purpose. Not too close to the wedding next Saturday, and it may get the crowd to disperse early."

We were quiet for a minute before I said, "Our sightseeing week is almost over."

Honestly, after the wedding was done, there was really no reason for me to stay. Macy would be leaving on Sunday, and Damian and Nic were leaving on their honeymoon on Monday, as soon as Damian's jet returned from taking Macy back home.

Since I'd canceled my plane ticket, it would probably be better if I headed back with Macy.

It would be kind of a waste for Dylan's jet to make another trip.

The two of us hadn't really discussed any kind of future plans to get together, but I trusted Dylan enough to know we *would* see each other. We cared about each other far too much to just walk away.

We had phone calls, video calls, and Dylan would be back at his beach house.

I just wished it wasn't going to be so hard to say goodbye.

It was going to rip my heart out, especially since we hadn't made any plans to see each other again soon.

Dylan stood, his arms securely around my body.

I wrapped my arms around his neck instinctively to keep my balance. "What are you doing?"

"Taking you to bed," he drawled in a sexy baritone. "Unless you have any serious objections to that idea."

I sighed.

I had so little time left with Dylan. I didn't want to spend it worrying about what would happen when we weren't in the same country anymore.

We'd work that out eventually.

While I was with him, I wanted to just enjoy every moment of it.

"Not a single one," I assured him and focused all of my attention on what pleasures he had in store for the rest of the night.

CHAPTER 28

Dylan

WHAT IN THE hell had I been thinking when I'd bought her that damn gown?

"Is everything okay?" Kylie asked softly as she sat next to me in the back seat of the Ghost on the way to the gala.

"Good. Yes. Everything is fine."

What else was I going to say?

I could hardly admit that I was regretting my decision to buy her a gown she loved, simply because it was probably going to draw every male eye at the gala.

The dress had looked perfectly fine on the mannequin.

I just hadn't been ready to see that same gown on Kylie or the way her curvy body filled out that damn garment.

If I wanted to be completely honest with myself, the dazzling blue color complemented her flame-colored hair and fair skin perfectly. Yes, she'd stand out, but Kylie Hart was going to be noticeable anywhere she went.

It was the deceptively innocent leaf patterns scattered in the cut of the dress that had nearly bowled me over when I'd seen her come down the stairs this evening.

All right. Yes. All of the important areas were covered with those sequined leaves—just barely. However, it was *the way* they were concealed that was totally unsettling.

Way too much bare skin and her entire back was exposed. The material clung to her shapely body, hugging it like a lover, and one wrong move in that dress would probably expose a part of her body that should not be uncovered.

I took a deep breath and let it back out again. To be fair, it was very chic, and if any other woman had been wearing it, I wouldn't have blinked an eye.

Seeing it on Kylie, however, had made me into a damn lunatic.

There was no denying that she looked stunning. I just wasn't crazy about the idea of every other guy at the gala ogling *my* woman.

Fuck! When in the hell had I become a possessive psycho?

I'd escorted women to social events who were wearing attire that was just as revealing.

Kylie looked sensual. Gorgeous. Elegant. Breathtaking.

I just hoped that I wouldn't want to punch every man who eyed her the way I would be.

"Are you sure you're okay?" she asked again, more hesitantly this time.

Christ! I was being a bastard to her, and she hadn't done a single thing wrong. I took her hand and squeezed it. "I'm fine, sweetheart. I'm sorry I had to go into the office today."

Damian had been unavailable, and we'd had a crisis at headquarters. It had taken me half the day to get things smoothed out.

While I planned on being at headquarters more this week, I'd hoped for one more day with Kylie before things got crazy.

"I told you, it was perfectly okay," she said adamantly. "It gave me a little time to catch up on work and make your picture collage. If you don't like it, I can take it down."

Was I really being such a prick that she thought I hadn't loved her gift?

Kylie had made it a point to have someone take our pictures everywhere we'd gone during the last week, and she'd put them together for me today. She'd gone out and gotten the frames and used my photo printer to put everything together.

The end result had been a large photo collection of the two of us that she'd put on the big wall in the kitchen.

We'd looked so damn happy in every picture, and I'd been touched that she'd taken the time to put it together.

"I loved it," I assured her. "It's in the perfect spot. I'll see it more often in the kitchen since I'm in that room a lot more often than others."

She sighed. "We haven't gotten to use the tennis court yet. That level is amazing."

I smiled. I'd planned that indoor tennis court before I'd even met Kylie. "Because we've been so worn out from all our other physical exercise," I said, using a tone of voice that would tell her I *wasn't* talking about our sightseeing."

She scooted closer. "I'd take *that* over tennis any day."

"Did I tell you how gorgeous you look tonight?" I asked.

"Actually, you haven't. Do you think the dress is too much?" she asked.

Shit! I shouldn't have let my overactive brain get in the way of telling her how stunning she was. "Not at all. I'm just worried I may have to chase all the lechers away from you."

She snorted adorably. "I feel good, and it's a beautiful dress, but I don't think your job will be that hard."

"Good, because I'll definitely have something else that is hard all night long," I grumbled. "And I won't be able to take my eyes off you."

"You're looking incredibly handsome yourself in black tie," she informed me. "I'll have the hottest escort at the gala."

I felt somewhat placated. "I do have an identical twin brother," I reminded her.

"No offense to Damian, but you're way hotter. Never once has he made my female hormones twitch."

I grinned, feeling even more appeased. "How is that possible when we look exactly alike?"

"You *feel* different," she said, looking like she wasn't quite sure how to explain. "Even though you look similar, your auras are different. Damian is a little aloof until you get to know him. You radiate energy, passion, and red-hot, sweaty, orgasmic sex. Maybe it's our chemistry, but I was attracted to you from day one. Yes, you were incredibly rude, but I was still…drawn to you. Maybe this is weird, but I could almost sense your pain, and it unsettled me."

I shook my head. "I was drawn to you, too. Those first few days, maybe that made me uncomfortable, too. So I wanted to scare you away. Fortunately for me, you aren't easily intimidated. I'm lucky that my balls are still intact."

"They felt just fine the last time I fondled them," she said in a low, sexy voice.

Christ! I'd thought my dick couldn't get any harder.

Apparently, I'd been wrong.

"Be careful, love, or you'll get more than you bargained for right here in the back seat of this car," I warned her.

I'd closed the partition up between the driver and us as soon as we'd gotten into the vehicle. Considering the fact that it was already dark, it wouldn't be impossible to—

"Not in *this* dress, or in *this* car. I'd prefer not to arrive to meet your family for the first time looking like I've just gotten quickie in the back seat of a Rolls," she said firmly. "No matter how hot that might be."

Bloody hell! She was right, but the gnawing instinct in the pit of my stomach was to somehow mark this woman as mine before those other tossers got any ideas.

I hated myself right now because this was essentially my damn fault for not having the discussion Kylie and I should have had a long time ago.

As of now, I'd done nothing to cement our future or make sure that every bastard out there knew that this woman was mine.

Not just for a week or two.

Not just for something short-term.

Not just as a girlfriend or a lover.

The way I felt about Kylie wasn't going to change, and I'd known that for some time now.

Granted, I *had* gotten the ball rolling on our future, but I hadn't shared those plans with her yet.

The truth was, maybe there was a part of me that didn't want to hear her say that it wasn't exactly what *she* wanted, too.

I'd wanted to make sure she trusted me enough to take that leap of faith since I still had a history of being an idiot to overcome.

Although Kylie had never blamed me for my past, it wouldn't be easy for a woman with trust issues to see me as that guy she could count on to stay.

I wished I had more time, more chances to prove to her that I was never again going to be that man she'd seen in an orgy picture, baring his ass for the entire world to see.

Unfortunately, I didn't have that luxury. Since we hadn't discussed our future and what we wanted, her first instinct after the wedding would be to go back to the States because her life was there. Her business was there. Most of her friends were there.

I was going to have to push my apprehension aside because letting her walk away was not an option.

"Kylie," I started, trying to ignore the dread that was lodged in my throat. "I know we haven't really had a chance to discuss what we're going to do about us after the wedding—"

"Let's not," she said in a rush. "Everything is going to be so crazy this week. Can we talk Saturday night after this is all over?"

"Of course," I assured her. "If that's what you want."

All right. So that hadn't really gone very well.

I wasn't sure if I was relieved or concerned because she was willing to wait until after the wedding to plan our future.

If we actually had one.

I let out a long breath I hadn't even realized I'd been holding.

Perhaps it wasn't a bad thing to give her a little more time to realize that I wouldn't go back to being an idiot.

I would never go back there, and I had no desire to slip into avoidance anymore.

While I couldn't say every single one of my demons was slayed, I'd killed off most of those little bastards, and if another rose up, I'd eliminate that one, too.

I wasn't that man crippled by post-traumatic stress anymore, yet I couldn't say I was the Dylan Lancaster I'd been before two years ago, either.

I was…different. Changed by my experiences and unable to go back.

And truthfully, I was all right with that.

I was warier, a little harder, and less likely to trust people I didn't know.

But I was also wiser and more aware of things I'd taken for granted before my life had been turned upside down.

Some of my priories were different, but that felt right, too.

At one point in my life, I'd always put Lancaster International first, just like Damian.

Now, also, just like my twin, my corporation wouldn't *always* come first in my life because I'd found someone who was more important than Lancaster International.

"Are we here?" Kylie asked as we pulled into the long driveway of Hollingsworth.

"This is it," I confirmed. "Are you ready?"

"As ready as I'm ever going to be," she answered. "Are you?"

I didn't have to ask what she meant. I hadn't seen my family since I'd taken control of my mind again, and what in the hell could I say to the people who had stood by me for way longer than they should have?

As we reached the circular part of the drive in front of the house, I could see Damian, Nicole, Leo, and Mum waiting for our arrival.

I squeezed her hand. "More ready than you'll ever know," I told her, beyond eager to finally take my place in the Lancaster family again.

CHAPTER 29

Kylie

I STOOD BEHIND DYLAN as we exited the car, giving him time to greet his family.

It was a pivotal moment for him and an important one since it was the first time he'd be face-to-face with them since he'd started treatment and decided to take back his life.

Damian and Dylan were dressed in nearly identical tuxedos, and the way they looked like almost mirror images of each other was even more striking when the two of them were standing side by side.

Yeah, I could see the differences, too, but they were subtle, and as the two men who looked so much alike faced each other, neither one of them looking like they knew quite what to say, my heart clenched.

I saw the struggle on Dylan's face, the desire to say a million things that he wasn't sure how to get out of his mouth.

It was finally Damian who reached out, wrapped his arms around his twin, and pulled his younger brother close.

I saw Dylan's eyes close as he hugged Damian back with just as much enthusiasm.

This family had waited way too long for this reunion, for Dylan to come back home again where he belonged.

After so much pain for all of them, watching Dylan being so readily accepted back into the family he loved so much was heart-wrenchingly sweet for me.

I assumed the blond guy who gave Dylan the same welcome was Leo, Dylan's younger brother. Some of his features were similar, but the stark differences in coloring between him, his mother, and his twin brothers made him stand out.

Dylan swept his petite mother into a long embrace, holding the elegant gray-haired woman like she was precious to him, which I knew she was.

I continue to watch as he finally stood in front of Nicole, not shying away from her as he said, "I owe you a very big apology."

Nicole, dressed elegantly in a striking red gown, shook her head. "I don't want your apology. It's not necessary. You're going to be my brother-in-law. Just give me a damn hug."

Dylan grinned. "I'd like that just as long as your soon-to-be-husband doesn't deck me if I do."

"Make it short," Damian grumbled good-naturedly.

Like the affectionate, compassionate woman she'd always been, Nicole threw her arms around Dylan's neck and hugged him like the brother she'd never had. "I'm so glad you're home," she told him.

"Me, too," he said as he hugged her back.

As he released Nicole, he took my hand and tugged me forward. I hugged Damian and Nicole before Dylan said, "Mum. Leo. This is Kylie Hart."

Leo stepped forward immediately with a mischievous grin. "I'm definitely getting a hug. Nicole didn't mention that her maid of honor was just as ravishingly beautiful as she was."

His smile reached all the way to his gorgeous blue eyes, and I instantly knew exactly why Nicole adored Leo.

"Get on with it, Leo," Damian grumbled. "No need to torture Dylan, too."

I wasn't quite sure what Damian meant, but the handsome blond scooped me up into his arms and gave me a warm hug.

"My turn," Isabella Lancaster said firmly once Leo had let me go.

As she put her arms around me, Isabella whispered, "Thank you for caring about my son and for everything you've done to help him."

"It wasn't me," I said in a hushed voice. "It was all him. You raised a very strong-willed, incredible son, Your Grace."

"None of that formal stuff in this family, Kylie," Dylan's mom insisted. "Call me Bella."

"I'm stealing my best friend away for a little while," Nicole said as she stepped forward and took my arm. "I have some people I want her to meet."

Isabella beamed and then winked at Nicole. "Take your time, dear. You two need to catch up."

I sent Dylan a quick wave as Nic dragged me inside, pulling me past the crowd in the ballroom and into a quiet room on the other side of the house that appeared to be a library.

"Tell me everything," she said as she closed the door. "Oh, my God, you look amazing, Kylie. I'm sure Dylan's eyes popped out of his head earlier."

"You look gorgeous, too," I told her. "And we went sightseeing all week. There's not much more to tell."

There was a radiant happiness vibe that surrounded my best friend that had never been there before. After all the heartache of losing her mom, I was ecstatic over the fact that she was going to be living in wedded bliss with Damian.

"There's plenty more to tell," she argued as she folded her arms and leaned her ass against a large oak desk. "I saw the way you were looking at Dylan when he and Damian were finally face-to-face. You were worried, and I swear I saw tears in your eyes. You never cry, Kylie. You're not just attracted to him. You're head over heels in love with Dylan Lancaster."

Dammit! I'd never been able to hide anything from Nicole, even when I really wanted to, which was right about now.

She was getting married. She didn't need to hear about my relationship with Dylan.

"Spill it," she insisted, her pretty blue eyes locked on my face.

I gave up. "I didn't mean for it to happen, but yeah, I fell for him. It was impossible *not* to fall in love with him. He's unlike any other guy I've ever met. He's the one who bought me this incredible dress. When we were in Harrods, I loved it, but I ran like hell when I saw the price. He had it delivered as a gift. A *gift.* Just because he'd noticed that I looked at it. In fact, every single thing I admired at that store ended up in my closet at his home. Who does that?"

Nic smiled. "They are a little overwhelming at first, but you'll get used to it. God, Kylie, it's obvious he's crazy about you, too. I thought he was going to tear Leo's head off when he told you how gorgeous you were and wanted a hug. Dylan looks at you in exactly the same way as Damian looks at me. Can't you see that?"

I shook my head. "We care a lot about each other, Nic, but I don't think Dylan is ready for any huge commitments. Not after what he's been through. I promised myself I'd be okay with that, as long as we gave this thing our best shot. He's definitely kept up his part of that bargain. Dylan gives without ever expecting anything back, and I know we aren't walking away from this entirely. It's just going to be really hard to leave him after we've spent so much time together."

Nicole lifted a brow. "What? You think he's just going to let you go, and you'll see each other once in a while? Not happening. Lancaster men aren't like that, Kylie. They love with their whole heart, and once they find the right woman, there is no one else for them. Their father was the same way, and Bella will never marry again, much less look at another man, now that her husband is gone. Do you really think Dylan is going to let go of the only woman he'll ever love?"

"He's never said that he loves me," I confessed. "I'm not sure that he does. You have to remember how much Dylan has been through, Nic."

"I realize that," she replied. "But I'm not so sure you two didn't meet at exactly the right time. I think you were both ready. You've certainly both been hurt enough times to appreciate each other."

"He's more than I ever expected," I said, my voice shaky. "He's…" my voice trailed off.

"Overwhelming?" she finished. "I know the feeling, but I wouldn't trade the way Damian loves me for anything else in the world. When he looks at me, I know he's seeing the one woman in the world that he wants. That he'll ever love. I'll take the possessiveness and insanity that goes along with that anytime."

"God, how do you handle the fact that there's nothing in this world that Damian can't buy?" I groaned.

"He can't buy everything," she mused. "The one thing he can't buy is my love, and when I gave him that, he's cherished it like it's the greatest gift I could give him. His money and power are a part of him, but it's just one part of a very amazing guy. It was hard at first because I didn't come from the same background, but it's just…money. And it is really convenient that he has a private jet that can take us anywhere," she said in a joking manner. "Not to mention a home that's pretty mind-blowing, and a Rolls that will take me anywhere I want to go. The thought of driving in London is a little daunting."

I gaped at her. "You really are okay with all that," I said. "It doesn't bother you anymore."

She shrugged. "Why should it? What am I going to do? Insist that he give up all of his money so we can take an Uber and budget how to afford everything?"

I snorted. "I suppose you're right. It's easier to elevate to his lifestyle."

"His money isn't going to change who I am," Nicole said firmly.

I nodded slowly. "You're right. I guess I never really thought past my own discomfort. Dylan and I just come from such different worlds."

"But you share the same heart," Nic said gently. "Which is all that really matters, Kylie. I have to get back to the gala, but think about that. All I want is for you to be happy."

I hugged her tightly before we made our way back to the enormous ballroom, my mind reeling as I surveyed the crowd.

There were food tables everywhere and an enormous dance floor.

I eyed the food and had just decided to head there first when a tuxedo-clad gentleman appeared next to me. "I don't think we've met. Would you care to dance?" he asked.

"Don't even think about it, mate," I heard Dylan growl from behind me. "This one is taken."

The stranger's eyes widened as he turned around. "Dylan? It must be you since your twin is marrying Nicole."

Dylan nodded sharply. "Nice to see you, Gerald, but Kylie and I have to be going. She's promised *all* of her dances to me tonight."

I bit back a smile.

Maybe the blatant possessiveness in Dylan's eyes should have terrified me, but it didn't.

Strangely enough, a thrill of satisfaction shot through my body because it was very clear that Dylan Lancaster was boldly claiming...me.

He took my hand and started to haul me toward the dance floor.

"Christ! You look way too sexy in that cock-hardening dress," he grumbled. "I want to punch any man who even looks at you."

"Then maybe it's a good thing that the only man I see is you."

He looked slightly less annoyed as he wrapped his arms around me on the dance floor. "That is rather fortunate for every other male at this event."

I laughed. "Dance with me, handsome."

It didn't take much convincing before he did exactly that.

CHAPTER 30

Kylie

"THIS IS THE most relaxing day I've had in a long time," Macy said as she took a long sip of her champagne.

"I love it," Nicole said with a sigh. "The best hen party day ever."

We couldn't exactly call this a simple party since we'd been celebrating together since morning in several different locations.

I smiled as I looked out at sunset over London from our pod on the London Eye, an experience I'd intentionally skipped with Dylan since we'd made plans to do this for Nic's bachelorette party day.

We'd spent the better part of the morning and afternoon at the spa before we'd moved on to an incredible high tea with plenty of scones, Nic's favorite.

Finally, we'd traveled here to the London Eye to take a private, thirty-minute champagne ride on the giant Ferris wheel. We'd intentionally picked the last ride of the night.

The pod was large, so we had plenty of space all to ourselves.

"I wonder what kind of stag party the guys had today?" I contemplated out loud. "Dylan isn't much of a drinker anymore."

Just like us, Damian had opted to keep his bachelor party to just his two brothers rather than make it a big party.

"I doubt it involves a bar," Nic pondered. "Not really Damian's thing, and Leo isn't a heavy drinker, either. Food would be my bet."

"I really hate to see the day end," Macy said in a wistful tone. "We won't have days like this together very often anymore."

"We'll just have to do a video conference date every week," Nic said adamantly. "I'm getting married, not going to prison."

Macy snorted. "Aren't those two things slightly similar," she joked.

"Not this marriage," Nic replied. "I'll be starting a new job as a corporate attorney once I get back from my honeymoon. It sounds like a challenge, so I'm looking forward to it."

"I'm happy for you," Macy said genuinely. "You're going to have a great life with Damian. I just don't think marriage is ever going to be for me."

"Never say never," Nic warned as she poured herself more champagne. "I thought the same thing at one time."

Macy shook her head. "My hours are crazy, and then I have the shelter volunteering, too. But I do like animals better than men most of the time."

I chuckled. "I can't even say that they won't keep you warm in bed every night because they can."

Macy beamed. "I can't recommend using a tiger or a bear for that job, but dogs and cats work perfectly fine."

"Okay, you two cynical single women," Nic said with a laugh. "There are a few things those animals can't provide, hot, sweaty sex being the first thing that comes to mind."

"Vibrator," Macy said. "When I'm not too exhausted to bother."

I snickered. "Which is almost always, I'm sure. Your schedule is insane."

"I don't mind," she answered. "I'm finally doing something I've wanted to do for as long as I can remember."

Maybe she didn't mind her hours, but her face was showing signs of stress. Macy's education to become a vet and then to pursue exotic vet status had been long and arduous for her. She was desperately in need of a break.

"I saw you talking to Leo at the wedding party dinner last night," Nic said. "You two probably have a lot in common."

Macy had gotten into London the night before last, and she'd finally met the rest of the family at the casual dinner at Hollingsworth House last night.

Macy's face lit up. "He's amazing," she said earnestly. "I've been a fan of his work for years. I wish I had time to get to his sanctuary and breeding center here. It's one thing to provide a home for exotic animals who can't live out their lives in the wild, but it's a delicate process to try to breed in captivity to preserve a species, so they don't go extinct. He's done some extraordinary things just to locate extremely rare species for his breeding program. Some pretty dangerous things, too. Those animals aren't always found in friendly territory or in an area where they care about conservation."

"He's starting another sanctuary and breeding program in the US," Nic said.

Macy nodded. "Out near Palm Desert. He offered to take me around after everything is built. It's a really ambitious project because there are so many natural habitats to set up, but I'm sure he'll be successful. He's already done it once here."

I grinned as I looked at the animation on her face, an expression I hadn't seen in a long time. "Am I sensing some hero-worship here?"

She made a face. "Probably. I've seen every documentary that's ever been put out about his missions. Unfortunately, there have only been a few, and they aren't easy to find since they were done by British television. They weren't exactly high profile."

"Leo never mentioned that those even existed," Nic said, sounding perplexed.

"I don't think he's after any kind of spotlight," Macy mused. "I think he only let a film crew follow him a few times for educational purposes and awareness."

"Sounds like him," Nic said with a nod. "Do you like him? If I wasn't thoroughly in love with my fiancé, I'd probably say Leo is pretty hot."

Like Nic, I wasn't attracted to Leo, either, but aesthetically speaking, he was definitely gorgeous. That wild blond hair, sinful blue eyes, and his very fit body made him a sexy sight to behold.

"I may have had a tiny crush on him at one time, after I saw his documentaries," Macy said, holding her thumb and forefinger together so there was just a small space in between.

"What was it like to see him in the flesh?" I asked.

"He's even hotter than he was on television," she admitted. "Nicer than I thought he would be, too. We mostly just talked about his work. You know I'm not good at small talk."

I gave her an inquisitive look. "Why would you think he wouldn't be nice?"

Macy poured herself more champagne as she answered. "He is a rich billionaire from an aristocratic family. Plus, he's accomplished some pretty incredible things at a very young age. That would usually add up to somebody with a very big ego. I guess I was just surprised that he was so down to Earth, and…nice."

"The whole family is like that," I said with a sigh. "Bella is so sweet. She's made me feel so welcome. For some weird reason, she thinks I'm responsible for some of Dylan's progress and recovery."

"I don't think she's wrong about that," Nic said, supporting her future mother-in-law. "Dylan said you even tried to teach him to meditate."

I chuckled. "I did try, and he's learned a few deep breathing techniques, but his full meditation was a fail. He said he'd rather keep his eyes open so he could watch me. Other than that, all I've done is support him, and listen when he wanted to talk. Over time, we just became friends and companions. It benefited me as much as it did him. He's a challenge as a tennis partner, and he took me to some fantastic places for dinner. Not to mention that amazing beach house that he's now purchased from the prince. So the relationship was far from one-sided."

Nic's eyes widened. "He actually bought that place?"

I nodded. "He said his friend was contemplating selling, and Dylan didn't want someone else to buy it. So he bought it himself."

"Okay," Nic said. "Now I know where I'm staying when I get back there to visit. Not that the purchase was really a big deal to him, but that house is so beautiful and relaxing. Once he's my brother-in-law, I can definitely ask him for a favor."

"He seems really nice. I think he'd loan it to you whenever you wanted," Macy said. "I'm still stunned by his donation to the animal shelter, and he and Damian told me last night that they've set up a recurring donation from Lancaster International. That's a really big deal for the shelter."

"Dylan didn't tell me that," I told her. "But I'm not surprised."

"Me, either," Nic said with a sigh.

"So," Macy said. "Dylan seems absolutely crazy about you, Kylie. Am I going to be coming back to England for another wedding?"

I nearly choked on my champagne. "God, no," I answered. "We haven't even talked about the future yet."

"I think you should pencil the wedding into your schedule, though," Nic told Macy.

I quickly filled Macy in on anything she'd missed, including Dylan's past, when Nic nodded at me in encouragement. After all, it wasn't like he was exactly hiding what had happened anymore.

"So don't start hearing wedding bells," I finished. "Dylan is still getting used to being a billionaire mogul again right now. He's not ready for a commitment."

"Are you ready for that?" Macy asked.

"I love him," I said with a note of hopelessness in my voice. "But his life is here, and mine is back in Newport Beach. He needs time. He was in a dark place for two years, through no fault of his own."

"Maybe that's all the more reason for you two to be together," Macy said thoughtfully. "It really sounds like you…heal each other."

I thought about that for a minute.

Did we?

"I know he's healed me," I admitted. "He turned all of my old insecurities around about men just by making me feel…special. And wanted. I trust him, and I haven't given a man my trust in a long time."

"I think you've healed him for the same reasons, Kylie," Nic said gently. "After what happened to him, do you really think he could hand over his trust to another woman easily? Maybe it was somewhat easier for him because he has family who showed him what trust and unconditional love was like, but still, he has no reason to trust a woman."

"She put him through hell," Macy agreed.

"I know," I said, my heart filled with pain. "I swear, if she wasn't dead, I'd bitch slap her into next week. I don't know how anyone could put a guy through that just to make her own life easier. I know she wasn't right in the head. Dylan told me. She didn't deserve to die, and neither did her child, but her cruelty still floors me."

"Me, too," Nic and Macy said at the same time.

"Sometimes, I feel helpless about what I can ever do to take that pain away," I confessed.

Nic smiled softly. "I think you already have just by being you. Just keep on loving him, Kylie. That will be more than enough."

I let out a long breath before I shared, "Since I love him more than I ever thought possible, it's the only thing I can do."

CHAPTER 31

Dylan

"I'LL ADMIT, IT was definitely an interesting evening," Damian commented as we hung out in the living room of his home. "I'm not sure whose idea it was to do an escape room, but it was entertaining. I never even knew it existed."

Since none of us were pub crawlers, Leo and I had decided to take Damian out to his favorite Italian restaurant, followed by an escape room experience that was run at an old tube station that had been abandoned.

"We made it out with plenty of time to spare," Leo pointed out. "Not too hard when you put three Lancaster brains on one mystery."

The three of us had needed to work as a team to follow the clues and solve the mystery to escape.

It had been extremely diverting, and doing it together had been the whole point of the entertainment.

"It was a great evening," Damian said. "Best stag party ever. I wonder how Nicole's hen day went. The ladies should be getting home shortly. She said she wouldn't be too late; then again, she and Macy did leave pretty early."

I knew exactly what they were doing, but I wasn't about to share. Macy and Kylie had worked hard to keep Nicole's day a secret, so Damian could find out all about it when Nicole told him about it.

"Only about thirty-six more hours, and you'll be a married man, Damian," Leo commented. "How are you holding up?"

"Honestly?" he asked without expecting an answer. "I'll be damn happy when she's finally my wife. Not that we need that piece of paper for the two of us to be committed, but it will be nice to make it official. I'm looking forward to the honeymoon, too. Nicole hasn't had a chance to do much traveling, so she's really excited."

"You're not nervous?" Leo questioned.

He shook his head. "Not at all. No second thoughts. There is no other woman for me."

Christ! I knew what that certainty felt like, and someday, when Leo finally fell hard for someone, he'd understand it, too.

I could tell that Damian was starting to get impatient, and since Nicole had nothing planned for tomorrow except any last-minute issues that came up, I was pretty sure my twin would be happy to tie the knot tomorrow if he could.

However, I doubted that idea was going to fly with Nicole or my mother.

In America, there probably would have been a rehearsal dinner taking place tomorrow, but Nicole had decided to skip that since it wasn't normally done here and had opted for the casual family dinner at Hollingsworth House the night before.

As expected, the wedding was a mix of traditions, but Leo and I had already been informed that the wedding party was standing, and that Nicole would be the last one down the aisle instead of the first.

Since Kylie had made it through the gala just fine, I had no doubt she'd feel completely comfortable at the wedding reception, too.

To be honest, she'd surprised me just a little at the gala. If she'd been nervous, it hadn't shown. She'd been able to converse with anyone who came her direction, and with so much charm and warmth that she'd never once needed to talk about the weather.

Maybe I'd forgotten about the fact that she was in public relations and that she did a lot of talking for a living.

She might have been apprehensive about saying the wrong thing underneath, but on the surface, she'd managed to charm every person who had crossed her path.

And yes, I'd been there to watch every single person who approached her—if I wasn't right beside her—because I'd circulated in that crowd most of my life, so I knew every single man present that might lay a hand on her.

"So, when is Kylie due back in the United States?" Leo asked.

Damian lifted a brow but stayed silent.

"I'm not exactly sure," I told Leo. "If I have my way, she'll be here for a while. We agreed not to talk about it until the wedding was over, but I know what I want. I've known for a while now. I'm just not sure how she'll feel about it."

"What do you want?" Leo questioned.

"I want her in my life for the rest of my life," I confessed.

"I could tell that you'd fallen for her," Leo informed me. "You have the same crazy look in your eyes when you look at her that Damian does when he looks at Nicole. But are you really ready to make that commitment, Dylan? You've been through a lot."

"I doubt very much if I'd be doing as well as I am right now if it wasn't for her," I shared. "I'd already started treatment when she walked through the door of that Beverly Hills home, and I was determined to get my head straight. But it's like Kylie grabbed me and yanked me out of that black hole way faster than I would have found my way out on my own. At first, she was incredibly diverting. Then, she was supportive. After that, she was a companion who listened. Finally, she was the woman I couldn't live without. There was never a moment when I wasn't physically attracted to her, but it was always a lot more than that."

"I think he's ready, Leo," Damian added. "I understand your concern, but we can't time the moment when the right woman comes along, and when she does, we can't lose her because the timing isn't quite right."

Leo frowned. "It's not as though I don't like her. I do. I just don't want to see you like that ever again. Christ! The last two years have been hell for you, Dylan. If I would have just known—"

"Don't, little brother," I said as I held up my hand. "I'll tell you the same thing I told Damian…no one could have helped me. I had to figure out that I was worth saving myself. You and Damian both tried. Mum did, too. I wasn't listening. Something inside me finally had to snap before I was willing to get help. I'm just grateful that we're all here together right now. The past is over, and I want to move on with my life. If Kylie decides that she's willing to take me on, I'd be happier than I've ever been in my entire life."

"And if she doesn't?" Leo asked with apprehension in his tone.

I shook my head. "Not an option. I'm in love with her. I'll find a way to be with her, no matter what it takes. I'm not going to let geography get in my way. I'll never believe that the two of us don't fit. I just have to find a way to put the connection together."

Leo shook his head. "Shit. No offense, but I'm glad I'm single. I have no desire to get that intense over a female."

Damian chuckled. "Your turn will come, eventually."

"Not if I can help it," Leo grumbled. "And most women think I'm crazy because I spend most of my time in remote locations. Me meeting a woman who actually understands why I do what I do is incredibly unlikely."

I frowned. "Maybe you should rein back your travel a little and relax. You're never in the same place for very long. I don't remember you even having a regular girlfriend. Have you? Did I miss it?"

"Two," he shared. "And there was nothing to miss. They didn't last long, so we never got to the meet-the-family stage. Neither one of them understood my obsession with saving species from the brink of extinction, or why, when I was a wealthy billionaire from an important family, I had passed on taking a role in Lancaster International. I guess in most women's minds, being a businessman would make a lot more sense than what I do."

"Damian and I have always understood," I told him solemnly. "You've always had something else that drove you, Leo, a passion that was different from ours but just as important."

Leo grinned. "But mine has never gotten me laid nearly as often as yours did," he joked.

He'd probably be surprised to know that I hadn't slept around quite as much as he thought. "Then maybe you should start spending a little more time in a location that at least has cell service."

"I will be, for a while anyway," he said. "I'm leaving for America after the wedding so I can finish getting my new facility set up there. The area isn't exactly a metropolis, but hot running water and a cell tower will be close enough."

"How's it going over there?" Damian asked.

"So far, so good," he said nonchalantly. "I have some issues to work out, but it's making progress."

"So, does that mean you'll call more often?" Damian questioned.

"As long as I have service, I'll call," Leo said and then turned his eyes back in my direction. "I'm behind you, Dylan, and I hope everything goes smoothly with Kylie. If you need anything, I'll only be a phone call away right now."

I swallowed the regret that rose up in my throat.

I'd missed so much time with both of my brothers.

Nothing had really changed between all of us, but that time void still remained.

"I'll be over to see your new sanctuary. Hopefully, Kylie will be with me."

"Nicole and I would like to come, too," Damian added. "We'll bring Mum."

Leo grinned. "Brilliant. I'll see if I can find a place to live that isn't too shockingly primitive."

Damian and Leo started discussing something else, but my mind wandered.

No matter how much I'd tried to put my future with Kylie out of my mind, it always rocketed right back there.

I had no idea when she'd want to leave to go back to the States, and I couldn't make her stay if she felt she *had* to go.

I'd leave and go with her in a heartbeat, but I'd already promised Damian that I'd stick around and work out of our headquarters here in London while he was away. I owed him that for dumping on him over the last two years. Hell, I owed him even more than that, even though that's all he'd asked for.

When I'd told Leo that I wasn't letting geography get in the way of my happiness, I'd meant it.

But what if it wasn't just a geographical problem?

What if Kylie wasn't ready for a commitment?

And if she wasn't, could I really blame her?

I'd wracked my brain for every single argument she could make and had come up with a solution for every single problem she might bring up.

Except one…

I couldn't make her love me and want to spend the rest of her life with me.

If she didn't, and that wasn't what she wanted, I was utterly and completely fucked.

CHAPTER 32

Kylie

"HAVE I TOLD you how beautiful you look today?" A sexy baritone voice said next to my ear.

I turned around and smiled at Dylan. He'd snuck up on me while my thoughts had been wandering during the wedding reception.

The ceremony had been perfect, and the weather couldn't have been better if we'd custom ordered it.

Nicole had looked radiant in her gorgeous ivory dress, with her hair swept up in an elegant arrangement that suited the vintage style gown.

The ceremony had been short, but achingly sweet, as Damian and Nicole had pledged their lives to each other.

I put my arms around his neck. "You've told me that a few times, but thank you...again."

The dresses Macy and I wore were simple but beautiful. They were deep blue with a sweetheart neckline and small, off-the-shoulder short sleeves.

My heart skittered as he grinned down at me and asked, "Care to stroll down to the lake? The crowd is finally starting to thin out. I think our duties are done here."

The reception had started right after the noon wedding, so everything was winding down.

I nodded. "Let me just dash inside and use the bathroom before we go."

Dylan had taken me down to the lake that was hidden in the trees once before, and it wasn't far, but I really had to pee.

I took a quick glance around at the remaining guests as I hurried toward the house, but I hadn't spotted Macy, Nicole, or Damian.

Oh well, it wasn't like Dylan and I would be gone long, and I had my cell phone tucked inside the silver wristlet I was carrying.

I headed for the bathroom right next to the library and quickly did my business, stopping to slap on a little more sunscreen from the small tube in my purse before I exited.

This part of the home was quiet and empty, so I stopped short, right outside the bathroom door, when I heard Nicole's voice as she said, "This just doesn't feel right to me, Damian. I really shouldn't sign these papers to sell ACM to Dylan without discussing it with Kylie first. We're partners."

My entire body tensed as I moved closer to the library door. It was partially ajar, but I couldn't see Nicole and Damian. They were obviously right behind the opening, near the library desk.

Are they signing paperwork?

It wasn't possible that I'd heard Nicole correctly, right?

She *couldn't* be selling ACM. *To Dylan?*

"You were never legally partners, Nicole," Damian said in a soothing tone. "Dylan is buying the entire company. He's going to do right by Kylie. You know he will."

How? Was he going to be magnanimous enough to give me my old job back?

I stood there, frozen, my entire life and everything I'd worked for crumbling beneath my feet.

Technically, it was Nicole's business to sell. We *hadn't* made a legal agreement yet, nor had I given her a penny yet, so I could hardly barge into the library and tell her she had no right to sell her business to Dylan Lancaster.

What I had saved toward a company of my own would only buy a tiny portion of interest in ACM, but I'd been okay with that since I knew I could keep paying Nicole for a bigger percentage over time.

Maybe I'd never get to the half-ownership she'd wanted to legally sign over to me for absolutely nothing at all, but I'd known that I could keep chipping away at acquiring more and more of the company I loved like it was my own.

That had been the solution I'd planned to present to Nicole once she was back from her honeymoon since there was no way I could just take half interest in ACM for free.

I'd been the one who hadn't wanted to be named as a legal partner until I'd worked out the details.

I'd known I was going to get pushback from Nicole because I would be the working partner in the future, but we could have haggled things out. Somehow. Now, because I'd hesitated to reach out for what I wanted, someone had snatched it away just when that goal had been so close I could almost taste it.

Why? What in the hell did he want with ACM? Yeah, Lancaster International was in the business of acquiring small companies that were floundering and building them up into huge, international companies. But ACM wasn't in financial trouble.

As he'd mentioned previously, our bottom line could be better, and there was huge potential for ACM to grow, but the company didn't need rescuing.

Had he seen an opportunity when he'd been helping me with some business issues?

Did he want to make ACM into an enormous, international PR company?

"Oh, my God," I whispered as I put my hand to my mouth.

"I'll do it," Nicole said in an unhappy tone.

The pain of Dylan's betrayal cut through my heart like it was being sliced by a red-hot knife.

He'd played me.

And I'd happily allowed myself to be played.

I didn't know his exact motivations, but did it really matter? He knew how much ACM and this partnership had meant to me.

Tears welled up in my eyes, and because I had no other option, I fled.

The partnership was never really mine. It was just a plan that had never been solidified. I'd never had the money to make it a reality.

I raced toward the front entrance, tears starting to trickle down my cheeks as I finally hit the door.

Run! Run!

I had to get away.

I wasn't about to confront Dylan Lancaster and let him feed me any more bullshit than he had already.

I'd talk to Nic later. We'd been friends for a long time, and even though I felt betrayed, it was her business, her possession left to her by her mom, to sell.

Maybe her intentions had been good, but since she was starting a new job as a corporate attorney, keeping ACM was just too much for her.

I'd just bolted out the front when I heard someone call my name. "Kylie! Wait!"

Leo.

He caught up to me just as I'd located the Ghost in the group of cars lining the driveway.

I pulled the car door open.

"I'm sorry, Leo. I have to go," I said with a strangled sob.

I hopped into the car.

"Not like this," he insisted. "What's wrong?"

I simply shook my head and pulled the door closed.

"I need to get back to the house, please," I instructed the driver.

"Yes, miss," he acknowledged, putting the car in motion immediately.

My pulse was still racing as I closed my eyes and tried not to hear the sound of Leo's voice still calling my name.

As the Ghost got further down the driveway, the sound of Leo's voice behind me finally stopped.

A million thoughts filled my head.

A million and one questions raced through my mind.

Why would Dylan mess with ACM when he knew damn well how much that company and partnership meant to me?

Why had he acted like he cared and given so much when he'd end up betraying me in the end?

Had it all been about the sex and only the sex?

Jesus! The guy deserved an Academy Award for those performances because I'd been pretty damn convinced that there was way more to our relationship than *just* hot sex.

Memories flashed through my mind.

Every thoughtful gesture.

Every time he'd told me I was beautiful.

Every time he'd told me that he cared about me.

Every look.

Every touch.

Nothing made sense except the pain of the heartache I was trying to live through right now.

I'd known that if I let Dylan Lancaster in, he'd have the power to destroy me.

I'd just never thought that it would ever happen.

I'd loved him.

I'd trusted him.

Shit! I'd wanted to spend the rest of my life with him.

No, he'd never said he was in love with me, but I'd hoped that someday, he'd end up falling in love with me, too.

This was the story of my life. I was sometimes fuckable, but *never* loveable.

God, had I really been stupid enough to think it would end any differently this time?

To make things even worse, I'd allowed myself to fall crazy in love, so it wasn't just rejection I felt. It was full-on emotional agony.

I swiped angrily at the tears on my face.

After my husband had died, and I'd taken a long ride on that emotional roller coaster through hell, I'd sworn I'd never cry over a man ever again.

And I hadn't.

Until now.

Dylan Lancaster had finally broken me, and I had no idea if I could ever manage to put the pieces back together this time.

CHAPTER 33

Dylan

I 'D BEEN MILDLY concerned when I hadn't seen Kylie come back from the house after ten minutes had passed.

I'd been a little worried when I'd walked through Hollingsworth and still had seen no sign of her after twenty minutes.

Once thirty minutes had gone by, and I'd walked the house and immediate grounds without finding her, I was fairly frantic.

Where in the hell could she have gone? She'd just gone to the loo, for fuck's sake.

She'd known I was waiting for her.

"Have either of you seen Kylie?" I asked Damian and Leo as I found them near the food tables, most of the guests now gone. "I can't find her, and she's not answering any of my calls or texts."

"Shit!" Leo cursed as he looked at me. "Why do I feel like I'm going through a serious case of déjà vu? I was just asking Damian why he thought Kylie had left in tears. It was almost the same as the time Nicole left so suddenly at the gala. Same tearful face. Same devastated expression."

Fear started to roar in my ears as I asked, "What in the hell are you talking about?"

"She left about twenty-five minutes ago," Leo answered. "She came flying out the door of the house crying. She told me she had to leave and then jumped into the Ghost before I could catch her."

"Kylie isn't the sort of woman who breaks into tears for nothing," I informed him.

"Well, she was definitely *weeping* today," Leo said defensively.

"Where would she go? Why would she go?" I said hoarsely.

"We were going to take a walk to the lake. She just went to the loo."

I pulled my mobile from my pocket and shot off a text to my driver.

His reply came back a moment later.

"She asked him to take her back to the house," I informed them. "They're nearly there."

I looked down as I got a second text.

"Shit! She asked him to stand by when they get there because she's going to want to go to Heathrow. What in the hell is she doing?" I growled as I texted him back.

Once he'd confirmed, I shoved the mobile back in my pocket.

She could very easily just call an Uber or a taxi. Asking my driver to stall and not take her anywhere wasn't going to buy me much time.

"I have to go," I told my brothers. "I'm not sure what happened, but she's going to be headed to Heathrow. If she hasn't answered my texts or calls by now, she obviously doesn't plan on doing it at all."

"What do you think happened?" Damian asked gruffly. "Kylie isn't the flighty type."

I raked a frustrated hand through my hair. "I have no idea. She was fine just minutes before. As I said, she just went inside to the loo before we took a walk down to the lake."

"Somebody had to have said something to her," Leo pondered. "She looked pretty upset."

Fuck! It was killing me not to know what was wrong with her. Kylie didn't get upset over nothing. I couldn't even see her getting distraught because of something someone said to her.

She would have come straight to me if someone would have said something offensive, and the fact that she hadn't talked to me had me *really* worried.

Everyone she really cared about was right here at this event.

Anyone she would want to talk to about a problem were all here, too.

Why in the hell would she just run away like that?

"Here," Damian said gruffly as he dug into his pocket. "Take the Ferrari."

He tossed the keys, and I caught them. "Thanks."

"Call us," Leo called after my retreating figure.

"And don't drive like a lunatic," Damian added.

Like I was actually going to take that advice?

Right now, my sole purpose was to get to Kylie before she had a chance to run any further away than she already had.

My drive from Surrey to London was made in record time, but as I pulled into the drive right behind the Ghost, I realized that Kylie must have packed even faster than I'd driven because she was at the end of the driveway with her bag and carry-on.

My driver was standing beside the Rolls like he had absolutely no idea what to do because I'd told him in my text not to take Kylie anywhere.

Apparently, she'd decided to take matters into her own hands and call for a ride.

I threw the vehicle into *park* and jumped out of the car, trying to force myself to be calm as I approached her.

"Going somewhere?" I asked, my voice rough.

She didn't say a word, nor did she even acknowledge my presence. Her head stayed down as she looked at her phone.

I scanned her face, looking for any hint of how she was feeling. She wasn't crying, but her eyes were red and swollen, and just knowing that she had *been* crying made an invisible vise start to tighten around my chest.

She'd changed out of her formal dress and into a casual sundress and a pair of sandals, obviously so she'd be more comfortable traveling.

Desperate, I plucked the phone from her hand, and quickly canceled the taxi she was waiting for, and then handed the phone back to her. "I'm not doing this at Heathrow like Damian did, so we're going to talk right now."

Christ! I wasn't going through the same scene that Damian had gone through with Nicole. I didn't have the patience for it, and knowing Kylie, she wouldn't bother to come find me. Judging by her expression right now, she'd board her plane and probably never look back if I gave her a choice.

I picked her up, threw her over my shoulder, and headed for the house before she had the chance to summon another ride.

I called for my driver to bring her bags inside as I jogged up the steps.

"What in the hell are you doing?" she squealed. "Damn you, Dylan Lancaster, put me down."

Well, at least she *was* speaking to me now, even if she was cursing at me.

I didn't stop until I reached the living room, where I finally put her back on her feet again. "Can you tell me what possessed you to take off like that? You took several years off my damn life. You didn't answer my texts or my calls. Nobody knew where you were. What in the hell happened?"

She folded her arms across her chest, her eyes flashing daggers at me as she answered, "You know what happened. Why didn't you just tell me that you were buying ACM instead of doing it behind my back? Were you even planning on giving me my old job back or just bringing in a whole new crew to build up some kind of super PR company?"

Christ! How had she heard about that?

I cleared my throat. "I wasn't planning on doing either one of those things." Did she really think I was out to steal her company? Why in the hell would I do that?

"Then why?" she asked with a choked sob. "Why would you do that to me? You know how much that company and that partnership means to me."

I raked my hand through my hair, so flabbergasted that she'd ever think I'd do anything to intentionally hurt her that I was feeling wounded myself. It was pretty damn obvious that she *didn't* trust me and that instead of asking, she'd just chosen to think of the worst possible scenario and run, just like she always did when she didn't trust someone.

"Do what?" I growled, so damn tired of not telling her exactly how I felt that I just gave up trying to dance around the topic anymore. "Yes, I was buying ACM from Nicole, not to steal it from you, but so I could give it to you as an engagement present—if you'd accept it. Nicole doesn't want or need to run that company anymore, nor does she think she has the talent to develop it for future growth. She's a corporate attorney, and she wants to go back to doing what she loves to do, what she's trained to do, but she doesn't want ACM to go to anyone but you. Apparently, you shot down her offer to simply gift you that partnership. So, I decided to buy the entire company and give it to you. Fuck the partnership. To expand internationally, you need control, not a silent partner you have to check with every time you want to make a decision.

Nicole said she'd be thrilled if you had complete control of the company. She doesn't want to own it, nor does she need it to keep her mother's memory alive anymore. The only reason she's hanging on to it now is for you."

I walked to the dining room table, plucked up the paperwork laying there, and handed it to her. "Read this copy of the contract yourself. The funds are coming from me, but sole ownership of the company will be yours. If you refuse, the sale won't be finalized. Whatever you heard was misunderstood or just plain incorrect. I would have hoped by now that you'd realize that I would rather die than hurt you, Kylie. Apparently, you *don't* comprehend that. Nor do you trust me."

I reached into the pocket of my tuxedo and pulled out a black velvet box. "If you need further proof, this is the ring I'd planned to propose with at the lake. I thought it would be a romantic spot to ask." I popped the lid open and heard Kylie's swift intake of a breath. "I had it custom made. It's not the traditional diamond center stone because I thought the emerald would look better with your skin color and that flame-colored hair, but I was willing to make any changes you wanted." I closed the boxed and shoved it back into my pocket. "I'll cancel the sale and transfer of ACM, and things will go back to exactly as they were before. Maybe it was a ridiculous expectation to hope that you'd trust a guy with my past in such a short period of time."

I turned my gaze to her face, taking in her wide eyes and astonished expression.

Christ! She really hadn't expected any kind of commitment, especially not a marriage proposal, apparently.

"Y-you wanted me to marry you?" she asked in an astonished, confused voice. "Why?"

I put my hands in the pockets of my tuxedo pants as I stood in front of her. "All of the usual reasons. I think it's quite obvious that I love you and don't want to spend another moment of my life without you in it." I took a deep breath before I continued, "I told you once that I was happy before Charlotte came along, but there was always some part of me that was restless, like something was missing from my life. That feeling is gone, Kylie, because that part of me that was missing was *you*. My heart, my very soul, has always been looking for yours, and now that you're here, that unsettled feeling doesn't exist. So don't ask me to stop trying to make you mine. It might drive me mad to be separated from you, but at least tell me there's a chance that you might trust me someday. That in the future, you might learn to love me like I already love you."

She was silent as a flood of tears started to fall down her cheeks, and her gorgeous eyes were so turbulent that I couldn't even begin to sort out all of the emotions I saw there.

Pain gnawed at my gut because I'd never seen Kylie cry this way, and her sadness ate away at me.

"Bloody hell! Don't cry, Kylie," I told her.

If she didn't feel the same way, it wasn't her fault.

She took a few steps and sank onto the couch as she whispered, "You're really in love with me and want to marry me?"

"I've just said so, haven't I?" I asked, the ache in my stomach intensifying. "I'm not sure why either of those things should be surprising. I haven't been trying to hide the way I feel about you, Kylie. I'm not the father who let you down and has stupidly ignored your existence unless it's convenient for him to acknowledge it. I'm also not your dead husband, who was idiotic and insecure enough that he needed more validation from another woman when he already had the very best a man could ever ask for. I'm not any of those other men who never recognized what they had, either. I'm just me, Dylan Lancaster, that man who has always been intelligent enough to know that if you were mine, I'd be the luckiest bastard in the world."

If I wasn't in agony already, I was certainly plunged into hell the moment that Kylie Hart, the woman whose glass was always half full, buried her face in her hands and started to sob like her entire world was falling apart.

CHAPTER 34

Kylie

WHAT IN THE hell had I just done?

Dylan Lancaster had laid his heart at my feet, and I'd been foolish enough to stomp all over it.

Looking back, it was ridiculous that I hadn't had *some* inkling about how he felt, and that I hadn't trusted my instincts enough to realize he would never hurt me.

Maybe the proposal was a little shocking, but Dylan wasn't a guy who did things in half measures.

I'd been so damn worried about guarding my own heart that I hadn't watched out for his.

"I'm so sorry," I said between sobs.

Dylan pulled me to my feet and into his arms.

I wrapped my arms around his neck and rested my head on his shoulder, furious with myself for what I'd just done to him. "Why did I do this? You deserve so much better than this, Dylan.

I get lucky enough to find this amazing relationship with the most incredible man I've ever known, and I manage to screw it up. Who does that? Who runs away without finding out all the facts? What idiotic female hurts a man who has done nothing but care about her? What in the hell is wrong with me?"

"Don't, Kylie," he said in a soothing baritone as his hand caressed my hair. "I know your history, and you know mine. We're both going to make some mistakes. You jumped to the wrong conclusion because you've been hurt so many times before."

I forced back a sob, lifted my head, and looked into his eyes as I said, "But I've never been hurt by you. You were right. You're not any of those other men. This has nothing to do with you, Dylan. You've never given me a single damn reason *not* to trust you. I love you. I've known that for a while now. When I heard Damian and Nicole in the library talking about selling ACM to you, I panicked. God, subconsciously, maybe I just wanted an excuse to run. I was so damn in love with you and so worried about what would happen after the wedding was over. You never said you loved me, but I've never said those words to you, either. Maybe I was just waiting for the other shoe to drop because it always does for me. And I needed a reason to go before *you* told *me* that you didn't feel the same way."

He searched my face as he asked, "Is that why you didn't want to talk about it on the way to the gala?"

I nodded. "I didn't know how I was going to handle a conversation about our relationship becoming much more casual. With me in the States and you here in London, I knew we couldn't have what we have right now."

"Oh yes, we can," Dylan said gruffly. "If you love me, and we want to be together, that's just geography, love, and we can work that out. I told Damian I'd be here for the next month while he and Nicole are traveling, but that I'd probably be living in the US after he gets back. I can handle my share of the work for Lancaster from the Los Angeles office with occasional trips back to London. I bought that beach house for a reason. You love it, and I'm hoping you'll live there with me."

"Dylan," I said, feeling dazed. "I don't want to take you away from your family. They just got you back. And have you ever tried commuting from Newport Beach to Los Angeles? It would be a nightmare with traffic."

"Twelve minutes by helicopter," he answered immediately. "And it's not like I can't get on my jet and go see my family."

Okay, so I forgot sometimes that quick transportation wasn't really an issue for him.

I fiddled with his bow tie as I considered, "It hasn't really been difficult to work remotely for me. We could spend time here, too. I am hoping that ACM will eventually be able to get UK contracts. I know I screwed up today, and I wouldn't blame you if you want to take a little more time now to think about that marriage proposal. But I do want you to know how much I love you, Dylan, and that there's no one else in this world for me but you."

My heart was racing as I waited for his reply.

"I told you that if you ran, I'd find you," he reminded me huskily. "Because there's no one else for me, either."

Tears were still trekking down my cheeks as Dylan pulled that gorgeous ring back out of his pocket, flipped the lid open, and slipped it onto my finger as he said, "Marry. Me."

My breath caught as the large center stone emerald, surrounded by smaller diamonds, shimmered on my finger. It was big, beautiful, breathtaking, and flashy, but not completely overpowering, and there wasn't a single change I'd want to make. "Is that a question?"

"No. I'm terrified to give you an option right now."

I smiled and started to wipe the tears from my face. "That seems fair enough, but I do trust you. It's not you, Dylan. It's me. I'll try to make sure it doesn't happen again. Maybe I just need time to get used to having a man like you. Sometimes, the way I love you is really frightening."

I wrapped my arms around his neck, my heart melting into a puddle as I saw the covetous, adoring way he was looking at me, even after I'd been such an idiot.

"You'll get used to it," he assured me. "Because I'm always going to love you back the same damn way."

My heart was so full that I could hardly take a breath. "We'll have to talk about you buying me the company, though. I'm not sure how I feel about that. I've always done everything on my own, Dylan."

"We'll discuss that later," he answered right before his mouth came down on mine.

I speared my hands into his hair and returned the fevered embrace.

My heart was galloping out of control when he finally released my lips and trailed his hot mouth down my neck.

My body was clamoring to be connected to this man in the most intimate way possible. "Fuck me, Dylan. Please. I need you."

I didn't give a damn about details, where we were going to live, or about my business.

The only thing I needed right now was him.

I shivered as his hands reached beneath my sundress and smoothed them up my thighs, finally reaching the point where he could hook his thumbs into my panties.

I kicked out of them once he'd pulled them down my legs and watched, my heart racing, as he liberated his very erect cock from his tuxedo pants.

He lifted me, and my back hit the living room wall with a small *thud*.

"Can't wait right now, love," he grunted. "Better next time."

My urgency was just as great as his as I tightened my legs around his waist. "Just fuck me, Dylan." I panted, my heartbeat thundering in my ears. "I. Need. You."

One sharp movement of his hips had him buried inside me as he growled. "You have me, Kylie. You always will."

My body responded wildly to the harsh, feral look on his face.

"Tell me," he demanded as he pumped into me. "Tell me you love me."

I leaned my head back against the wall and closed my eyes as his mouth devoured the sensitive skin of my neck. "I love you, Dylan Lancaster. I love you."

Right now, I needed him like this.

Fierce.

Uncontrolled.

Demanding.

Greedy.

"Again," he commanded with a groan.

The frantic coupling had my climax building already.

I speared my hands into his hair and gripped the locks to ground myself.

"I. Love. You," I cried out.

His hands gripped my ass harder. "Don't ever run from me like that again. It nearly killed me, woman."

"I won't. I won't," I promised as I dropped short, heated kisses on his face.

Dylan was my life, and I knew I'd think twice before I ever did anything to hurt him again.

It might happen unintentionally in the future, but the haunted look on his face when he'd assumed I didn't love him would be tattooed into my memory forever.

There was nothing I wouldn't do in the future to make sure I never saw that expression again.

"Christ! I love you, Kylie. I'll never be able to get enough," Dylan rasped against my skin. "You're fucking mine."

"And you're mine," I replied fiercely as I nipped his earlobe.

Unable to hold back any longer, my orgasm seized control of my body.

Dylan followed me soon after and captured my last lusty moan by slamming his mouth down on mine for a frenzied kiss.

We stayed just like that for a few minutes, our foreheads on each other's shoulders as we recovered our senses.

Finally, when my lips could form the words, I said, "Let me stay with you, Dylan. Let me love you. Let me be there for every happy moment of your life and the difficult ones, too. No more running away."

"Thank fuck!" he said fervently. "I'll never take that love for granted, sweetheart. I lived too damn long without it."

"I feel exactly the same way," I murmured as he started to carry me toward the bedroom, my legs still wrapped around him.

I was completely convinced that no matter what happened in the future or how we ended up working things out, Dylan would always make sure that I knew I was totally and completed loved.

CHAPTER 35

Macy

I DROPPED MY CELL phone on the desk in the library, my heart so heavy I couldn't move out of the chair.

There weren't very many of Damian and Nic's wedding guests left outside, so I'd gone in search of a quiet place to make a call to the sanctuary to check on Karma.

The aged Bengal tiger had been sick for a long time, but I'd thought she'd linger long past the time that I was due back in the United States.

Now, I wasn't sure I'd get there in time to be there with her when she died.

It shouldn't really matter. It isn't like I've never lost an animal before.

Tears began to trickle down my cheeks, and I didn't bother to check them since I was alone.

The problem was, I got way too emotionally attached to some of the animal patients I cared for, which was an issue I'd always tried to improve on.

I tried to stay more detached, more clinical, but Karma had always been special.

She'd been extremely abused when she'd come to the sanctuary, and because one of her legs had been deformed, she'd needed a lot of care.

Maybe the two of us had bonded because we'd sensed each other's pain. She'd been extremely wary about trusting anyone, but she'd eventually come around. At least for me, she had. She just wasn't all that crazy about anyone else, especially men, which I completely understood.

I'd comforted her.

She'd comforted me.

Yeah, maybe I'd crossed a few professional lines by hanging out with Karma way more than I should have, but I didn't regret that. She'd seen nothing but torture and pain for most of her feline life. She'd deserved a little peace and contentment in her older years.

"Macy?" a concerned baritone voice said from behind me.

I swung around in surprise.

Leo Lancaster.

I swiped at the tears on my face, embarrassed. He was the last person I wanted to find me crying over a crippled tiger.

Not that he wasn't a nice guy, but Leo was into science and preservation. I couldn't see him being the type of guy who would understand.

"Hey," I said weakly. "Do you need to use the library? I can go—"

He frowned. "You're crying," he said, stating the obvious. "Is everything all right?"

God, I loved that sexy British accent of his, and the fact that he looked like the subject of every woman's wet dream didn't hurt, either.

I shrugged. "Sorry. I just found out that I'll probably lose a patient before I can get back to California. I was a little upset. I've been working with her for a long time."

He put his hands into the pockets of his tuxedo. "Dog? Cat? Ferret?"

Um...maybe I'd neglected to tell him what type of veterinarian I was. "Bengal tiger," I confessed. "I'm an exotic animal vet."

He raised a brow. "A little larger than I was expecting and a bit wilder. Probably not as easy to give a cuddle to, either."

"Actually, Karma is very affectionate. She came to us after being abused for most of her life. Her leg is deformed. It was crushed. She's always needed a lot of care, and we bonded pretty hard, even though I shouldn't have let that happen. Maybe it sounds really stupid to be that attached—"

"It doesn't," Leo interrupted. "I understand, Macy. I've had losses that crushed me, too."

I looked at his face, but I saw no sign of anything except compassion in those gorgeous blue eyes of his.

"I really wanted to be there with her when she died. She doesn't really trust anyone else. I thought she'd make it at least a few more weeks. She's twenty, and she's been fighting cancer for a long time," I explained, my voice cracking with emotion.

"Come here," Leo said and opened his arms.

Generally, I'd be the last woman to throw myself into the arms of a male stranger, but I felt so lost, and Leo looked so...comforting.

He immediately wrapped his powerful arms around me, and I snapped.

I started to cry, a great big ugly cry that I couldn't stop.

"We'll stop and pick up your suitcases from Damian's place, and I can get my jet ready to fly," he said in a soothing baritone once my sobs slowed down. "I was planning on leaving for the States tomorrow, but there's nothing stopping me from going now. We can try to get there before she's gone."

I pulled back to look at him. "You'd do that? Seriously?"

Every moment counted, and leaving earlier than tomorrow could make a difference.

"It's not exactly an inconvenience," he assured me.

God, I really wanted to take him up on his offer, but I didn't even know Leo Lancaster. He was just another wedding guest—the new brother-in-law of my best friend.

Yeah, we'd chatted about the work he'd done as a wildlife biologist, but flying alone with him could be…uncomfortable, and I was the queen of awkwardness when it came to men.

I was a lot less ill at ease with animals.

But Leo had been so…nice.

It's a twelve-hour flight. You'll be sleeping for most of it. What's the worst thing that could happen when you'll hardly see each other?

And it was highly possible that I could be home with Karma when she passed, which was something I desperately needed.

I hadn't been ready to say goodbye when I'd left for London.

I hadn't thought I needed to do it.

I blinked as I continued to look up at him and saw the sincerity in his gaze.

God, he was tall.

He smiled as he said, "I've been out in remote locations for a long time, so I'm not sure how much civilized conversation I can make. I've been a bit of a loner."

I stepped back from him. "That's okay. We'll be in bed." My cheeks flushed. "I mean, we'll be…sleeping."

Oh, Good Lord, Macy, stop talking.

If I had to talk to Leo Lancaster, I was far better off sticking to wildlife biology.

I had no doubt he was joking about not being a good conversationalist. He was cultured, polished, and had seemed perfectly comfortable chatting with a variety of people at the reception.

I, on the other hand, was the epitome of social anxiety at its worst.

Put me in a clinical setting with my animal patients, and I could talk to any other professional just fine.

Toss me into a crowd of people I didn't know, and I had no idea what to say most of the time.

I didn't have Nicole's sophistication as a corporate attorney or Kylie's gift of communicating as a PR expert.

It's just twelve hours. Think about Karma.

I plastered a smile on my face and said to Leo, "I'm ready to go whenever you are."

He nodded and led the way out of the library.

EPILOGUE

Kylie

Three Weeks Later...

"**I**T'S MUCH TOO early to be out of bed on a Sunday morning, sweetheart. What are you doing?" Dylan asked curiously.

I looked up to see my handsome fiancé wandering into the kitchen in nothing but a pair of black boxer briefs.

My heart skittered as his gorgeous green-eyed gaze caught mine.

Jesus! Would I ever get used to the way Dylan made my heart race every time he walked into a room?

"Making British pancakes," I informed him. "I thought maybe we could start having a Pancake Sunday once in a while. Your mom taught me how to make them last week when I was visiting her in

Surrey. I just asked for the recipe, but somehow, before I knew it, we were cooking a batch together. She was really enthusiastic about it."

Dylan reached for a bottle of water in the fridge, took the cap off, and took a sip.

I added, "I think she's hoping you'll get me pregnant as soon as possible."

I turned my head in surprise as Dylan coughed after nearly choking on his water.

"Christ! You can't just do that to a man when he's trying to drink," he grumbled.

I snorted. "At least you're hearing it secondhand. Bella isn't really all that subtle."

He took one more gulp before he set the bottle down and raised an eyebrow as he looked at me. "She never has been. And what exactly did you tell her?" he asked.

I smiled at him. "What could I say? I could hardly tell your mother that you're practicing like a champion every single day, sometimes several times a day, for that future event."

He moved up behind me and wrapped his arms around my waist. "Will that event be in our future?" he asked hoarsely as he kissed the side of my neck.

Children were something Dylan and I hadn't talked about…yet.

"You tell me," I said as I stopped mixing the contents of the bowl in front of me and turned around to face him. "My vote would be *yes*, but I'd like to get married and be a couple for a while first. Right now, I just want to be with you."

He grinned down at me. "I was hoping it wouldn't be *no*. But if it was, I'd be okay with that, too. I have you, and that's always going to be more than enough."

I wrapped my arms around his neck with a sigh. "I think we can take a little while to figure out how that's going to happen. I would have been okay if your answer had been *no*, too."

"I'd be happy to teach you exactly how it happens," he offered.

I shook my head. "I'm going to feed you first, and I told your mom we hadn't talked about it yet."

"She'll be absolutely relentless," he warned. "Damian said she hasn't stopped hinting at grandchildren since the moment she realized that he was crazy about Nicole."

I smiled. "I think I can handle the pressure. I'll just keep reminding her that I'm not even married yet."

"A problem I hope we can remedy pretty damn soon," he rumbled. "Do we have a date yet?"

Dylan was definitely his mother's child. He was just as relentless about setting a date for our wedding as she was about getting grandchildren. "Late spring?" I asked.

He shook his head. "I'd have to kidnap you and take you to Vegas if it's going to take that long."

I laughed. "Honestly, I don't think I'd resist, but your family wouldn't be happy. If we do it sooner, it won't be outdoors. It would be way too cold."

"We can have a very nice wedding indoors. There are an endless amount of places in England to choose from, Kylie. We don't have to do it at Hollingsworth just because Damian and Nicole did. In fact, I wouldn't mind doing something different, so our wedding is unique," he said thoughtfully.

"I'd really like that, too," I said. "Let me check out some venues online and see if I can go take a look."

"Take me with you when you narrow the list down to places you want to see in person," he requested.

My heart squeezed inside my chest. "I wouldn't ever go without you. Now let me finish those pancakes."

He reluctantly let me go and went to the coffee maker. I watched as he put my favorite brew into the machine.

God, it amazed me that Dylan never really thought about doing things for me. He did it as automatically as he would do it for himself.

"You do know that you don't have to cook for me, right?" he asked. "You're busy, too. I told you I could hire someone or just have a chef come in for evening meals."

I did still cook for Dylan every evening, but I did it because I wanted to, not because I felt like I *had* to. "I want to," I told him. "You take care of me all the time. I like doing the one thing you can't do well for yourself. I do like to take care of you, too."

I smiled as I glanced over at the enormous bouquet of roses that Dylan had given me Friday night.

It wasn't the first time he'd brought me flowers, and I knew it wouldn't be the last.

He did so many thoughtful things for me, and even though it wasn't easy to find anything I could do for a man who had everything, I tried just as hard to remind him that I loved him and thought about him every single day.

I grabbed the boiling kettle from the stove, put Dylan's favorite tea in the small teapot, and poured the water over it so it could steep.

He came up beside me and put my mug of coffee close enough so I could reach it. "You take care of me just by being here with me," he informed me. "Anything else you want to do is a bonus."

He deserved as many of those bonuses as he could get, as far as I was concerned.

"This is almost ready," I told him as he took a seat at the island. "After last night, I think you need sustenance."

He shot me a sexy grin. "You do realize that I'll be completely refueled after this."

"That was the plan, handsome," I teased.

He shot me a heated look before he asked, "Did you make a decision about letting me gift ACM to you? If not, I'm going to be shopping for another appropriate engagement gift."

Oh, Lord. That could be frightening. "There's so much I want to do with ACM, starting with a UK office so I can go international. I think I'd need help from a brilliant business mind for consultations," I told him.

"Then I guess it's convenient that you have one of those extremely close at hand." His voice was nonchalant, but his expression was pensive. "I'll be there with you every step of the way, sweetheart," he vowed as he rose and walked around the island to me. "Not that you really need me, but I'll be here if you do. Are you saying you're going to reach out and grab what you want?"

I nodded. "Yes. It's kind of ridiculous not to accept. We are going to be married, you are Dylan Lancaster with more money than God, and ACM means a lot to me." I turned the heat off the stove, jumped into his arms, and hugged him. "Thank you for the most incredible engagement gift a woman could ever receive."

I pulled his head down and kissed him, my heart dancing because I'd actually been lucky enough to find this man I loved so damn much and who would do anything to make me happy.

"Thank fuck," he grumbled. "I wasn't looking forward to trying to find another gift that would make you as happy as ACM."

"I love you, Dylan," I told him. "Anything else is just a bonus for me, too. But I think we should clear one thing up."

"I love you, too, sweetheart," he replied. "What do we need to clarify?"

I looked into his eyes as I told him, "I *already* reached out and grabbed *exactly* what I wanted, and I'm looking at him. ACM is important, but not as vital as the guy I want to spend the rest of my life with."

"I might have missed that whole grabbing part," he said in a husky tone. "Would you like to grab me again just so I remember what that was all about?"

I shook my head. "You're already mine, Dylan Lancaster, and I'm not letting go. A repeat is impossible, but after we finish these pancakes, I'd be more than happy to remind you that I'm yours."

He shot me a wicked grin as he tightened his arms around me. "Bloody hell, woman," he growled, his eyes filled with sensual anticipation as he started to lower his head to kiss me. "If *that's* your plan after we refuel, I think we're going to need to make a few more batches of those pancakes."

The End

Please visit me at:
http://www.authorjsscott.com
http://www.facebook.com/authorjsscott

You can write to me at
jsscott_author@hotmail.com

You can also tweet
@AuthorJSScott

Please sign up for my Newsletter for updates,
new releases and exclusive excerpts.

Books by J. S. Scott:

Billionaire Obsession Series

The Billionaire's Obsession~Simon
Heart of the Billionaire
The Billionaire's Salvation
The Billionaire's Game
Billionaire Undone~Travis
Billionaire Unmasked~Jason
Billionaire Untamed~Tate
Billionaire Unbound~Chloe
Billionaire Undaunted~Zane
Billionaire Unknown~Blake
Billionaire Unveiled~Marcus
Billionaire Unloved~Jett
Billionaire Unwed~Zeke
Billionaire Unchallenged~Carter

Billionaire Unattainable~Mason
Billionaire Undercover~Hudson
Billionaire Unexpected~Jax
Billionaire Unnoticed~Cooper

British Billionaires Series

Tell Me You're Mine
Tell Me I'm Yours
Tell Me This Is Forever

Sinclair Series

The Billionaire's Christmas
No Ordinary Billionaire
The Forbidden Billionaire
The Billionaire's Touch
The Billionaire's Voice
The Billionaire Takes All
The Billionaire's Secret
Only A Millionaire

Accidental Billionaires

Ensnared
Entangled
Enamored
Enchanted
Endeared

Walker Brothers Series

Release
Player
Damaged

The Sentinel Demons

The Sentinel Demons: The Complete Collection
A Dangerous Bargain
A Dangerous Hunger
A Dangerous Fury
A Dangerous Demon King

The Vampire Coalition Series

The Vampire Coalition: The Complete Collection
The Rough Mating of a Vampire (Prelude)
Ethan's Mate
Rory's Mate
Nathan's Mate
Liam's Mate
Daric's Mate

Changeling Encounters Series

Changeling Encounters: The Complete Collection
Mate Of The Werewolf
The Dangers Of Adopting A Werewolf
All I Want For Christmas Is A Werewolf

The Pleasures of His Punishment

The Pleasures of His Punishment: The Complete Collection
The Billionaire Next Door
The Millionaire and the Librarian
Riding with the Cop
Secret Desires of the Counselor
In Trouble with the Boss
Rough Ride with a Cowboy
Rough Day for the Teacher

A Forfeit for a Cowboy
Just what the Doctor Ordered
Wicked Romance of a Vampire

The Curve Collection: Big Girls and Bad Boys Series

The Curve Collection: The Complete Collection
The Curve Ball
The Beast Loves Curves
Curves by Design

Writing as Lane Parker

Dearest Stalker: Part 1
Dearest Stalker: A Complete Collection
A Christmas Dream
A Valentine's Dream
Lost: A Mountain Man Rescue Romance

A Dark Horse Novel w/ Cali MacKay

Bound
Hacked

Taken By A Trillionaire Series

Virgin for the Trillionaire by Ruth Cardello
Virgin for the Prince by J.S. Scott
Virgin to Conquer by Melody Anne
Prince Bryan: Taken By A Trillionaire

Other Titles

Well Played w/Ruth Cardello

Printed in Great Britain
by Amazon